MW00653912

# MURDER at the STROKE of MIDNIGHT

The Sisters, Texas Mystery Series

Book 14

## BECKI WILLIS

Copyright © 2023 Becki Willis
Clear Creek Publishers

All rights reserved. No part of this publication may be reproduced, distributed or transmitted in any form or by any means, without prior written permission.

This is a work of fiction. All characters, businesses, and interaction with these people and places are purely fictional and a figment of the writer's imagination.

Editing by SJS Editorial Services
Cover by Diana Buidoso dienel96

ISBN 13: 978-1-947686-23-6

# CONTENTS

# 1

The night was cold and dark. Even the moon tucked itself beneath a thick cover of clouds. Needles of sleet fell from the sky, pinging against the sidewalk. In Naomi, Texas, few people ventured out on a night like this. Even the Christmas lights strung along the businesses dared to twinkle in the night.

A lone figure braved the elements, swaddled in a wet overcoat and soggy knit cap. The person walked in the shadows, avoiding the weak glow from the sparsely placed streetlights.

A power glitch rendered most of the businesses dark. Here and there, a storefront window revealed battery-operated candles glowing from within. One shop had a twinkling Christmas wreath hung on its door, its lights no doubt powered by batteries.

As the prowler neared the circle of dancing lights, a turn of the head kept their face shrouded in shadow. They moved, instead, to stare at the restored old building across the street. *New Beginnings Café and Bakery* wasn't dark.

The person grunted. Genny Montgomery had that sort of charm. She probably willed the lights to stay on. They shone like a beacon in the night, beckoning one and all to take comfort in their steadfast glow.

A fresh shower of sleet and rain blew in with a hearty gust. Dormant leaves and bits of debris, once settled along the roadside and in the gutters, rallied for the chance to fly in the wind. The burst of current coaxed a piece of paper from its post and slammed it against a store window, narrowly missing the person on the sidewalk.

*It could be a sign,* the person mused. Pun intended.

Peeling the slick paper from the glass, they dared moving nearer to the streetlamp, just enough to read the words on the poster.

**NEW YEAR'S EVE MASQUERADE BALL**
**December 31, 9:00 pm - 1:00 am**
**The "Big House"**
**Corner of 2nd and Main**

**Dancing * Live Music * Prizes for Best Disguise**
**Hors d'oeuvres & Non-Alcoholic Beverages Served**

**Presented by The Sisters High School Drama Club**
**Hosted by Troupe Over the Hill and Brash & Madison deCordova**
**See any Drama Club or Troupe Over the Hill member for tickets****
****TICKETED EVENT. No tickets sold at the door.**

*What do you know. It* is *a sign,* the person smirked. It was a sign of destiny. The perfect opportunity to carry out 'The Plan.' *Yes. New Year's Eve. There's still time to orchestrate the perfect plan.*

The thought brought a smile to the prowler's face. The cunning sneer was nothing less than chilling.

No pun intended.

The downtown streets may have been empty, but not everyone slept. Across the railroad tracks in Juliet, Madison deCordova took full advantage of the power still flowing to the Big House. There was so much to do before the ball, and so little time to do it.

"We should have said no," she muttered to herself as she replaced red bows with silver.

This was the last garland to transform. Over the next two days, all traces of Christmas would be gone, switched out with sparkling gold and silver. The drama club had chosen the palette, hoping the color scheme would inspire million-dollar dreams for the year to come.

"I *like* my Christmas decorations," Madison continued to grumble. "I'm not ready to take them down, but I just couldn't say no. Blake knew that. He knew good and well I would cave."

That was the problem. Her son was a charmer, no doubt about it. When he turned up the volume, something in her just melted. His smile and mischievous blue eyes were as hard to resist at eighteen as they had been when he was four.

She jumped with surprise when Brash's voice spoke from the doorway. "Are you talking to anyone in particular? Or just grumbling in general?"

"Grumbling in general. I still don't know how we were suckered into this."

"Yes, you do," her husband replied. One word said it all. "Blake."

Madison dusted off her hands and met him halfway, turning her face up for his kiss. "I'm glad you're home. It looks nasty out there."

"It is. Power's out in half of Naomi. The roads are

starting to freeze over."

Maddy sighed. "We can't ever have a white Christmas, but we can have ice and sleet."

Brash chuckled as he wrapped his arms around her. "We live in the wrong part of the country for a white Christmas," he reminded her.

"I know. But just for once, I wish I could see snow at Christmas time."

He touched the tip of her nose with his finger. "We don't live in a Hallmark movie, either. Besides, I thought the day was perfect, just like it was."

"It was! I didn't mean it wasn't wonderful. I just..." She gave up, snuggling in closer to him as she asked more about the weather conditions. As chief of police for the two towns most commonly known as a collective 'The Sisters,' Brash was the first to inspect roads and general conditions during a storm of any kind. Tonight was no exception.

"I'm glad you're home," Madison said, squeezing his waist. "You know I can't sleep without my brood under one roof."

"You're like a mother hen. But you know your flock is about to fly away."

"I don't need reminding of that fact, thank you very much."

"You know it's true. In just a few months, all three of our children will graduate and be ready to go out on their own."

Madison stepped out of his arms, mumbling a protest. "Why did I marry a man with a daughter the same age of my twins? There's no slow progression of adjustment. Just *bam!* Just like that, they all fly away at once!"

"Most flocks do that, Maddy. As parents, it's our job to give them roots first and then wings."

"Stop being so right," she said with a frown, "and

help me put this last garland back on the mantel."

After doing as requested, Brash again pulled her into his arms. "What's wrong, sweetheart?" he asked. "It's not like you to grumble so much. Does this party cause you that much stress?"

"Yes and no. Part of it brings back memories," she confided, "and not the warm, fuzzy kind. Gray and I used to host parties, and we even had a costume ball once. It was so much fun because it was informal and cozy. But then as he changed, so did our entertainment style. He wanted to impress clients. And Annette, being the meddling mother-in-law that she was, insisted on grand, formal affairs. Sometimes, it was easier to just let her take care of it. Like a dutiful wife, I just smiled and served fancy, catered appetizers and flutes of champagne." She sighed, thinking of her first marriage. She and Gray had been so happy at first, but financial success had changed him. By the time he died in an automobile accident, their marriage had already disintegrated.

"I'm sorry. I didn't know, or else I would have told Blake no."

"It's okay. A masquerade ball actually sounds fun." Madison lay her head upon his chest. "It's just that..."

"Just that what?" he prodded.

"I can't shake the feeling that something is going to go wrong."

"It will be perfect, sweetheart. You're worrying for nothing."

"You do remember our wedding reception, right? A guest fell over dead, actually *poisoned*, right there in front of everyone."

"That was a one-in-a-million disaster. Nothing will go wrong with this party."

She was unconvinced but wanted, oh so hard, to believe him. "Blake does call me a dead body magnet, you know," she whispered skeptically.

"Maybe the New Year will change all that," he encouraged her.

"Maybe."

Yet somehow, she couldn't bring herself to believe the thought.

"Whew! What a messy night!" On a ranch outside of Naomi, Cutter Montgomery removed his cowboy hat before opening the back door, inadvertently slinging water onto the faithful dog waiting for his return.

"Sorry about that, Deogee," he mumbled. He bent to rub the devoted pet's head before ushering them both inside. The canine had been with him for a long time. Cutter had called him Dog at first, until one day, he reminded his furry friend that he was a D-O-G and was not allowed in the house. D-O-G became Deogee, and on cold nights like this, the loyal outside dog became an inside pet. There was a cozy bed in the corner of the mud room just for him.

Cutter tugged his feet from the clutches of sodden, mud-caked boots. Inspecting the soggy soles of his socks, he peeled them off, as well. Genny would give him grief if he tracked footprints across her clean floor.

His jeans were every bit as wet and caked as his boots, so he shucked those, too. He emptied his pockets into one of the baskets his thoughtful wife provided for this very use and threw his clothes into the washer. The socks were well past their original white color, thanks in part to previous washings with denim. The everyday wear of being a firefighter/rancher/welder didn't help much, either. Without concern, Cutter added detergent and turned on the machine. He set his boots into a rubber tray to drip dry.

A single light shone in the kitchen, meaning Genny had already gone upstairs for the night. She always left a light on for him when he was late getting in. At this hour, he hoped she was sound asleep, and both girls were down for the night.

Cutter moved through the house as quietly as he could, finding his way in the dark until he reached the master bedroom. A quick, hot shower restored feeling to his near-frozen limbs and brought his core body temperature up.

As he slid beneath the covers, Genny stirred. He could see her tussled blond hair by light of the gas-lit fireplace across the room.

"Are you just getting in?" she asked sleepily. "What time is it?"

"Close to two. I didn't mean to wake you."

Fighting a yawn, Genny shook her head. "I tried waiting up, but I guess I fell asleep."

"I told you not to wait on me. I never know how late I'll be when I'm paged out."

By habit, Cutter pulled her close and spooned his long body around her shorter one.

"What was it? A fire?" she asked, wiggling in closer.

"A downed tree. Knocked out power to a few houses along Mason and to parts of downtown."

"As long as no one was hurt..." she said around another yawn.

"No, but there was one stranded motorist," Cutter told her. After the slightest of hesitations, he added, "It was Shilo Dawne. I had to give her a ride."

At mention of the name, he felt his wife stiffen ever so slightly in his arms. He ran a light hand across her stomach, hoping to ease her. As he trailed fingers over her hip, his touch became a caress.

"What was she doing out at this time of night?"

"She didn't say." Cutter frowned, still bothered by

the flimsy excuse she had given. Something about visiting a friend and losing track of the time. Yet something in her voice told him that was only a partial truth. He had to wonder if the unnamed person was a married man. None of his concern, of course, but Shilo Dawne was an old friend and deserved better.

"Really? That's odd."

"What's even more odd is that she was walking. Said her car had stalled about a quarter mile on the other side of the tree. She was soaked to the bone, so I gave her a ride while Rob and Tank cut up the tree."

Her body had relaxed under his touch but tensed again. "Genny, darlin'," he murmured in her ear, "you know you have nothing to worry about. You know I never returned Shilo Dawne's feelings. And that I've *never* loved anyone but you. You and the girls are my world."

"I know. Really, I do." Genny reached backward to caress his jaw. "But ever since she's come back to town, she seems determined to somehow put herself in your path."

"I told you a long time ago, she was always like a pesky fly buzzing around. She was friends with my sister." His caress turned bolder, warming them both. "And if you remember, *you* were the one who encouraged me to be nice to her. 'Take her feelings into consideration,' you said. 'Give her a chance.' You practically threw us together."

"That was before we were involved," she defended herself.

"Genny, darlin'," he told her in a throaty voice, "I was involved the first time I saw your smile. And when I saw those dimples of yours, I knew I was a goner." His fingers worked under her pajama top. "Now," he murmured into the curve of her neck, "let's quit talking about pesky flies and talk about us."

Genny rolled over to face him. “I have a better suggestion,” she countered, sliding her arms around him. “Let’s not talk at all.”

# 2

Temperatures warmed overnight, making the morning commute easier than expected. Icy patches still clung to the bridges and spots of pavement shaded by trees, but nothing new had fallen over the last few hours.

Still, Genny couldn't shake the feeling that something bad was in store.

She ran through a checklist in her head. Cutter was staying at home this morning with the girls. Weather conditions were better than they had feared but still too iffy to risk getting their infant daughters out. The almost-twins were less than three and four months old and didn't need another cold. Between the two, Genny sometimes felt as if the Montgomery girls kept the pediatrician in business.

So far, no one had called in sick for their morning shift at *New Beginnings Café and Bakery*. On a morning like this, that was definitely a plus. She had prepped for breakfast the evening before and had the menu for the day planned and posted. With any luck, the day would go smoothly, and she could leave after the noonday rush.

Assuming, of course, there *was* a rush.

Genny wouldn't admit it, but she was more worried about her new competition than she let on. *New Beginnings* was a wildly popular eatery in the sister cities of Juliet and Naomi and, until now, had enjoyed almost no competition. *Montelongo's* was a favored Mexican restaurant in town but offered a completely different menu from hers. Gas station delis, traveling food trucks, and the local donut shop gave the community options yet posed no real danger to Genny's restaurant.

Then came *Fresh Starts*.

While Genny insisted there was room enough for them both, she had to admit she had noticed a dip in her bottom line since the breakfast and lunch specialty shop held its grand opening. Her most loyal customers refused to visit the new business, but curious patrons had checked it out. She couldn't begrudge them for it, but she did miss some of her regulars during the normal rush.

Yet in Genny's opinion, the worst danger came from out-of-towners depending on an internet search to find her somewhat-famous restaurant. *New Beginnings* was an unusual name for an eatery—more reflective of her new start in life than of her made-from-scratch menu—and could be easily confused with *Fresh Starts*. Genny had no doubt that entrepreneur Anastasia Rowland knew that when choosing a name for her latest venture. She already owned several successful cafés in the Houston and Galveston areas, but this was her first foray into the Brazos Valley. Genny saw it as both a compliment and a challenge that she chose to invade her territory.

The Montgomerys still weren't certain that Anastasia wasn't responsible for the string of troubles that had plagued *New Beginnings* of late. Complaints by the two towns' nemesis Myrna Lewis were nothing new, but threat of a lawsuit by the unknown Lawrence Norris was something else. Despite efforts by the owners to meet reasonable demands, negotiations had fallen through on several occasions.

If greed was the man's motivation, he seemed to have unlimited pockets when it came to lawyer fees. To Genny, it seemed that something more fueled his determination, and she suspected that Anastasia Rowland was behind it.

She continued reviewing the list in her head as she pulled into the café's parking lot. She needed to put the final touches on a promotion she was offering for the New Year. She wanted to believe she always offered her customers a great deal, but this was the first time since the eatery's inception that she had to do a large-scale campaign. That alone told her something.

Genny punched her code into the back door's keypad. The rich aroma of freshly perked coffee and the yeasty goodness of homemade coffee cake greeted her, meaning her morning crew was already hard at work. She truly did have a great group of employees. She was excited to be giving them New Year's Eve off this year, even if it meant putting an end to their traditional party for the entire community.

The original plan was for Cutter and Genny to spend the holiday at home with their new little family, but a change of venue for the drama club's big fundraiser changed that. Now, their best friends were the impromptu hosts of the event, and the couple wanted to show their support. They would bring the portable bassinets with them so the girls could sleep, allowing the new parents to spend time with their babies while still attending the party.

Thoughts of their almost-twin daughters brought a tender smile to Genny's face. She and Cutter had wanted to start a family as soon as possible after they married, but their best efforts had failed. Facing the news that Genny might be unable to conceive, fate led them to a young mother-to-be. Wanting a better life for her unborn child than what she could offer, she asked the couple to raise her child as their own. They immediately took steps to set up the private adoption. They were still adjusting to the idea of becoming parents when Genny discovered she was six weeks pregnant.

They had named their dark-haired, olive-skinned daughter Hope because she had given them the opportunity to be parents and hope for a future as a family. They named their blond-haired, fair-skinned daughter Faith, for it was faith that pulled them through and never allowed them to give up.

The many adjustments had been challenging. Not only were she and Cutter still learning to co-exist as a couple, but now they were the parents of two infants. Juggling parenthood, two careers, and the erratic schedules that came with it wasn't easy, but so worth it. Genny had never been happier in her life.

*Happy*, she reminded herself as she grabbed an apron off the hook and greeted her employees. *I'm happy. So why does something feel so 'off?"*

"Hey, boss lady." Thelma, her longest and most faithful employee, returned the greeting. "I wasn't sure you'd be in first thing or not."

"Cutter could stay with the girls, so here I am."

"One day," the third woman in the room replied with a dreamy smile, "I hope to marry a man just like yours. Handsome, devoted, and good with children."

"First, Dierra girl, you have to start dating," Thelma reminded her.

"That's true," Genny seconded, weaving her way between the two women to gather ingredients for biscuits.

The three worked together like a well-oiled machine. Thelma checked the baking coffee cake, while Dierra whipped up a pecan icing to pour over it. Genny set to work preparing her famous made-from-scratch biscuits. Conversation flowed between them as easily as the hints of cinnamon floating in the air.

"What about that man I saw you talking with just before Christmas?" Genny asked as she piled flour into a mini pyramid, wallowed a hole at the top with her fist, and broke eggs into the dip. "You seemed awfully cozy at the Christmas parade."

The younger woman tried hiding her flushed face. "I don't really know him. He's just in town for the holidays."

"What's his name? Does he have relatives here?" Thelma asked. Not many people came to The Sisters unless they had friends or family in town. Now that *Home Again* wasn't filming their reality television show here, it wasn't exactly a tourist destination.

"His name is Kelvin. He mentioned visiting an old friend."

"Maybe this Kelvin will decide to hang around after the holidays, and the two of you can spend more time together," Genny said.

"Maybe," Dierra responded. She sounded hopeful.

Like an over-protective mother, Thelma wanted to know more about the man. "What's he do for a living?"

"He's a freelance reporter for various newspapers, blogs, and even a magazine or two. I think his specialty is travel and, uhm, maybe food."

The way she hesitated over the words put Genny on alert. "Oh?"

Dierra was hesitant to explain. "I think he's doing an article on *Fresh Starts*." Her tone brightened as she added, "I suggested he stop in here, too, for a more well-rounded article."

"And is he?" Genny hated the hopeful note in her own voice. It certainly couldn't hurt to have her name and café mentioned favorably in the media.

"I think so, although we haven't talked in a few days. He said he'd be back before the New Year, and time is running out. Maybe I'll hear from him today, and I'll remind him to drop in."

"I'd like to meet him. It looked like the two of you were having a good time together."

"I know I did," Dierra admitted.

"The masquerade ball tickets are good for two. You could invite him to come with you."

The twenty-something-year-old blushed again. "I don't know him well enough for that."

"What better way to get to know him?" Thelma pitched in. "It sounds like the perfect first date to me. Music, dancing, free food. And if you don't like him, you can ditch him in the crowd before the clock strikes midnight, and you're forced to kiss him." She clucked her tongue. "Nothing like kissing a toad, even if I do plan on bringing my husband with me, warts and all."

As her two employees chattered on about the ball and what they planned to wear and who they hoped to see there, Genny's mind wandered. Had Anastasia Rowland invited the columnist to town, or had the entrepreneur's latest café garnered that much attention? More importantly, should Genny be worried?

She had little time to fret over Anastasia's interview. A truck arrived with a delivery that was two items short. By the time they sorted through the items, found the discrepancy, and put away the rest of the order, it was time to greet the first customers of the day.

By mid-morning, Genny was ready for a break. She welcomed the sight of her best friend as she came in from the brisk wind.

"Have time for a cup of coffee?" Madison asked as she slid out of her coat and stuffed it in the booth seat beside her.

"I'll make time!"

Genny was gone just long enough to bring two steaming cups of coffee and a square of coffee cake for them both. As she slid into the opposite seat, Madison eyed her with a knowing look.

"That bad of a morning?" she presumed.

Genny frowned. "Aside from Christmas, that bad of a week. Maybe of a month."

"This thing with Lawrence Norris still getting you down?"

"Yes, but that's only part of it. It seems like if one thing goes wrong, everything does. There was a mess-up on this morning's delivery, one of my warming ovens is on the fritz, and Joey didn't show up to wash dishes. It's almost a good thing we weren't busy!"

Madison sipped her coffee, reading between the lines of her friend's troubles. "Business still off?"

Genny shrugged. "A little. It comes with the time of year when everyone's busy with family or on a tight budget. For some people, the holidays are the only time they actually eat at home. But even with the curve of the holidays, business has slowed down more than usual."

"I'm sure it's just until the new wears off of *Fresh Starts*. Believe me," Maddy said, savoring a bite of her coffee cake, "nothing compares to your homemade creations."

"But homemade takes time, and people are always in a rush these days. They can pop into *Fresh Starts* and come out with a pre-made breakfast before I get fully started."

"You have quick options, too, you know. But there's a huge difference in your bakery case and theirs. Theirs is filled with generic, mass-produced pastries. Yours is filled with unique, handcrafted pastries that come from your own recipes. And as for the rest, your dishes are custom made the way diners want them. Trust me. The new will wear off, and you'll be as busy as you ever were."

The thought didn't seem to cheer her friend.

"Genny? Isn't that what you want?" Madison prodded.

"Honestly, I don't know what I want anymore. On the one hand, of course I want to be busy and successful and know I can provide the best for my employees."

"And on the other hand?"

Genny toyed with the handle of her coffee cup. "On the other hand, being that busy takes a lot of my time, and that's one thing I'm woefully short on these days."

"I thought you'd finally gotten the hang of giving Trenessa more responsibilities. She is your manager, after all."

"I know. And she's done a great job. Plus, I've been very pleased with Dierra's baking skills and Ann's prowess in the kitchen."

"But?"

"But it's my restaurant and my recipes. I feel like I should be the one preparing them."

Madison reached out to cover her friend's hand with her own. "You can't do everything by yourself, Genny. Especially now that you're a wife and mother."

"I know. And I know it's a problem that all women with both a family and a career have to face. *You* face the same issue, and you and Brash have been married just a few weeks less than Cutter and me. Neither of us has seen our second anniversary yet."

"True. But it does help that I have three teenagers, versus your two infants."

"You may have acquired Megan as a teen, but

Bethani and Blake were once infants, just like Hope and Faith. You made it look so easy."

Madison's laughter twinkled in the air. "Oh, how quickly you have forgotten! I was a complete mess, and I didn't even work at the time. Don't you remember how many times I called you, crying and at my wit's end? You flew in many a weekend to help with the twins."

"I know I have a great support system. Between you, Cutter's mom and sisters, Bethani and Megan, and, most of all, a wonderful husband, I have no room to complain. But sometimes, it's just so overwhelming, especially with everything else that's happening."

"I think you have a touch of the postpartum blues," her friend diagnosed. "It's perfectly normal, especially at this time of year, and even more so with the stress you're under. Give it time, Gen. I promise it will get better. And if it doesn't, you should talk with your doctor."

"I have," she confessed. "She gave me some pills, but I don't think they work. If anything, they make things worse." Genny ran her fingers through her bouncy blond curls. "Between not getting enough sleep... running back and forth to the doctor... seeing empty seats during what should be the busiest times of the day... dealing with Lawrence Norris, Myrna Lewis, Anastasia Rowland, and now Shilo Dawne... I just don't know anything anymore."

Madison frowned. "Hold on. Two questions. Myrna Lewis? What's she up to now? And that, by the way, only counts as one question."

Genny sighed. "Myrna is just being Myrna. Mean and spiteful and talking trash about me all the time. Did you know she owns the building where *Fresh Starts* is located? Apparently, she thinks if she spreads enough rumors about me and my restaurant, it will ensure a long and healthy bottom line for her rental property."

"No, I didn't realize that. But everyone in town knows what a bitter, spiteful old hussy she is. Not many people pay her much mind."

"We can hope," Genny muttered behind the rim of her cup.

Madison allowed them both a sip of coffee before crossing her arms on the table and leaning forward. "Question number two. Shilo Dawne?"

When her friend squirmed in her seat, Madison all but gasped. In a whisper, she hissed, "Genny! You aren't seriously jealous of her, are you? That's ridiculous!"

"I know," she claimed, yet she looked doubtful. "I know Cutter never felt the way about her that she did for him, but still..."

"Still, *what*?" Madison pressed. "Your husband is utterly and completely in love with you. I've never seen a man more devoted to his wife and children than he is. Okay, maybe Brash," she corrected herself, "but that's beside the point. We both are blessed with men who love and adore us. You can't be serious about seeing Shilo Dawne as a threat."

"Not a threat, exactly. Just another complication. Ever since she came back to town, she's... different."

"Different? How?"

"I always thought she and I were friends. Sure, I was her employer, but we got along well, and I thought we parted on good terms. She said she wanted to get a good education and make a better life for herself, and I could hardly fault her for that."

"Plus," Maddy was quick to put in, "she could see that Cutter wasn't interested in her. She knew staying would bring her nothing but heartache where he was concerned."

Genny didn't disagree. "In a lot of ways, our stories are a lot alike. We both left this town to make new lives for ourselves. We both left because of men. We both came back." She fiddled with her cup again. "I'd like to think I came back a better person. On the surface, I see some of the same improvements in Shilo Dawne. She definitely has more confidence in herself. Plus, she has a promising career as an accountant."

"Even if it's for a rival business?" Everyone was surprised when *Fresh Starts* brought in a hometown girl to act as the general manager and accountant for the eatery.

"Maybe *because* it's for a rival business. There was a certain look of—I don't know, maybe challenge—in her eyes when she told me about her new job."

"It was probably more like pride. You always encouraged her to reach for her dreams."

"Yes, and I'm proud of her for making them come true." Genny tried her best to sound convincing.

Madison knew her too well. "As long as those dreams don't include your husband?"

"Exactly. It seems like every time we turn around, there she is. She goes out of her way to come over and speak to us when she sees us in town."

"Are you sure she's not just being friendly?" Madison asked gently. It sounded like her friend was being overly sensitive.

Or, maybe not, if Genny's next words were true. "Not when she has to put her hand on his arm or come up and hug him. Every. Single. Time. She all but ignores me. She just swings her long, dark hair—she knows he always said it was prettiest when it was down—and looks up at him with adoring puppy-dog eyes."

"You mean the same look Cutter has when he looks at you and the girls?"

Genny ignored her and went on. “It’s to the point that people are starting to notice. And it’s making Cutter uncomfortable.”

“By now, Cutter should be used to adoring females. He’s been a major heartthrob for all females in this town from age two to ninety-two.”

“Yeah, well, most people know to look and not touch. Shilo Dawne didn’t get the memo,” Genny sulked. “Oh, and guess who conveniently got stranded at one o’clock this morning and needed a lift?”

“Brash said something about a stalled car. That was her?”

“Yes. And Cutter, being the gentleman that he is, gave her a lift home.”

“What was she doing out in weather like that, especially at that time of the night?”

“She didn’t say, but does it matter? She called Cutter to come to her rescue.”

“I think you’re forgetting one very important thing,” her best friend reminded her.

“And what is that?”

“*You* are the one Cutter came home to. The one he’ll always come home to. He loves you, Genesis Baker Montgomery. Don’t ever forget that.”

Genny’s smile was weak. “Thanks. I know I’m being ridiculous.”

Her gaze turned to stare out the window. “It’s just that...”

“I know,” Madison agreed quietly. “It’s like the quiet before the storm, and I don’t mean the weather.”

“You feel it, too?” her friend whispered.

“Most definitely.”

Genny suppressed a shiver. “What do you think it is?”

“I don’t know. But it’s something, and I don’t think we’re going to like it.”

# 3

"Oh, great," Genny moaned a few moments later. "We may have our first answer. Here comes Myrna."

"If we ignore her, do you think she'll go away?" Madison asked hopefully.

"My guess is no. Her beady little eyes are laser focused on you."

Myrna Lewis' shrill voice shattered the peaceful atmosphere in the restaurant. "Madison deCordova!"

With a sigh of dread, Madison turned to give the obnoxious woman a lukewarm greeting. "Can I help you, Myrna?"

"As a matter of fact, you can. And you can start by taking down those god-awful posters around town! There are three—*three*, mind you!— right in the middle of my rosebushes!"

Everyone knew that the rotund woman took far more pride in her lawn and garden than she did with her own appearance. Now, for instance, a red and black plaid shirt peeked through the gaps of her fuzzy purple jacket where the belt couldn't quite encircle her shapeless waist. Completing the atrocious ensemble were aqua sweatpants and a pair of men's black rubber boots.

"I guess last night's storm must have blown them there," Madison surmised.

"Don't be blaming the weather for you littering the town. I demand you take those posters down this minute!"

"First of all, they aren't my posters. They belong to and were placed around town by the school's drama club. Secondly, you can't demand any such thing. It's not your place."

"Then I'll *make it* my place at the next city council meeting!" she threatened.

Madison shrugged. "The event will be over by then but help yourself."

Myrna gave both women a hateful glare. "You two think you're so special. You think you have both towns under your spell. Well, just wait. Your time is coming." She wagged a stubby finger between them. "Mark my words. Your reign is coming to an end, so you'd both better be ready for the fall."

"'Tis better to have reigned for a moment in time," Genny pretended to quote, "than to have forever lived in the shadows."

"How dare you act all high and mighty after the stunt you pulled yesterday!" Myrna huffed. "You had no reason to threaten Anastasia Rowland that way. Look around you!" she sneered. "This place is nearly empty. That's because *no one eats here anymore.*" She raised her shrill voice, pounding the words into the table with her finger.

Neither woman took the bait. "Or," Madison pointed out, "it could be because it's ten thirty in the morning."

"That," Genny added, "or seeing you in here has ruined everyone's appetite."

"There's no one in here to see me!" Myrna countered.

Without a word, Genny indicated the plate glass windows, Vanna White style.

"Just wait," Myrna repeated with a glower, pushing her short, round body back toward the door. "Your time is coming."

As they watched her waddle out to her car, Madison frowned. "What was she talking about? What stunt did you pull with Anastasia?"

Her best friend of thirty years squirmed uncomfortably in her seat. "It wasn't as bad as she made it sound. At least, I don't think it was. Has Granny Bert called you about it yet?"

"No."

Genny touched her chest in relief. "Oh, good. Then it wasn't grapevine worthy."

"Now I'm really curious. What happened?"

"I ran by the grocery store on my way home to pick up a few things. The sidewalk was already slick, and the wind was blowing like crazy, so people were running in and out as quick as possible. I did the same thing. I didn't bother with an umbrella. I jumped out of the car, pulled a cap over my head, and ran inside," Genny explained. The more she talked, the more agitated she became. "But when I go back out, another car has pulled up so close to mine that I can't even open the driver's door. So, I load the groceries in from the other side, go back inside, and ask them to request that the owner of a silver Audi move their car."

"And?"

"No one comes forward. So, I go back out, thinking maybe they've already moved. Nope. There it still sits, squished up next to mine. I go back in, but this time, I slip on the sidewalk."

"Oh, no! Were you hurt?"

"I was too mad to be hurt! My bottom got all wet, I scraped my palm, and I think I saw a couple of high school boys laughing at me. But I pull myself up, wipe off, and go back into the store. I ask the cashier to repeat the request. Still, nothing. So, I wait. I wait, and I wait, and I wait—"

Her animated rendition of the story was so unlike Genny, Madison had to frown. Maybe those pills *did* make things worse.

"—and finally, the owner of the Audi waltzes up to the front. Guess who it was?"

"Anastasia?"

"Exactly! And you know what she said? She said she had heard the first announcement but was at the back by the refrigerated section and wanted to pick up 'a few more things.' She had a full basket, and most of it was items from the *front* of the store!" Genny was still fuming over the incident, a day later. "She made me wait, freezing my wet heinie off, while she buys out half the store!"

"I guess you said something to her?"

"Of course I did. I told her she was rude and selfish, and inconsiderate of others, especially in weather like that."

Again, Madison frowned. "That doesn't sound at all like you, Genny. You hardly ever lose your temper."

"I know, I know. But I've been such a wreck lately. And like I say, I think the pills make me more aggressive. But I was cold and miserable, and I just wanted to get home to my babies, and *she* stood between me and them! And then, *then*, she had the audacity to say she needed to check out before she moved her car. She said it was too miserable out there to get out in it a second time."

Madison could see where the story was going. Downhill, for certain.

"I told her this would be my *third* time out in it, thanks to her not parking correctly. I told her if she didn't come out right then and move her vehicle, I wasn't responsible for any dents or dings I caused when getting into my own car. She gave me an insulting look up and down, more or less saying I couldn't squeeze through a freight elevator."

"And I guess there were people in there to hear your exchange?"

"Because of the weather, not as many as normal. But of course, Myrna was there, and of course, she couldn't keep her mouth shut. She said I was being mean to Anastasia because she was taking customers away from me, and I might as well put a 'For Sale' sign in my window. Anastasia just stood there, still unloading her basket, until I stalked out of the store. I had just reached our vehicles when she came running out, waving her keys in the air."

"So, what happened?"

Genny wound down with a sigh. "She moved her car, I crawled in mine, and I went home. Not one of my finer moments, but not the *stunt* Myrna claimed, either."

Madison studied her friend with new concern. She had known Genny most of their lives. The two of them had gone through the best and the worst of times together, but this was nothing like the sweet Genny she loved so dearly.

Genny had finally calmed down, and Madison didn't want to rile her again. She changed the topic by wagging her fork and saying airily, "I forget. Does Myrna hate me because she hated you first, or was it the other way around?"

"Does it matter? She hates us both and is determined to get even. But in answer to your question, I'm not sure what we did wrong to begin with, are you?"

Madison thought back to when she first returned to The Sisters and somehow ignited Myrna's eternal wrath. "The goat incident, maybe? The one Bethani videoed and posted on social media."

"Oh, that's right. Followed by the Darla incident."

"The death of her sister only sealed our fate," Madison agreed.

"Not to make light of Darla's death, but that's hardly the only thing Myrna holds against you. Or us, I should say."

One by one, they ticked off some of the points of contention between the women.

"With Myrna," Madison summed it up, "there's always a long list of grievances."

Genny nodded. "I think the biggest one is that neither of us is intimidated by her. And since we're best friends, her hatred encompasses us both."

"Kudos on the quote, by the way. Shakespeare?" Madison's eyes twinkled in jest.

Genny's dimples finally appeared. "Close enough," she quipped, and both women burst out in giggles.

It was good seeing her friend laugh again, but Madison inwardly vowed to keep a closer eye on her friend's mood in the future.

Able to leave early in the afternoon, Genny had been home for less than an hour when a call came across Cutter's radio. The couple sat on the floor with the girls, marveling over every coo their brilliant daughters uttered. Genny was too busy blowing raspberry kisses into Faith's little tummy to hear the dispatcher's words clearly.

"Sorry, babe, but I should go," Cutter said, already unfolding his long legs. He kissed the top of each baby's head before he stood. "There's a potential gas leak in downtown Naomi."

Genny looked startled. "Not the restaurant, I hope."

Was this what all the bad vibes had been about?

"Not ours, anyway. It's at *Fresh Starts*."

"Oh, no. By all means, go." No matter the situation, Genny wished no ill against her competition.

"Hopefully, it won't take long. Love you." He kissed her goodbye as he radioed back to say he was enroute to the station.

"Well, kiddos, it looks like it's just us girls," Genny said to her babies. Spotting a pile of hair bows nearby, she smiled. "Want to play beauty shop?"

*Fresh Starts* was already closed for the day. Only three members of the staff were still inside but as a precaution, firefighters asked them to step outside while they checked for danger.

After a thorough sweep of the interior, one of the firefighters declared, "All clear."

Shilo Dawne was the first one through the door and the first to approach Cutter. She looked unnaturally pale.

"What was it, Cutter? The smell was so strong. Are you certain we aren't in danger?" Her fingers pressed through the thick bunker gear to grasp his arm.

"I'm sure. Probably just residue off one of the burners." He motioned toward the gas stove, deliberately making her hand fall away.

His old friend wasn't easily dissuaded. "You're sure? Because I feel a bit lightheaded."

"Maybe you should step back outside and get some fresh air," he suggested. "I need to get a signature from your boss, and then we'll be out of your way."

"I can sign it," she said. She sidled up close to him, peering over his arm to the clipboard he held.

Even through the thick coat, he could feel the way she pressed herself against him. Cutter used exaggerated movements to force her back a step.

"Okay. Sign here and here."

When Shilo Dawne hastily did as told, he frowned down at her. "Don't you want to read it first? It says you agree with our findings and release the department of all responsibility."

"No need. I trust you explicitly. I just trusted you with my life, didn't I?" She moved closer, looking up at him with wide, adoring eyes. "You said we were safe, and I believed you."

"I see no reason to believe otherwise," he replied, tucking the clipboard under his arm. He touched the brim of his hat in parting. "Have a nice day." His gaze swept around the room to encompass them all. "Happy New Year."

Cutter headed outside to his truck, only to hear Shilo Dawne's voice calling his name. The other truck had already pulled out, leaving only the chief behind.

"Yes, Shilo Dawne?" he asked, trying to keep the irritation out of his voice. Even though he stopped, he didn't bother turning around to face her.

"I just wanted to thank you again for last night." She caught up with him easily enough, dancing around to stand in front of him. "Thank you for taking me home."

"Just doing my job."

"It feels like you're my own knight in shining armor," she gushed, hugging her arms around her. She no doubt knew that the pose was good for displaying the cleavage above her low-cut neckline. "First, that little fender-bender in town last week. Then rescuing me last night when my car stalled." She smiled, pretending to shiver from the wind, all the while knowing it made her clinging sweater dance with the motion. "Now today, saving me from a gas leak."

"It was hardly a fender-bender, Shilo Dawne. A brushed bumper, at best. And we didn't save you from a gas leak. Nothing registered on our meter."

"But every time I call, you come." She put her hand on his arm again. "I just want you to know how much I appreciate it."

"I'm the fire chief. Like I said, it's my job. I do the same for everyone who calls."

She looked up at him through lowered lashes. "Still, it's nice to know you still care." She twisted her arms in front of her, shifting so that her cleavage was better displayed, should he look.

He didn't. Cutter moved to go around her as he took off his helmet and shook his hair free.

"You're leaving, just like that?" she pouted. "The least I can do is offer you a cup of coffee. It's awfully cold out here, don't you think?"

She probably shivered again for effect, but he didn't look her way. "That's okay. Genny always has a cup waiting for me when I get home."

"I guess it's the grandmotherly instinct coming out in her."

Cutter recognized the jab for what it was. Genny was eight years his senior, and Shilo Dawne was trying to make her sound old.

"Genny and I hope it's at least twenty years or so before we're grandparents," Cutter replied smoothly, forcing himself to laugh off the insult. He kept walking until he reached the engine. "Have a good New Year."

"Oh, I'm sure I'll be seeing you before then," the dark-haired beauty said with confidence.

Cutter crawled up into the driver's seat, unconcerned if she heard his muttered, "Not if I'm lucky, you won't."

Hoping he might look back in his rearview mirror, Shilo Dawne put an extra swing in her hips as she returned to the café. She failed to notice the silver Audi that had just pulled up.

"Shilo Dawne! What was that fire truck doing

here?" Anastasia demanded. "Is everything all right?"

"Everything's fine, just fine." She waved her hand as if not to worry, but her boss still looked concerned. "We thought we smelled gas, so I called the fire department," she explained. "Just to be safe, of course." She offered her best smile. "They gave us the all clear."

Her boss looked first at her and then at the truck fading in the distance. Looking back at the younger woman, she said, "I'd like to see you in my office."

Shilo Dawne told herself there was nothing to worry about, but she couldn't help but feel like a child being called into the principal's office. Anastasia had a disconcerting way about her, noticing every little detail of those around her with her all-seeing pale green eyes. It was downright spooky, the way she could see in her peripheral vision. *Like a fly,* Shilo Dawne thought. She had probably seen enough of her conversation with Cutter to know Shilo Dawne was still hopelessly in love with the man.

She followed behind her boss dutifully, ignoring the curious eyes of the two employees still there.

The kitchen was clean, and everything done, but she couldn't resist making a show of generosity. "You two go on. I know you've had quite a scare. I'll close up here." As an afterthought, she added, "And good job today, especially on the quick evacuation."

Luckily, Anastasia was well in front and didn't see the confused expressions on the faces of her other two employees. There had hardly been a scare and not much of an evacuation, either. Shilo Dawne insisted she smelled gas and called the fire department. Unconcerned, the others had continued cleaning up. When the firefighters suggested they step outside, they had done so in conjunction with their last duty of the day, which was taking out the garbage.

Shilo Dawne wasn't about to tell her boss as much.

Leading the way into the office, Anastasia closed the door and motioned for her manager to take a seat. "The gas leak was a false alarm?" she asked, taking her own place behind the desk.

"Thankfully, yes. Mario thought he smelled gas, and I had a bit of a headache, so I thought it best to have things checked out." The lie fell easily from her lips.

"Hmm. Didn't something similar happen last month? Although, if I remember correctly, that time you thought you smelled smoke."

"Uhm, it seems like maybe I did. I really don't recall."

Anastasia solemnly regarded the younger woman. "Shilo Dawne, this has to stop."

"I'm— not sure I know what you're referring to."

"Yes, you do. You're inventing excuses for that good-looking firefighter to come here. But in doing so, you're sending an unspoken and unnecessary signal to our customers. You're suggesting our premises are not safe. This has to end. Now."

"I only want to make certain our building and our customers are completely safe," Shilo Dawne protested.

"I had the building thoroughly checked out before I began remodeling. I am no novice as a businesswoman. I would never throw money into a project that was unsafe."

"Of—Of course not."

"Shilo Dawne, you are a very creative and talented young woman. I don't blame you for being attracted to Mr. Montgomery. I'd dare say we all are. But creating these flimsy excuses to see him are not working, particularly when they put a mar on my café's reputation. I won't allow it. Do I make myself clear?"

The brunette nodded, but the only thing she truly

heard was that her boss was attracted to Cutter, too.

"Good. I have no doubt you can think of many ways to draw the man's attention but making *Fresh Starts* a target is not one of them."

"Yes, ma'am."

"Very well. Lock up, and I'll see you in the morning."

Shilo Dawne didn't appreciate the way her boss simply dismissed her, but she did as requested.

She stewed all the way out to her car. The one she pretended had stalled on the other side of the downed tree last night.

If Anastasia Rowland thought she was going to make a play for Cutter Montgomery on her own behalf, she had better think again.

*Has she forgotten I do her books?* Shilo Dawne sulked. *She said it herself. I'm very talented, and I've already found a few questionable entries. I'm not sure what she and Doyle Nieto are up to, but I'm not certain it's legal. The same can be said for her and Kelvin Quagmire. I haven't decided if they're lovers only, business partners only, or a little of both. But there's something between them, that's for sure.*

Starting the engine, Shilo Dawne contemplated further. A cunning smile crossed her face. *Anastasia also pointed out how creative I am. If she messes with my man—and yes, Cutter Montgomery is my man, whether he knows it yet or not— I may have to make a few* creative *adjustments to the books. Anastasia Rowland does not want to mess with me. Not when it comes to my job, and not when it comes to the man I've loved my entire life.*

# 4

Bertha Cessna, best known as Granny Bert to the entire community, spoke around the straight pins she held in her mouth.

"Be still," she chided, "or one of us is going to be bleeding before this is over."

"I still don't know how you talked me into this," the man before her complained. "What's wrong with wearing starched jeans, leather vest, and a monogrammed shirt to the party? I always wear jeans and vest to a dress-up party."

"This is a masquerade ball," she reminded him for the third time. "If you wear a monogrammed shirt with the initials 'SP' and a pair of boots with your signature on them, everyone is going to know it's you. Now hush up and turn around."

Sticker Pierce growled out his complaint. "There's a half million people who wear boots with my signature on them. I own a western wear company, remember? My boots are our number-one seller."

"So let someone else go in disguise as the almighty rodeo king Sticker Pierce," Granny Bert grumbled, unimpressed. "You're going as an English dandy, and that's that. If you'll be still for just two minutes—two minutes is all I ask! — we'll be done here."

"I still can't believe you're making me wear velvet," the crotchety old cowboy complained. "If anyone from the rodeo circuit sees me, I'll be a laughingstock."

"Is that supposed to be a pun?" she asked. "You raise the best rodeo stock in the business, and here you are complaining about being part of it."

"My stock breeds fear in their competitors, not laughter."

"You're just full of puns tonight, aren't you? Stock. Breed. Fine, then. Wear one of your championship belt buckles and just go as yourself. The handlebar mustache will give you away, anyhow." She threw her hands up in the air and huffed with exasperation.

"Come on, Belle. Don't be that way. I'll be quiet and get gussied up as a dandy if that's what you want." He tried to capture her in an embrace, but she twisted away. "As long as I have the prettiest girl in town by my side, I don't care what I wear."

"It's been a long time since I was a girl, you old coot. And flattery won't do you any good. If you want to go as your ornery old self, then go that way."

"Belle—"

"My name is Bertha," she reminded him.

"You'll always be my Belle," he told her with his still-charming smile. "Come on, sweetie, what do you say we bring the New Year in right? Marry me."

"That ship sailed a long time ago, Sticker Pierce, and you know it. We're too old to get married."

"No one's ever too old to get married," he argued.

"Or too young, from the looks of some of your wives," she snorted.

"I told you, Belle, none of them ever held a candle to you. You'll always be my first love."

She allowed him to capture her in his arms and snuggle in for a kiss. "That may be," she said, softening just a bit. "And you may have been mine. But Joe was my last love, and I won't sully his memory by helping you break the legal limit on how many wives a man can collect." She swatted him away. "Now. Are we going as a matched set, or will I make a solo appearance to this shindig?"

The former rodeo champ sighed. "When you put it that way..."

He stood still while she measured, tucked, and pinned. He decided having her arms around him was worth wearing a velvet vest, even if his old rodeo buddies laughed at him.

"There!" she proclaimed after another tuck or two. "All done. Now you can take me out for dinner. The girls will meet us there."

"By girls, I don't suppose you mean my two little precious great-granddaughters?"

"Not Hope and Faith, and you know it. I mean Sybil and Wanda." She gave him a challenging look. "Why? You have something against my oldest and dearest friends?"

"No, not as long as Wanda doesn't get too tipsy. The woman doesn't know how to hold her alcohol," he groused.

"Or her medicinal weed, but that's a story for another day."

"One I probably don't want to hear," the cowboy said, helping her into her coat. "I assume we're going to *Montelongo's*?"

"Of course. It's half-price margarita night."

A plate of enchiladas and two margaritas later, Wanda Shanks was definitely tipsy.

With most of the conversation centered around the

upcoming ball—all three women were founding members of the newly formed Troupe Over the Hill—Wanda made a sudden announcement. "Our last acting gig was so much fun, I'm writing a play about it."

"That wasn't exactly an acting gig," Sybil reminded her. "We were helping Madison with a case."

"We wore sheets and pretended to be ghosts. That's close enough to acting for me!"

Wanda held her glass up in a toast and tried taking another swig. Finding it empty, she stared into the salt-rimmed goblet with a frown. She tried another sip, but only a drip trickled out. A second examination didn't help. Her eyes weren't communicating with her mind.

Soon enough, she was distracted by another thought. "Say. Did we ever get paid for that gig?"

Granny Bert answered from across the table. "We got a free week's vacation out of it, we helped Maddy get to the bottom of a so-called curse, and we helped put criminals behind bars. That was payment enough."

"Oh. Right." With a sudden smile, the eighty-something-year-old remembered, "And I scored some Mexican vanilla. Don't forget that part."

Sybil patted her friend's hand in pacification. "Yes, Wanda, you got your vanilla."

"Mexican vanilla makes me happy," she babbled, her puffy face set with a goofy smile. "These margaritas make me happy, too."

"Oh, brother," Granny Bert muttered. "She's definitely had enough alcohol for one night."

The smile disappeared, replaced by a frown. "You know what *doesn't* make me happy?" Wanda whined. She waved a finger toward one of the booths against the wall. "That woman right there."

Since Wanda couldn't see that her glass was empty, Sybil doubted she could see across the room, but she asked just to be polite. "Who is it?"

"Genny's arch enemy, that's who!" she said in a loud voice. The outburst drew curious stares from nearby diners.

"Who are you talking about?" Granny Bert frowned.

Wanda blinked to clear her vision. The third time her eyes closed, they were slow to open again. The tequila was definitely taking effect. "Yep. That's her, all right. The woman trying to put our sweet little Genny out of business."

Her companions turned to see Anastasia at a nearby booth, deep in conversation with the man across from her.

"Who's that fella with her?" Sticker asked.

"Her business partner," Granny Bert supplied. "I think his name is Nieto."

"Nieto." Wanda tried the name out on her lips. "Nieto, Nieto, Nieto. That's neat-O." She giggled at her own joke. "Get it? Neat-O?"

"We get that you need to go home and sleep off your margaritas," Granny Bert grumbled.

Wanda ignored the suggestion and continued, "I don't think Miss Fancy Britches thinks he's so Neat-O. She looks mad."

"She does sort of looked peeved," Granny Bert agreed. "Maybe things aren't as rosy at *Fresh Starts* as they want everyone to believe."

"They sell *roses* there?" her tipsy friend asked in amazement. "I thought they sold breakfast! I thought she was trying to ruin Genny's business." Her face crumpled with despair. "I should go over and apologize. 'Tis the season to forgive, you know. Sybil, help me up."

"I'll help you up, all right," Sybil agreed. "Up and out to the car. It's time we get you home, Wanda."

"I'll help," Sticker offered, already pushing back his chair. "Belle, you finish eating. I'll be right back."

Granny Bert watched her friends half-pull, half-push a very tipsy Wanda Shanks toward the door. They steered her the long way around, careful to avoid the booth where Anastasia and her companion were still in a heated discussion.

"I swear, I can't take that woman anywhere!" Granny Bert grumbled aloud.

She abandoned her unfinished meal to study the couple in the booth. Granny Bert didn't do subtle. She openly stared at them hoping, trying to listen in on the conversation. When she only caught bits and pieces, she resorted to reading lips and body language.

For once, Wanda was right. The business owner was clearly unhappy with something her partner had said or done. She caught words like 'idiot' and 'scheme.' It was easy to see the way she ground out the words. Don't. Push. Me.

Was that Nieto man threatening her? Or was it the other way around?

Before Granny Bert could hear more, the man threw his napkin on the table and stormed from the room.

"Just when it was getting interesting, too," she mused aloud. "And look at Ms. Rowland over there. Cool as a cucumber, acting like half the restaurant isn't staring at her."

"Belle?" Sticker returned in time to hear his date speaking aloud. "Are you talking to someone?"

"Myself," she confirmed. "I like talking to a smart woman, and I like hearing a smart woman talk."

Amused by her answer, he asked, "Having a good conversation?"

"Fair. We were discussing what happened over at that table. Mr. *Neat-O* stormed out, and Ms. Poised and Polished looks like nothing even happened."

Cutter's grandfather took his seat at the table. "You should have seen him outside. He burst through the doors like a bull out of the riding chute."

Granny Bert nodded her gray head. "He did look mighty upset."

She gathered her coat and purse, but Sticker didn't notice.

"What's eating at you?" Granny Bert asked.

"Who said something was eating at me?"

"You're twirling the ends of your handlebar mustache. You do that when you're deep in thought."

"I reckon so," he admitted. "Truth told, something odd did happen outside. You know that man who's giving Cutter and Genny so much grief? The one threatening to sue them?"

"Lawrence Norris." She spat the name.

"Him. He was outside, apparently waiting for Nieto to come out. They had a few heated words, Nieto pushed Norris away, and they both stormed off in opposite directions."

"That is odd," Granny Bert agreed. "You think they know each other?"

"It sure looked like it."

They both turned to look at Anastasia Rowland. Unaware of their scrutiny, the woman daintily dabbed at her mouth and stood in one smooth, graceful movement.

"I don't know what's going on around here," Granny Bert said, "but I don't like it."

When the Big House was built in 1918, the entire third floor was designed to be a ballroom. The masterfully crafted wood floor, polished and glossed to perfection, covered the huge, open space. It represented the height of elegance and confirmed Juliet Randolph Blakely's prominence in the community. Tucked into the two corner turrets at the front of the mansion, tastefully decorated sitting areas flanked either side of the grand ballroom.

Fast forward to the twenty-first century. A formal ballroom was a bit over the top for Madison's tastes, even for a stately old mansion that dominated an entire city block. When the *Home Again* crew remodeled the house for a reality television show, they kept the hardwood floors intact but gave the space a more functional use. The ballroom became a game room, and one of the turrets transformed into Bethani's bedroom. When Madison married Brash, the other turret became Megan's room.

For the masquerade ball, the clock turned back in time. The game room was cleared, and the space looked, once again, like the grand ballroom it was meant to be. Strings of twinkling lights crisscrossed the vaulted ceiling and framed the many windows in the space.

"See, Mom?" Blake said, standing back to inspect their handiwork. "I told you it would all come together."

"It does look great," Madison agreed.

"And you gotta admit, the club came through and did their part."

"I agree the drama club did a good job up here, but this is far from doing your 'part,'" his mother corrected. "If you remember, when you talked us into this whole scheme, you promised you had it all covered."

"We do, we do," the blond teen assured her. He draped an arm across her shoulders and flashed his best smile. "When have I ever let you down? You know you can always count on your number one son."

"You're my only son," Madison said, poking him in the side. Being his most ticklish spot, she knew it would make him squeal like a girl. "And there's still a long list of things for you and your friends to do. When you're done up here, you can start moving furniture out of the formal parlor."

"That's where you old folks are dancing, right?" he teased. "Two flights of stairs can be hard on the joints. I figure we'll get this floor, and y'all will get the ground floor."

"Watch it, buster. It's not too late for me to nix this whole thing, you know," she threatened in jest. "And don't think for one minute that you kids will have this ballroom to yourselves. Not only will there be chaperones up here, but most of the ticketholders are looking forward to seeing the grand ballroom back in use. And," she said with another pointed jab of her finger, "for the record, your father's knee may pop once in a while, but it's more from playing professional football than from age."

Even though Brash wasn't the twins' biological parent, he and Blake shared a strong father and son bond. The teen referred to his stepdad as Daddy D, but in the ways that mattered most, Brash was his father. It didn't mean Blake had forgotten his late father, but long before Grayson Reynold's death, the two had grown apart. He and Brash had things in common that he and his real dad never shared.

Bethani had been slower in accepting her mother's love for another man. As a typical 'daddy's girl,' it somehow felt like a betrayal. The teen grudgingly realized how happy her mother was with Brash in her life, and even Bethani had to admit he was a pretty great guy. Now, less than two years later, they were truly a family.

"Just kidding you, Mom," Blake assured her. "But seriously, if you need help with your wheelchairs, I'm here for you." Before she could jab him again, he ducked away with a merry laugh.

As the lanky teen bent to pick up boxes from the floor, he assured her, "Besides, we've got the most important thing covered."

"And what would that be? Decorating? Parking? The music? Making certain there's enough seating for people when they're tired of dancing?" Madison listed only some of the things demanding attention.

"Nah. I mean the *most* important thing. The food!"

Bethani had just topped the stairs and heard her twin's declaration. "Leave it to the Bottomless Pit to think food is the most crucial part of the evening," she smirked.

"You're right. Something to drink is important, too," Blake agreed. He did a quick dance step, ending with a fancy twirl. "A guy can work up quite a thirst with moves like that."

His sister couldn't resist goading him. "He can also work up quite a few laughs. Is that all you got, bro?"

"Hardly. I've been polishing up on my dancing skills. That, dear sister, is only a small sample of what you'll see on New Year's Eve."

Bethani rolled her baby blue eyes. "All I can say is... keep polishing!"

Madison interrupted their banter to ask her daughter, "How was work, sweetie?"

"Long." Over the Christmas break, Bethani was putting in extra hours at *New Beginnings*. "The drama club may say they've got the refreshments covered, but they're just being *dramatic*." She threw her brother a disgruntled look. "What they didn't pay to cater from *New Beginnings*, Aunt Genny threw in for free. So, guess who has to do most of the prep work and early baking?" She tapped her own chest.

"Hey, why are you complaining?" Blake asked. "You're getting paid, aren't you?"

"Yes, but it has to be done in between customers.

And guess who I had the pleasure of waiting on today? And by pleasure, I mean absolute torture."

"The only person I know who invokes such scorn is Myrna Lewis," Madison guessed, "but I thought she was boycotting the café?"

"Unfortunately, that's only at breakfast and lunch. Since her beloved *Fresh Starts* is closed in the evenings, she ventured into enemy territory tonight."

"I suppose she was her usual charming self," her mother stated wryly.

"You know it. She complained about everything. And, if that wasn't enough, guess who else came in?"

"Miley Redmond?" Madison guessed. She was Bethani's nemesis, the same way her evil father Barry was Madison's.

"I think she's away for the holidays, thank goodness. No, I meant that Norris guy. Not Chuck. The mean one."

"Lawrence," Madison said. The name left a bad taste in her mouth.

"He didn't even ask if Aunt Genny was around. He marched back to her office and banged on the door. When he found it locked, he stormed back down the hall. I had a tray of coffee and Gennydoodle cookies in my hand, and he almost made me drop it. Some of the coffee splashed on him—like one tiny drop!— and he went ballistic. He said it gave him all the more reason to sue. And, naturally, that big 'ole toad Myrna Lewis heard it all and egged him on."

"I'm sorry, honey," Madison said, tucking a strand of her daughter's long, blond hair back into its ponytail. "Sounds like it wasn't a very good night."

"Hardly. But at least toad lady left me a tip. A whole whopping quarter." Bethani pulled the coin from the pocket of her jeans. "Luckily, she was with her husband who is a good and decent person and the complete opposite of her, so he left a ten." With an exaggerated sigh, she said, "I'll never understand what he sees in her."

"I think the same thing about your boyfriend," Blake said. "Trenton's a smart guy, so what's he see in you?"

"Hardy-har-har. You think you're so funny. Too bad it's only your looks that get the laughs." She pulled her hair free of its rubber band and shook it loose. "I'm headed to the shower. It's been a long day, and tomorrow promises to be the same. At least it's the last one. Maybe I can sleep in on New Year's Eve."

Madison looked skeptical. "I'm not so sure about that. There's still a lot to do for the ball."

"I'm not even in the drama club," she protested. "Why do I have to help?"

"Because you're part of the family, and that's what families do. We pitch in and help one another."

The teen rolled her eyes again, muttering as she marched off to her room, "I knew I should have been an only child!"

# 5

The last two days of December had long been heralded the busiest days of the year. It didn't help that New Year's Eve was often seen as a holiday. From a business standpoint, that meant one less day to run end-of-month and end-of-year reports, pay bills, take advantage of last-minute tax breaks, send correspondences, and to wrap up all loose ends for the year.

For Anastasia Rowland, the list seemed endless. She owned multiple businesses, so it multiplied the reports and the paperwork and the end of the year details. It was even more challenging this year, since she was spending most of her time in The Sisters. Until her newest store was properly up and running, the apartment above *Fresh Starts* made a cozy home away from home.

At least the commute, she liked to say, wasn't bad.

Being a city girl from Houston, it was difficult being stuck in a small town over the holidays. There was absolutely no *decent* form of entertainment here. No black-tie events or festive cocktail parties. No high-dollar charity galas designed specifically for those who had money to burn and the desire to burn it in public.

No concerts or theaters. Not decent ones.

There were events, of course. Local churches had potluck dinners and Christmas pageants. The elementary school presented their annual Christmas play. The Sisters High School held a holiday band concert. Various clubs and organizations had bake sales, bazaars, raffles, and their own versions of holiday parties.

Like a dutiful business owner, Anastasia made donations to every cause that came calling, but the only one that even remotely caught her interest was the upcoming masquerade ball. Held at the impressive mansion everyone in town called the Big House, it was certain to be the only event that promised a flair of refinement.

Anastasia wasn't a snob. She had worked hard to get where she was in life. Her appreciation for the finer things had been an acquired taste and heightened with each phase of her success.

As a smart businesswoman, she knew when to keep her opinions to herself. There were some things a successful entrepreneur never waded into: murky water, politics, religion, and the rituals of small-town Americana.

No matter how amateurish or unimaginative the event, Anastasia knew to smile, make a donation, show up in support of the community, and pretend to enjoy herself. She would have preferred the mandatory schmoozing be done at cocktail parties and high-end galas—even boardrooms were preferable to barns—but as the owner of a small eatery in a small town, she had to work with what she had.

Her financial adviser had questioned her sanity when she announced she was opening a location in The Sisters. Even between the two towns of Naomi and Juliet, the combined population barely topped two thousand residents. It didn't have the lure of the coast or the shores of a highly acclaimed lake. There was no state park, no fabled hiking trails, and no majestic mountains. No breathtaking fall foliage, even if springtime bluebonnets and wildflowers ran a close second in beauty. At first glance, there was nothing to draw tourists, aka customers, to the area or to a new eatery. Particularly an eatery that didn't serve the standard fare of chicken-fried steak, hamburgers, and barbecue.

But Anastasia had a knack for picking just the right location for one of her businesses, and she insisted that Naomi, Texas was the place.

Doyle Nieto had approached her with the idea over the summer. She and Doyle were co-owners of upscale restaurants in Houston's The Galleria and at The Woodlands Mall in The Woodlands. Both areas were highly trafficked, well-established, and often considered upper end. So, when he mentioned opening a bistro in a small town that she had never even heard of, Anastasia's first instinct was to laugh.

The clientele in Naomi was quite different, he quickly explained, but the area held promise. He then pulled up an impressive list of some of the community's best-known residents. The up-and-coming rock band known as Cowboy Candyband. World famous artist Jean Applegate. The late soap opera queen Caress Ellingsworth and her longtime partner, movie star John-Paul Noble. Rodeo legend Sticker Pierce. His son-in-law, Heisman trophy winner Tug Montgomery. Former pro-football player and college coach Brash deCordova, who now served as chief of police and who was married to Madison Reynolds, owner of *In a Pinch Temporary Service* and the former star of the HOME television network's mega hit, *Home Again*.

"I know you're familiar with the show," Doyle had

insisted. "A young widow with two teenage twins is left penniless and moves back home to live with her grandmother. The grandmother is like the town matriarch and inherited a huge old mansion from the town's founder. The old lady sells it to the granddaughter for a song and dance and then contacts the network to have it restored. The grandmother's a piece of work, herself. Eighty if she's a day, just stepped down from being the mayor, likes to sky dive and travel in her motor home and meddle in other people's business. A real firecracker. Anyway, she cons master carpenter Nick Vilardi into taking on the project. She even convinces him to do it all for free, getting sponsors to donate their products. Kiki Barretta decorated the whole place, if you can believe it."

"The interior decorator with her own show? The one who did Senator Abel's fabulous new home here in Houston?"

"That's the one. But the most impressive part of all this is the ratings the show garnered. Off-the-chart numbers for the network. Trending stories on every social media platform you can think of. Adoring fans all over the nation, glued to the screen for every episode. There were even buses with adoring fans pouring into town."

"Wait a minute," Anastasia had said. "I think I remember that. I didn't watch it until I heard all the chatter about it among my customers. It was like a home remodel/soap opera type of show, wasn't it?"

"I don't think it started that way, but it ended up like that. A lot of the show was filmed at *New Beginnings Bakery and Café*, a hot spot for locals. The owner was best friends with the homeowner, and so their stories overlapped."

Anastasia nodded. "I remember. The handsome chief of police, this Brash guy, was involved with the homeowner. And the hot firefighter had a thing for the café owner."

"Yes, that's right. The firefighter married the baker, and the chief of police married the homeowner. And then, at their wedding—"

"A guest fell over dead!" Anastasia recalled with a gasp. "And then there was that picture that circulated around of a shirtless, very muscled, very sexy bridegroom... *That*, I definitely remember!"

"The point is," Doyle Nieto had said, "this little out of the way town, smack-dab in the middle of ranching country and cotton fields, is filled with interesting people who, for whatever reason, manage to capture the fascination and devotion of the public. I don't have to tell you how rare—how powerful— that is. And I see no reason why we shouldn't get in on that fascination."

"But that show aired two or three years ago. Even the infamous wedding was... what? At least two years ago?"

"A year and half. But I have it on good authority that something big is about to happen in The Sisters. That's why I think we should seriously consider opening a restaurant there."

"You said it yourself. That *New Start Café—"*

*"New Beginnings,"* Doyle had corrected.

"Whatever. The café is the hot spot in town. It's already established and already a tried-and-true media sweetheart. What makes you think we could compete with that?" Anastasia had asked.

Doyle's eyes had glittered with a chilling light she could only describe as unadulterated greed.

"I have a plan," he told her.

Now, just a few months later, *Fresh Starts* was in business. Things were running smoothly, and the business was good, given the demographics. Yet they weren't great, and Anastasia strived for greatness. The 'something big' Doyle told her about hadn't happened yet. In fact, she had heard little about it. Her partner insisted it was in the works, but she remained skeptical.

For his part, Doyle seemed to be more vested in this café than he was in the others. He was more like a silent partner in their other ventures, but he had taken a particular interest in this new project of theirs. Several days a week, he either commuted back and forth to Houston, or he booked a room at the town's only bed and breakfast, *The Bumble Bee*.

Doyle didn't seem as anxious as Anastasia to achieve greatness. He urged her to be patient and give it time. Rome, he would tell her, wasn't built in a day. He knew she hated the phrase, yet it didn't stop him from saying it. Often. He always followed it by assuring her he was still working on his plan.

Part of having a successful partnership was learning to trust the other and believing that they shared the same desire to succeed and prosper. Anastasia called on that mantra now, convincing herself that Doyle had the bistro's best interest at heart. He apparently knew something she didn't—something 'big'— and she needed to be patient and wait for the pieces to fall into place.

Anastasia had never been good at waiting. Nor had she been good at puzzles. She liked her pieces nice and straight, so that she could align them or rearrange them as needed. She liked clean, simple, and straight.

Right now, their business was anything but.

Doyle had become a curve. She sensed he was veering away from their tried and-true business plan and headed off in an unknown direction. For now, she had to trust him, but it didn't mean she had to like it.

Shilo Dawne Nedbalek was an angle. She was an exceptional manager and accountant, plus she had experience in food service. Yet there was a sharp edge to the young woman. Anastasia couldn't help but feel the young woman had some sort of ulterior motive. Something around the corner that could take them all by surprise. A hostile takeover of this location wasn't out of the question, but Anastasia didn't think so. She hadn't pinpointed the problem yet, but Shilo Dawne was definitely working an angle.

Myrna Lewis was a circle, and Anastasia didn't mean her shapeless figure. The woman was nosy and obnoxious and extremely self-centered. Everything always came back to her. Myrna credited herself for bringing the business to town. She credited herself for allowing them to lease the building she owned. (At an inflated price.) She credited herself for their success and mistakenly took it to mean she had a stake in their business operations. Everything always came back to her. A circle.

Lawrence Norris was so crooked, he was like a great-big question mark. She had no idea how the man fit into the puzzle. She didn't even know who he was. He simply showed up in the parking lot one day, making vague threats to 'expose' her. Over the past few weeks, his threats had escalated. He claimed to know something that could ruin her and her business, though he was vague on the details. Knowing it could be a variety of things, she had reluctantly agreed to his demands.

And then there was Kelvin, the boomerang. She kept tossing her old lover aside, yet he kept coming back. They had gone into the relationship with an agreement to keep it casual and un-entangled. Their time together was pleasant but temporary. Anastasia had kept her end of the bargain. Kelvin, on the other hand, had fallen in love with her. He couldn't— wouldn't— accept that she didn't feel the same way. Like a boomerang, he returned to her side. He pledged his undying love and loyalty and begged for a chance to prove his devotion.

Anastasia didn't need curves. She didn't need angles. Question marks and circles were unacceptable. And boomerangs were an encumbrance she didn't need nor want. Her strict standards demanded neat, simple, and straight.

"I don't have time for this," Anastasia said aloud. Her voice held impatience. "I have reports to do, a business to run, and a party to attend. The rest will have to wait for the New Year."

# 6

On New Year's Eve, the old mansion on the corner of Second and Main glowed with thousands of twinkling white lights. Merry bulbs sparkled from every ridge, every eave, every balcony, and every turret. The draperies were pulled aside in most of the front rooms, showcasing each room as they glowed from within. The elaborate chandeliers sparkled like diamonds and danced in reflection off the gold and silver decorations.

The masquerade ball was originally set for a much smaller venue. When those plans fell through, Blake sweet-talked his parents into offering the Big House as an alternative. The upside was that it doubled the number of tickets sold and made the event that much more profitable.

The downside was that people kept pouring into the old mansion. Tickets were inspected and surrounded at the door, yet looking at the crowd, Madison would swear there were more people here than anticipated. But it was for a good cause, she reminded herself. The ball would fund the club's dream trip to attend a Broadway play.

Plus, she had to admit it was fun seeing all the fancy

dresses and snappy suits the people wore, not to mention their creative masks. Sequins and glitter sparkled under the lights. Due to the cost of tickets, not as many teenagers attended as did the older generation. For many of them, it was the opportunity to see the Big House in all its grandeur again and to attend one last ball there. In years past, Juliet Blakely and her parties at the mansion were legendary.

Brash came up to his wife and murmured in her ear, "It looks like everyone is having a good time."

"Definitely!" Madison agreed.

"Here, I brought you some punch."

"Thank you, kind sir."

"Anything for my beautiful date. If I haven't already said it, you look amazing in that dress."

She reached up to kiss his cheek. "You may have mentioned it a time or two."

"Bears repeating. You look ravishing."

"Ravishing, is it?" There was a twinkle in her eyes.

"Ravishing," he said with heated promise, his hand possessive upon her waist.

"You look rather dashing yourself. Think anyone would notice if we disappeared for a little while?"

"Don't tempt me, woman."

"Maybe they won't know who we are. We are in costume, after all."

"This monkey suit definitely *feels* like a costume," Brash agreed, adjusting the red satin vest beneath his tuxedo. "Remind me why I'm dressed like this?"

"Because this is a masquerade party, and it's the exact opposite of the jeans and starched shirt you normally wear, even when you're on duty. Plus, the red matches my dress."

"And this ridiculous red and gold mask?"

"It accents the red vest and the gold tie. It makes you look dapper."

He was clearly amused. “Dapper? I don’t think anyone has ever referred to me as dapper before.”

“Maybe you never wore a dapper outfit like this before,” she quipped.

“Well, you’re right about that,” Brash agreed with a chuckle. “You know who else looks *dapper* and completely out of his element?”

He nodded, and Madison followed his line of sight. “You’re right. I doubt Sticker Pierce has *ever* worn a velvet vest and silk cravat before! If it weren’t for the handlebars, I might not recognize him.”

“Your grandmother even got him to wear a top hat.”

“The things we do for love…” she mused.

She watched the elder couple as they danced. Granny Bert wore an elaborate gown of gold brocade. Madison had never seen the dress before, but something about it looked familiar. In deference to her height over that of her dancing partner, her grandmother wore slippers on her feet. Her hair, enhanced by a wig, was piled gracefully upon her head. A dramatic, sequined mask of gold added the finishing touch.

“They both look amazing,” Madison agreed.

“I see a lot of great costumes. Did you see Vina? In all the years she’s been our dispatcher and clerk at the department, I’ve never seen her dressed up like this. She’s always been secretive about her age, but now I’m thinking she may be younger than we all thought.”

Madison laughed. “Makeup and the right clothes can do wonders!” she assured him. Her laugh mellowed to a smirk. “And of course, I’m sure you noticed your officer’s costume.”

“Otis? He’s on duty tonight. So is Schimanski.”

“I’m referring to Misty Abraham, as if you didn’t know.”

“Hmm. Was she wearing a green dress?”

"She's wearing a stunning blue dress, and you know it!"

"Oh, was that her?" Brash asked innocently.

Long before Madison came back to town, Brash and Misty had dated. When the voluptuous blonde was hired into The Sisters police department almost two years ago, Madison couldn't help but feel a small twinge of jealousy.

In a wry tone, Madison said, "Your eyes may not have made it past her daringly low neckline."

"Oh, you mean the woman with the feathered mask."

"You noticed the feathers, did you?" she teased, not fooled by his innocuous expression.

"They were a little hard to miss. And, yes, I'm referring to the feathers, not the... other."

"Nice save, Mr. deCordova," she chuckled.

"What about that woman there in the red dress? I can't decide who that is."

"I see a dozen red dresses."

Brash discreetly motioned to one of the swirling couples. "She's dancing with the man wearing a full Batman mask. Can't tell who he is, either."

"I think that may be Anastasia Rowland. I have no clue who the man is."

"What about the guy over there by the window? The one in the full mask? He doesn't seem to be interacting with anyone."

Madison glanced at her husband. "You think he's up to something?"

"I never said that."

"You don't have to. I know that tone."

"I just don't recognize him is all. I haven't seen him talking or dancing with anyone, and his build is unfamiliar, so it's hard to place who he is."

"It could be anyone," she pointed out. "Someone

from Riverton, since that was the original venue location. Or it could be a relative visiting for the holidays."

"Maybe," he murmured. "You haven't unlocked any doors, have you? I double-checked all the bedroom doors, especially those to our suite and your office."

Madison gave her husband a sharp look. "Are you saying you think he's up to no good?"

"I'm saying this is our home, and we've already had one leftover guest after a party."

Madison shivered with the memory. "Kalypso."

"I don't want a repeat performance. That one was much too close for comfort."

"Maybe we should keep an eye on that man," Madison worried. "You know I've been apprehensive about this whole thing. Maybe he's the reason."

"I think it has more to do with the colossal effort it took to pull this off, no matter if the drama club and Troupe Over the Hill did pitch in."

"Or," she countered, "with the fact that our track record for hosting big events hasn't gone too well. First an international spy trying to kill me after Genny's wedding reception, then Nigel being poisoned at ours."

Beneath his mask, Brash flashed a smile. "Look on the bright side. This isn't a wedding reception."

"Still, I think you should keep an eye on that man."

"Don't worry, sweetheart, I am. There's a couple of others I have my eye on, too. Call it an occupational hazard, but I'm not comfortable when I see a person wearing a mask other than for health purposes."

"I agree. But there's one person wearing a mask that you don't have to worry about. King Arthur in full garb, a mask, and a crown. Lots of shimmer and shine, and maybe a touch of glitter."

Brash hadn't seen her assistant yet, but he identified him simply from her description. "Derron."

"You know it." Madison chuckled. "He lives for the opportunity to dress up."

Spotting him now, Brash said, "I'm surprised to see who his date is tonight."

"I think it's sweet. Not many younger men would bring their eighty-something-year-old housemate to a New Year's Eve party."

"Just promise me you won't let Miss Wanda get a hold of any alcoholic beverages tonight."

"I'm more worried about the teenagers getting a hold of it," she admitted. "You know kids."

"I also know Wanda Shanks. As much as I like the old dear, she can be a handful, even sober."

Madison's eyes found the woman in question. She had squeezed her generous body into a very tight gown made of green velvet. It, too, looked vaguely familiar, but Madison knew she had never seen her or her grandmother in those dresses before. At the risk of popping the seams from her fancy gown, Miss Wanda was doing a lively dance with the young man who rented her spare bedroom.

"What do you say we join the party and dance, Mrs. D?" Brash suggested, presenting his palm.

"I think that's a wonderful idea, Mr. D."

After two dances, Madison needed a breather. She saw her grandmother sitting on a settee against the wall and went to join her.

"Where's your handsome date?" Madison asked.

"Out there dancing with someone. Probably Jolene Kopetsky, but at this point, my feet hurt so bad, I don't even care," the older woman admitted. "I forgot that I can't wear flats."

"No matter, you look lovely tonight."

"Thank you, Maddy. You do, too."

"I can't believe you coerced Sticker into wearing that suit! He looks quite dashing, I must say."

"He does clean up good for an old man," Granny Bert agreed, her eyes finding her date on the dance floor. They lingered with appreciation for a moment before she turned her gaze back to her granddaughter. "I'd say this shindig is a rousing success, wouldn't you? I had no idea so many people would turn out."

"I didn't, either, or I wouldn't have agreed to host it," Madison mumbled.

"It's as crowded as an angry ant hill in here. People moving around every which way."

"There're several people I don't recognize. It feels a little weird, having complete strangers in your house."

"Who's the man in the phantom of the opera get-up?"

"No clue. Or that man there in the full venetian mask. He looks a little suspicious, don't you think, just standing there on the sidelines?"

"Well, then, maybe you should ask him to dance."

"Why? I just said he looks suspicious."

"All the more reason to dance with him and find out who he is."

"That's more your department than mine. We both know you can con a drowning man into buying water from you."

Her grandmother was pleased with the comment. "Why, thank you, dear." She picked at the folds of her dress, pretending to be modest.

"By the way, I know I've never seen you in that dress before, but the fabric looks so familiar."

"This old thing? Why, it's been hanging at the house for years!" Behind her mask, Granny Bert's eyes glittered with amusement. "Of course, it was hanging over my windows," she admitted. At her granddaughter's quizzical look, she explained. "I took a cue from Scarlett O'Hara in *Gone With the Wind* and made use of my draperies."

Madison laughed at her grandmother's ingenuity. "*That's* where I've seen this material before! It used to be one of your living room curtains!"

"The things were outdated, anyway," Granny Bert said. "I bought some light, airy ones. Wanda did the same thing."

"I love it!" Madison said, clapping her hands together in glee. "I thought her green dress looked familiar, too."

"What's a couple of women our age need with a ball gown we'll never wear again, anyway? No one wears a fancy dress down at the VFW Hall."

"That's very creative of you."

"Thank you. And now, if my feet can take it, I think I'll do a little creative snooping with that masked man over yonder."

"Granny..."

"You can thank me later," the older woman said with a saucy grin.

Pulling to her feet, Granny Bert revealed a slight wince before she straightened and made her way into the formal living room. She avoided bumping into dancers as she pushed through the crowd.

"Hello, there," she said to the masked man. Her tone was friendly and upbeat, but she allowed a slight quiver to creep into her voice as she said, "I don't suppose you'd do an old woman a favor and have a twirl out on the dance floor." She put a hand to her chest, sounding sad and just a bit breathless. "Everyone else has a partner, but my husband passed years ago. It looks like you and I are both alone tonight, and this will probably be the last ball I ever attend. The doctors said... Well, never mind what they said. Tonight's about celebrating, and I'd like to celebrate with a dance."

The man stiffened, his eyes looking startled. After a moment's hesitation, he nodded and offered his hand.

At first, Granny Bert thought she wouldn't learn anything by dancing with him. She dangled several leads, but he wouldn't take the bait.

"Oh, my, you're a lovely dancer!" Granny Bert gushed. "Where did you learn to waltz?"

"Lessons," he said simply. So far, all of his answers had been short, one-word replies.

"Where are my manners? I didn't introduce myself. My name is Belle." She smiled as she gave him her alias. "And you?"

"This is a masquerade ball, is it not?" he said. "I thought our identities were meant to be kept secret."

"I suppose so. I just love secrets, don't you?"

"They have their merits," the man agreed.

"I'm having the best time, trying to decipher who's who. Even with their masks on, I can still tell who some people are. For instance, see that man over there in the overalls and nice jacket? He's wearing a mask over his eyes, but I know who he is because he always wears overalls. The jacket and mask don't do much to hide his identity." She didn't mention that he was her brother Jubal. "But I can't quite figure you out. Now, don't help me. Let me figure it out on my own."

His eyes looked amused.

"Do you live here in The Sisters?" Granny Bert asked.

"No."

"Do you *work* here in The Sisters?"

His hesitation was brief. "Not as my full-time job."

"Ah, a working man. I like that," she said with approval. "Does your wife work, too? It seems to take two incomes these days."

"Not for me. No wife."

Keeping the conversation going, Granny Bert continued, "Tell me, how did you hear about tonight's ball?"

The man shrugged. “Word of mouth. And I saw a poster in town.”

“You’ve been here a few days, then.”

“Why would you say that?”

“The event sold out almost two weeks ago.”

Her dancing partner’s face may have been covered by a mask, but Granny Bert saw the way his eyes followed Misty Abraham as they glided past her.

“Lovely woman,” Granny Bert said. “And such a beautiful gown.”

“Yes, it is.”

“Looking at her, you’d never believe she was a police officer, would you?” she added slyly.

She felt her partner stiffen. He jerked his eyes away from the buxom blonde as if looking at her would burn his corneas.

Too soon, the song came to an end. The man thanked Granny Bert for the dance and wished her a Happy New Year. Before she could press for another dance, he disappeared into the crowd.

A large decanter of water lured Granny Bert to the nearby refreshment table. She was on her second cup when Madison approached.

“Uh-oh. You’re frowning. It was a bust, huh?” her granddaughter asked sympathetically.

“Not completely,” Granny Bert countered. “I found out he’s a man of few words, and he has something to hide.”

“How do you know that?”

Her grandmother relayed much of the conversation, but Madison was unconvinced. “How does that add up to he’s hiding something? A lot of people don’t like small talk.”

“He’s not staying at the only hotel in town, he’s allergic to bees, he doesn’t have family in the area, and he’s doing some sort of work as a sideline.”

Madison frowned. “I thought you said he was a man of few words.”

“You gotta read between the lines, girl.” She shrugged before offering an explanation. “He said he heard about the ball from a poster. If his family told him, he would have said so. We’ve been out of tickets for a while now, so he’s probably been in town for a couple of weeks. He’s not staying at the local bed and breakfast, though. When I mentioned the Bumble Bee, he looked around like we were being swarmed. He had no idea it was a place to stay, and there was raw panic in his eyes.”

Madison bobbled her head with each answer, trying to follow her grandmother’s logic. As loath as she was to admit it, it made sense. “If you deciphered all of that during a brief dance, do you know what it is he’s hiding?”

“Now, *that’s* something I don’t know,” Granny Bert admitted.

“How can you be sure he is, then? His mask is a little freaky, but it doesn’t mean he’s hiding anything.”

“True. But when I told him that the hot blonde in the blue dress was a cop, he tensed up like a long-tailed cat in a room full of rocking chairs. The minute the song ended, he shot off like a bottle rocket.” Granny Bert drained the water from her glass. “Not sure what it is, but the man is definitely hiding something.”

# 7

The party was well underway, and spirits were high. At eleven o'clock on the dot, those who signed up for the contest had removed their masks and were judged for best disguises. Granny Bert and Sticker had won a prize for their portrayal of a proper English lady and her dandy, and Derron had won for having the most extravagant disguise. There were a few more winners yet to be announced, and then the big countdown would begin. Out with the old year, and in with the new.

"I can't believe so many people showed up," Cutter told Genny as they stood in an out-of-the way alcove, enjoying a moment of peace.

"I know. It was a sellout, but usually some of the ticketholders don't show up. I think every single person showed up with a date and possibly smuggled in an extra or two."

"I don't know about that," her husband countered. "Faculty members were in charge of the doors, just in case the kids wanted to slip their friends in."

"Either way, it's been a big success."

"You know, at first, I thought you were being a little over the top wanting to hire a sitter to stay in the room with the girls. But with so many people milling about, I'm glad we did."

"Even though we're in the house, the girls are tucked away in the back bedroom suite. Anyone could go in there."

"I get it, babe. Good call."

Genny gazed out at the crowd. With the music temporarily halted, people were visiting in small clusters, enjoying refreshments, or stepping out onto the porches and balconies for a breath of fresh air.

"There's so many people I don't recognize. I don't know whether it's the masks or the fact that some of the guests are from out of town, but it makes me doubly glad we hired a sitter," she said.

"Did you notice how a few people didn't take off their disguise, even when it was time to reveal their identity?"

Genny bit her lip. "Makes you kinda nervous, doesn't it?" she murmured.

Cutter ran a hand along her arm. "Are you still worried something bad is going to happen?"

"The night's not over yet."

"The worst thing to happen so far is that the appetizers are going fast. The trays are almost empty."

"I know," Genny murmured, casting a worried look toward the refreshment table. "I'm thinking about going to the kitchen and seeing what I can throw together."

"I think you've done enough, Genny darlin'. They can resort to chips and dips once the rest is gone. I *know* Blake has a good store of those."

Genny chuckled affectionately. "That boy," she said with a shake of her head. Blake was known for his insatiable appetite.

He nodded to one particular woman filling her plate. "I did notice that Anastasia Rowland has returned to the table several times. Obviously, she's a fan of your food."

"That, or she's trying to steal my recipes."

"Genny, I thought you were determined to turn over a new leaf in the New Year. You said you wanted to be more charitable toward your competition."

"I do," she said sincerely. Then her dimples appeared as she made an impish admission, "But there's still forty-five minutes left in the old year."

Cutter laughed at her reply. As always, he was caught up in her blue eyes and her wide smile. "You know I love you, don't you?"

Genny leaned in to kiss him. "I love you, too."

A ding from the baby-monitor app, installed on both their devices, interrupted their kiss.

"I should go check on them," Genny said, "in case they both wake up. The sitter's not used to twins."

"I'll come with you."

"That's not necessary."

"I want to. I don't want to spend the stroke of midnight without you by my side."

"You're so cheesy," Genny teased.

"I'm just addicted to my girls. All three of them." He winked.

A quick diaper change, and both girls were sleeping peacefully again.

"I could have taken care of it," the sitter assured them. "You didn't have to leave the party."

"We know," Cutter admitted with a grin. "But we couldn't resist peeking in on them one last time this year."

They dusted kisses on top of the girls' heads and left the room holding hands. "It's getting close to midnight," Cutter noted.

"We still have a little while, and I want to run by the kitchen to see if there's anything I can do."

"They hired servers to do that, you know. Trust them to do their job."

"I won't be long," she promised.

"If you're not out here five minutes before midnight," he warned, "I'm coming after you."

Genny smiled at her husband as they parted. "I'll be here."

Over a hundred years ago, Juliet Randolph Blakely had designed the mansion to reflect her social standing in town. As such, the original design and decor had been sophisticated, formal, and quite elegant. When Madison became the owner, however, the style was too fancy and impersonal for her tastes. After the remodel, the mansion became a charming blend of old and new, melding the best of both centuries into a comfortable, livable space.

Only a few rooms were left untouched, but the formal parlor and the dining room with its famed mural were among them. The rooms were seldom used by the family but tonight, the pocket doors between them were pushed aside to create one large, seamless space. That space was now filled with revelers. Along the back wall of the dining room, refreshment tables held a variety of beverages, cookies, and the last of Genny's appetizers.

As his wife continued to the kitchen, Cutter took the hall leading back to the party. He glanced down at his vest and jacket, making certain Hope hadn't left baby drool there. Not that it mattered. He was the father of infants and proud of it.

Not watching where he was going, he bumped into a woman heading toward him, presumably to the powder room he just passed.

"I'm so sorry!" he apologized. He put out his hands to steady the woman, belatedly looking to see who it was. A hint of dread slipped into his voice. "Shilo

Dawne."

If her bright smile was any indication, she didn't notice his lackluster reply. "Hello, Cutter. You know, we have to stop meeting like this, or people will start to talk!" She giggled, not looking the least bit worried. Tonight was an alcohol-free party, but maybe she had smuggled some in. She acted tipsy.

"I'm sorry. I should have been watching where I was going."

When he tried removing his hands, she held them in place by her own.

"No worries," she gushed. "I've been wanting to talk to you all evening. I wanted to thank you, again, for coming to my rescue the other night."

"Like I said, it's in the job description," Cutter said with a tight smile.

"You could have had one of your subordinates take me home, but you took it upon yourself to make sure I was all safe and sound. I truly appreciate it."

"Again, no problem."

"At least let me give you a proper hug!"

"That's not—" He got no further as she launched her arms around his neck. "Necessary," he finished lamely.

"Of course, it is! You're my hero, as always!"

She pressed herself against him, closer than was appropriate. Cutter tried to step back, but she had him in a tight grip.

"I would have done the same for anyone," he said, trying to pull her arms away.

Shilo Dawne pulled back just enough to give him a sultry look. She knew the move thrust her bosom up and against his chest. "You mean I'm not special?"

He refused to take the bait. "You've always been a good friend to me."

"Then, why not give an old friend a proper hug?"

Her boldness took him by surprise. This was

nothing like the girl he had once known. The Shilo Dawne who left town was a friendly, well-liked girl. Sure, she had dressed in odd outfits she made or knitted herself, even when they weren't in style. And she definitely had a quick temper, one that was often directed at him. Genny said it was because he didn't seem to notice the girl and her attempts to flirt with him. He had seen her as a little sister type and was fond of her, but his feelings for her had never been romantic.

But *this* woman. This new Shilo Dawne was nothing like the girl he remembered. She was more confident and self-assured than before, which in itself was a good thing. Yet she overestimated her skills of seduction, particularly with a happily married man. For all her polish and shine, this new Shilo Dawne was abrasive.

With an iron grip, Cutter removed her arms from his neck.

"I've tried to be polite," he told her firmly. "I've tried to give you the benefit of the doubt. But it's time to be blunt. This has to stop, Shilo Dawne. I love my wife. I love my life. And, frankly, you're embarrassing us all with your relentless behavior."

The brunette stared up at him, obviously blindsided by his rejection. "Be—Behavior?"

"This," he said, waving to the space that had finally opened up between them. "Your too-long body hug. The way you disrespect my wife by ignoring her and throwing yourself at me."

"Throwing myself! *Throwing* myself?" she repeated in a quiet rage.

Cutter's voice remained firm. "The first hug—when you came back into town, and we saw each for the first time— was sufficient. The other hugs. The casual touches. The 'accidental' brushes against me. Those were uncalled for."

Fire flashed in Shilo Dawne's eyes. She stepped

back and held her spine rigid as she glared at him.

"I'm sick of you treating me like a kid, Cutter Montgomery. Like I'm nobody and not worthy of your attention. But you'll regret it. Before I'm done, you'll be sorry for not taking me seriously!"

She whirled around to leave. Cutter stepped aside, assuming she would make a haughty sweep into the hallway. Instead, she marched past the refreshment tables and hit the door into the butler's pantry with a forceful bang. The space connecting the dining room to the kitchen wasn't intended for public access, but Cutter figured she needed a quiet place to cool down.

*Man, was she mad!* Cutter chuckled at her full-blown hissy fit. Without another thought to her childish behavior, he wandered over to speak to a friend.

He was still standing within hearing distance a few minutes later, when Shilo Dawne came out of the pantry with a bellow of rage.

"That woman is a lunatic!" Shilo Dawne cried. "She attacked me!"

Her hair was mussed, the sleeve of her dress was torn, and there was a red imprint on her cheek. Tears bubbled in her eyes.

"Who?" one of the partygoers asked, rushing to her aid. "Who did this to you?"

"Genny Baker Montgomery, that's who! She's mean and bitter and jealous because of the special friendship I have with Cutter. She—She—She *hit* me!" the brunette said with a loud sob.

Around them, people gasped and came to help the distressed 'victim.' One man found a chair and pulled it up for her to have a seat. A woman hurried to bring her water. Rumors flew around the room.

Cutter quietly slipped down the hall and entered the kitchen from the other side, concerned for his wife. He knew Genny was struggling with stress and the adjustment of motherhood. He knew she had talked to her doctor and was taking a prescription drug for PPD. A drug that only seemed to make her mood worse, not better.

But his sweet Genny attacking Shilo Dawne? He wasn't buying it.

He found his wife in the kitchen, adding the final touched to a tray of appetizers. She had a satisfied smile on her face, the smile intensifying when she saw his approach.

"Oops. Is it five 'til already?"

"No. I, uh..." Cutter stuttered to a halt. His wife was calm and relaxed. He hated to ruin it by relaying a jealous woman's accusations. "Did, uh, Shilo Dawne come in here?"

"No. I haven't seen her since early in the evening. Why?"

"Uhm, no reason. Someone was looking for her and thought she came this way."

"Not that I saw." Genny took off her apron and nodded to the counter. "What I *did* see was enough to scrounge up one more tray of goodies. Now, let's hurry out to hear the countdown. I promised you I wouldn't miss it."

Cutter wanted to delay the inevitable for as long as possible. Why ruin the very first minute of the New Year? Once they went out those doors, people would be pointing and talking, accusing his sweet wife of something malicious. Something Shilo Dawne had lied about out of pure spite.

"You know what? Why don't we celebrate midnight in here, just the two of us?" he suggested, slipping his arms around her waist.

"I like the sound of that." She smiled and put her arms around his neck. "Let's hope this year holds better and brighter things."

At the front of the old house, the crowd started the countdown.

*Nine!*

*Eight!*

*Seven!*

*Six!*

He wouldn't break her heart now. Instead, Cutter smiled back at her and said, "No matter what the year holds, always remember that I love you, Genny darlin'."

*Two!*

*One!*

As a collective, the front rooms erupted in cries of, "Happy New Year! Happy New Year, everybody!"

Genny and Cutter whispered the sentiment to each other and sealed the wish with a kiss.

"I should get this tray out there," Genny said, wiggling from his arms, "before people start to leave."

"They haven't done the main giveaway yet," he reminded her. "But I'll take the tray out for you."

Surveying the messy countertop, she nodded. "I suppose I should clean up."

There were other people assigned to clean-up duty, but if cleaning the kitchen kept her in here longer, he wasn't about to remind her of the fact. Cutter would go out first, see what nonsense Shilo Dawne was spouting, and sort out matters best he could.

"Are you sure you don't mind?" Genny reached for the cutting boards and knives to carry to the sink.

"Not at all."

One of the knives started sliding. "Ouch!" she cried in surprise. A sharp butcher knife nicked her hand on its way to the floor.

"Are you okay?"

"Yeah, I think so." She had to set everything down to examine her hand. It immediately started to bleed.

"I'll go find something to put on this. You go on with the tray."

Cutter looked worried. "Maybe I should take a look at it."

"It's not that bad, honestly. It burns more than anything because there was lemon juice on the knife. You go on."

"Are you sure?"

"Positive. Believe me, I've done more damage with a knife than this!"

He still looked concerned. "Clean it good before you put on a bandage."

"I will. Now, scoot."

Madison and Brash had shared the stroke of midnight at one another's side. When the crowd called the time, Brash crushed her lips in a hearty kiss.

"Happy New Year, sweetheart. I love you."

"I love you, too." Maddy whispered. "Here's to a great year."

The sensation of impending doom had lessened, pushed now to the back corner of her gut. But as she noticed a cluster of people at the back of the formal dining room, their voices heated, and a woman seated among them, the sensation eked forward.

*Had someone fallen,* she wondered. Was this the premonition she had felt? What if someone sued them?

Before her imagination could create more toe-curling scenarios, someone pulled Brash away, asking a how-to question about the light show taking place out on the lawn.

Blake quickly replaced him at her side.

"Happy New Year, Mom."

"Happy New Year to you, too, sweetie," she said

with a warm hug. "I have to admit, it's been a great party."

"See, Mom?" he grinned. "You worried for nothing!"

"Most of the crowd is still here, and the party is going strong. A lot could still happen."

"You worry too much," Blake assured her.

"I'm a mother. It's in the job description."

"Yeah, well, I'm the emcee for this event, and it's in my job description to get up there and draw another name for a door prize. It's the last one before the big giveaway."

Madison watched him push through the crowd and bound onto the stage. Blake was a natural when it came to performing. Whether it be on the stage, behind a microphone, or on a baseball diamond, he did everything with a flourish. She enjoyed listening to her son as he engaged the crowd with his easy-going charm.

Whatever the ruckus was taking place at the back of the dining room earlier, it seemed to be settled now. Cutter had come from the butler pantry to speak with the seated woman and the small crowd gathered around her. Soon, everyone had dispersed.

As co-hostess, Madison knew she should have checked things out for herself, but she fully trusted her friend to handle any emergency that arose. She also knew she needed to pop in upstairs and see how things were faring in the grand ballroom. Throughout the evening, the crowd had alternated between the two dance areas. Even the older generation hadn't been thwarted by two sets of stairs. Seeing the grandeur of the famed ballroom again was worth whatever aches they suffered in the morning.

*Which, technically,* she acknowledged, *it already is.* The striking of the clock ushered in more than a new day. It ushered in a New Year.

*Hostess duties can wait*, Madison decided. She needed a breath of fresh air. With luck, she could catch the fireworks finale.

Since everyone she passed along the way wanted to thank her for the party and wish her a wonderful New Year, it made the closest route the slowest. The quicker route was through the formal library turned office on the far front corner of the house. No one should be on that side tonight, so the door normally reserved for clients of *In a Pinch Temporary Services* offered a straight, quick path to prime viewing.

All she had to do was make her way through the front parlor, unlock her office, and cross through to the door. It was cold out but not enough to bother with a coat.

Damian Green, the father of Blake's best friend Jamal, had outdone himself creating an extravaganza that blended an electronic light show with actual fireworks. As a rocket flared across the sky and erupted into fantastic sparks, followed immediately by another, and then another, Madison watched the night sky come alive with lights. Before the last sparks faded, thousands of electronic lights echoed their sparkle.

"Wow," Madison said aloud, awed by the stunning display. "Damian is a genius."

Caught up in the beauty of the celebration, she wasn't watching where she stepped. A well-worn path surrounded the perimeter of the mansion, winding around the numerous porches and flowerbeds to create a complete, if not oddly shaped, circle.

When designing the display, Damian was careful to keep the path free of lights, stakes, and electrical cords. Yet as Madison moved toward the front of the house, her foot snagged on something lying across the pathway. She stumbled and almost fell.

She caught herself before she fell upon the very bloody, very dead body of Anastasia Rowland.

# 8

She had done it again. She had discovered a dead body!

Panic crept into her lungs as she stared down at the grotesque sight. It took her brain a moment to process what she was seeing with what she should do next. There was no doubt that Anastasia was dead. Her head was cocked one way, her neck the other. Her eyes stared blindly up at the sky.

A sky that, just moments before, had seemed magical.

Madison knew she couldn't yell for help. It might create panic and a mad exodus for the gates, putting guests in danger.

*Think, Maddy, think.*

She didn't have her cell phone with her, but she could go back to her office and use the house phone to call Brash's cell.

With a final look at the poor woman lying at her feet, Madison forced her legs into action. Her hands shook as she entered her security code, but she managed to open the door and get to her desk phone.

Brash picked up on the first ring. "Maddy? Is everything all right?"

"No, it's not. We have a problem."

His voice sharpened in alarm. "What's wrong?"

"I've lived up to the nickname Blake gave me. Again."

"What? You mean—Who?"

"Anastasia Rowland."

She could almost *hear* Brash rake his hand through his hair. "Can you tell if it was a natural death?"

"Hard to know with all the blood."

He cursed under his breath. "Where are you?"

"I'm in my office, but she's out on the walkway, near the azalea bushes. It's the only shadowy spot in the yard, so be careful where you step."

"Okay, I'm headed that way." From the sound of his voice, he was already in motion. "Call Cutter and ask him to meet me out there. I'll call Vina. She'll tell Abraham and notify the other two deputies."

"I'll meet you there."

"Are you okay, sweetheart? You can wait in the office if you like."

He couldn't see it, but Madison shook her head. "I feel like someone should be out there with her, you know?"

"I won't be far behind," he promised before hanging up.

After calling Cutter, Madison took a moment to gather her courage. A few deep breaths helped.

By the time she reached the pathway, Brash was kneeling beside the dead body.

"It definitely looks like murder," Brash muttered, using a small but powerful flashlight to scan the immediate area. Call it an occupational hazard that he actually carried a flashlight in his tux. He glanced up as Madison approached. "Is this how she was when you found her? This looks like a partial footprint here. Did you step in the crime scene?"

"I almost fell across her!"

"So, that's a *yes*?" he asked the rhetorical question wryly.

Cutter skidded to a stop when he saw Brash crouched on the ground and Madison standing over him. "What's wrong?" he asked. "Is someone hurt? Do I need to page the paramedics?"

"Even the paramedics can't help her now," Brash answered. He moved just enough to clear Cutter's field of vision.

"That's—That's Anastasia Rowland!"

"Yes, and it appears she's been murdered. There's a knife protruding from her chest."

"Wait," Madison interrupted. "What knife? I didn't see a knife earlier."

Both men asked a question at the same time.

"Are you sure?" Brash asked.

Cutter's head popped up. "*You* found her?"

Answering Cutter first, she turned her palms upward in a sheepish gesture. "Who else? I seem to have an uncanny knack for this."

"Maddy!" Brash's voice was abnormally sharp. "Did you or did you not see a knife when you found her?"

"I—I don't think so. No, I know I didn't. At first, I thought she had fallen and hit her head. There was red all around her. I thought it was her dress. Then I realized it was blood and plenty of it. I would have noticed a knife." She stared down at the woman on the ground. Seeing her in the muted light of Christmas bulbs was bad enough. Seeing her under the harsh glare of the mega-watt flashlight was so much worse.

A nibble of doubt crept into her mind. What if, in the dim light and the shadows, she hadn't been able to see the knife? Stumbling upon the woman had taken Madison by such surprise, her mind went numb. All she had seen was red. Red blood. Red material. The two reds appeared intertwined, pooling and flowing all around Anastasia's lifeless body. Was it possible she was mistaken?

"I *think* not, anything," she amended on a whisper.

The sound of swishing skirts proceeded Misty Abraham as she sprinted barefoot across the lawn, holding her hemline and high heels in her hands. Her once neatly coiffed hair was in disarray and an impressive amount of cleavage spilled from her bodice.

No one noticed.

"Vina said there's been a 10-67. Who was it?"

"Anastasia Rowland," Brash replied in a tight voice.

"The owner of that new bistro in town?" Her eyes automatically went to Cutter. Everyone knew it was in direct competition with *New Beginnings*.

"That's the one," Cutter confirmed.

Officer Abraham peered around them to see for herself. "She was stabbed?"

"Maybe."

Brash's answer surprised her. She gave him a sharp look. "But there's a butcher knife sticking out of her chest! Why do you say *maybe*?"

The lines around his mouth were tight. "Because Maddy was the one to find her, and she doesn't remember seeing a knife. She went into the house to call me and by the time I arrived, this is what I found." He motioned to the weapon.

Misty turned to stare at Madison. There were times when Maddy suspected the officer still had feelings for Brash and held a touch of animosity toward his wife. Tonight was one of those times.

"Don't remember, or didn't notice?"

Madison bristled at the derisive way she asked.

"It was dark," Madison defended herself. "I wasn't expecting to stumble across a dead body. I saw the blood and the unnatural angle of her body. Her eyes were open and staring upward. I noticed the red dress splayed out around her and how the gravel on the path was disturbed." She added the last details without looking at the scene. "I noticed how this was the only shadowy spot in the entire yard. I noticed how she was missing one shoe. I did not notice a knife."

At mention of the shoe, Misty's eyes darted to the victim's bare foot. It was a detail she had missed on her first perusal.

Brash's knee popped as he stood. "We need to secure the scene and keep potential witnesses from leaving the premises."

"Vina's on it," Misty said.

"Of course she is," Brash said around a tight smile.

"She asked Blake to lock and set the alarms on all doors," the officer went on. "So far, no one's noticed. But when they do, they're going to ask questions, and then they're going to panic."

"We don't have to tell them what happened, just that there's been an incident, and we need their cooperation."

"I can round up some of the fire department," Cutter offered. "My radio's in the kitchen. I also need to check on Genny. She cut her hand, and I want to make sure she's okay."

"Was it deep? Does she need stitches?" Madison asked in concern.

"I didn't see it, but she said it was nothing. I still want to check."

Cutter loped off toward the furthest side of the sprawling mansion. It took him past the firework display but away from the party inside. He knew the door code and could go directly into the kitchen.

Brash and Misty were deep in conversation, discussing a plan of action.

It left Madison with nothing to do but stare down at

the dead woman and wonder how—and if— she had somehow missed the knife sticking from her chest.

Cutter let himself in through the kitchen door. The room was much busier now than it had been when he left. With the appetizer trays now empty and only chips and dips available, the clean-up crew had removed the fancier serving pieces. They were now cleaning, washing, and straightening the aftermath of the party.

Cutter scanned the room for his wife, spotting her stashing wares into the plastic totes she used for catering.

"Genny!" he called. Intent on reaching her, he didn't bother greeting anyone along the way.

"Where have you been?" She sounded impatient. "You won't believe what happened! And... why do you look like you just ran a mile?"

"Because I probably did. Genny, I need to talk to you. Let's go in there." He motioned to the laundry room off the kitchen.

"If you're here to tell me about Shilo Dawne's ridiculous accusation, I already know." She propped her hands upon her curvy hips. "Can you believe her?" she huffed.

"Look, let's talk in there. How's your hand?"

She held it up, showing off the wide bandage across her palm. "Been better, been worse. But—"

Before she could say more, he took her other hand and pulled her along, inspiring a few curious looks from the kitchen helpers.

"*What* is going on?" his wife demanded in exasperation.

Cutter shut the door behind them and pulled her to the center of the room. He didn't want anyone eavesdropping on their conversation.

"There's been an incident," he said.

"I just told you, I know all about it. Shilo Dawne claims I assaulted her and tore her dress. The worst part is, there are some people who actually believe her!"

"Shilo Dawne is being mean out of bitterness and revenge. But this isn't about her. Something else has happened."

"I'm almost afraid to ask. What now?"

Cutter lowered his voice. "There's been a murder."

Genny clutched her injured hand to her chest in dread. "Who? What happened?"

He hesitated slightly before saying, "It's Anastasia."

Genny gasped, and her eyes widened. "Anastasia? Anastasia Rowland? Wh—Where? How? I just saw her thirty minutes ago."

He jumped on her response, hoping it held a key to her murder. "Where did you see her?"

"By the refreshment table. You saw her, too," she reminded him, even though she was wrong about the time. Still in a daze, she saw the nearby bench and plopped down. "How did this happen? And here, of all places! On New Year's Eve!"

"Maddy found her on the far pathway, between the corner porch and the main one."

"*Maddy* found her? How horrible! Why does this keep happening to her?"

"Maddy hoped to see the last of the fireworks, so she went out her office door with the intentions of making it back around to the front. Before she got there, she stumbled across Anastasia's body lying in the path."

"That's horrible. I may have had a few issues with the woman, but I never wished her any harm! This is just horrible," Genny kept repeating.

"I agree."

"How did it happen?"

"It hasn't been determined yet. Maddy insists all she saw was blood at first. She went inside to call Brash and by the time he got there, there was a knife in her chest."

"A knife?"

"A long butcher knife, similar to the ones you use."

A cold dread seeped through Genny's bones and settled somewhere in her gut. Her eyes slid toward the closed door and to the kitchen beyond. "Cutter," she said lowly. Nervously. "There's something I should tell you. You know—You know the knife I was using when I cut my hand?"

"The one that fell and hit the floor?"

Her voice fell to a breathless whisper. "That one. It was a long butcher knife." Worry watered in her beautiful blue eyes. "When I went back to pick it up and wash it, it... it was gone."

"What do you mean, it was gone?" The same sense of dread was contagious, making her husband go pale.

"I thought someone saw it there and put it in the sink, but most of the cutlery is washed, and I still haven't found it. It—It's mine from the restaurant. Cutter," she whispered, as the dread hardened into pure fright. "What if someone stole the knife and tries to frame *me* for her murder?"

# 9

It wasn't the opening act anyone had hoped for in the New Year.

All those outside were asked to return inside the house. It didn't take long for rumors and speculation to spread among the crowd, especially when they discovered that all exits were locked.

The teenagers were the first to be released. Officers asked only if they had heard or seen anything suspicious that evening. Thinking one of their classmates had done something wrong, and they were all being blamed for it, they ratted a few out by confessing they saw such and such making out, or smoking a cigarette, or that, yes, one of them had cheated on their last test so that they maintained a passing grade and could attend the party.

Their parents were the next to be interviewed and released.

By then, everyone knew something was terribly wrong. The other two Sisters deputies joined Brash and Misty on the scene, along with several members of the fire department, two deputies for River County that Brash requested, and an ambulance.

Madison closed the draperies to shield the moment

the ambulance loaded Anastasia's body into the box, but many saw enough to draw their own conclusions, particularly when the ambulance pulled away without running lights and sirens.

Vina personally escorted the rest of the partygoers into Madison's office, two by two, to be interviewed. Brash chose his most trusted employee to do the job because there was something so no-nonsense about the woman that most people were in awe of her, if not outright afraid. Few people dared cross her. Even fewer had the nerve to tell her a lie. As she led them to speak with either Chief deCordova or Officer Abraham, she gave each a spiel about being honest and transparent during their interview. Her piercing eyes warned that if they disobeyed, they had her to deal with.

After their interview, Officer Schimanski escorted each person out the side entrance, where fire department personnel made certain they exited the property via the gate rather than the lawn. More firefighters and two county deputies stood guard over the crime scene.

For those left waiting, the festive mood had turned gloomy. Some took it worse than others.

"They're treating us like prisoners!" one man complained. "Keeping us locked inside, escorting us to the gallows one by one, telling us we can't re-enter the property. I know my rights, and I demand to be released!"

"Hush up, Raymond Grouchy-Pants," Granny Bert told him. "None of us like it, but that's no reason to get nasty."

Someone else pointed out, "They won't even tell us what happened! The least they could do is tell us why they're holding us. All Perry will say is 'you'll know soon enough.'"

Otis Perry guarded the front door and glared out at

the crowd with silence.

Thirty minutes into the interviews, someone leaked the news.

"I just got a call!" Deanna Gleason announced breathlessly, waving her phone in the air. "B—er, I mean, my friend," she said, catching her blunder, "had her interview. She said someone died, and they asked if she heard or saw anything that could be helpful. They didn't come out and say it was murder, but why else would they ask that? They asked if she personally knew the person."

Amid the gasps and cries of surprise, Vanessa Hutchins demanded, "And? Don't leave us hanging! Who did she say it was?"

"That new woman in town, the one who opened that breakfast place!"

More gasps circled the room, followed immediately by speculation and rumors.

"That Rowland woman? The one who wants to put Genny out of business?"

"I heard she's trying to buy *Montelongo's* and get a monopoly on the food industry here in The Sisters."

"This is hardly a metropolis," Vanessa Hutchins pointed out in a wry tone. "Having a monopoly here won't make anyone rich."

"I told you something was up!" Raymond Grouchy-Pants claimed.

"I *liked* that place!" someone else wailed.

"Who could have done this?" another asked.

While suspicions and accusations abound, Granny Bert huddled with her crew.

"He brings up a good point. Who *could* have done this? Who had a motive?"

"It's usually the spouse," Virgie Adams pointed out, "but I don't think she was married."

"Boyfriend?" Sybil suggested.

"If you mean the one in the Batman mask—he had quite the bod, by the way—" Derron said, "I don't see him in the crowd."

"Maybe he took his mask off," Wanda suggested.

Her housemate smirked. "Like I said, he had great abs. Believe me, he's not here."

"We'll have to take your word for it," Granny Bert said. "The rest of us are too old to notice things like that."

"Speak for yourself!" Wanda protested.

Ignoring her friend, Granny Bert went on, "What I did notice is that there were at least three men who wore masks that hid their faces. I saw all three after the reveal, still wearing them. None of them are here now."

"Good catch, GB," Derron congratulated her.

"We need to find out who those men are and why they were here."

"Belle?" Sticker interrupted. "Don't you think Brash and his officers will find all that out? He's a good investigator. Let the boy do his job."

Virgie's husband Hank gave the other man a look of pity. "You don't know these women at all, do you? Reasoning with them won't do one lick of good."

"Of course not. This is where we shine!" Wanda claimed. "We're Madison's back-up team. The senior division of *In a Pinch*."

"Madison isn't a private detective, you know," Sticker pointed out needlessly.

"No, but everyone seems to think she is," Virgie responded. "That's why most people hire her."

"It's true," Derron confirmed with a nod of his stylishly cut blond hair. Even straight out of his helmet and mask, it fell with precision around his handsome face. "Ninety percent of our clients hire us for services normally performed by a PI. It's become our specialty."

Sticker was determined to point out, "No one's

hired her yet. We don't even know for sure what happened. I think y'all are putting the cart before the horse."

Granny Bert's actions belied her image as a proper English lady. She propped her hands upon her brocade-covered hips to glare at her date. "Sticker Pierce, if you can't be supportive, you can at least keep your mouth shut, like Hank here. Do you go into a rodeo unprepared? Do you get on a horse without checking things out? No, you do not. So don't you lecture us on doing some prep work. It's never too early to start oiling the saddle and getting the cinch tightened up."

The grizzled old cowboy put his hands up in surrender. He caught Hank's eye and sent him a wink. Clearly, both men adored their women enough to put up with their bossy attitudes.

She turned back to address the circle. "Now, let's get back to business. Who did we see Anastasia Rowland talking to tonight?"

"I only saw her dancing with Batman," Derron said.

"That's because you had the hots for the other man," Wanda complained. "You were watching him, not her."

"Was anyone watching Anastasia?" Virgie asked. "Did any of us see her dancing or talking to someone besides Batman? It was so crowded in here, it's not like we had a clear view of the whole room."

"I saw her dancing with the drama teacher and a couple of other people. Was that the mayor wearing the black cape with the black and gold mask? She was dancing with him," Sybil offered.

"And with Reggie Carr, that scoundrel who was just elected to the city council," Granny Bert said. "How he got enough votes to win is beyond me!"

Hank spoke up, "He had Joel Werner backing him."

His wife sounded surprised. "The one who stirred up all that trouble before? The one who tried taking Brash's job?"

"That's the one."

"We may circle back to that one later," Granny Bert said. "Anyone else notice her movements this evening?"

"I saw her at the refreshment table several times," Wanda said. "I bumped into her when I went back for seconds—okay, thirds—" she amended when she saw that look from Granny Bert. "Maybe fourths, on those little stuffed shrimp. Those were delicious, with just the right blend of—"

"Wanda, dear," Derron said, putting his hand on her arm, "focus. This is about Anastasia, not the shrimp."

"Sorry. I get sidetracked when it comes to a food. Anyway, she seemed to be fond of the gingersnap cookies. Genny's are the best, you know. Soft and chewy, not like their name implies." Wanda caught herself before anyone else could pull her back on track. "My point is, maybe someone poisoned her."

"Then why aren't there dead bodies all over the place?" Virgie said. "That plate was empty every time I went up there."

"Okay, maybe she was allergic to one of the ingredients. Like Nigel was allergic to the shrimp at Maddy and Brash's wedding reception."

"Doubtful, but I guess possible," Derron said, trying to be supportive of her ideas. Sometimes the old gal made it difficult.

In a quiet voice, Sticker spoke. "I saw her talking to the Phantom of the Opera guy. It looked like a heated conversation."

Granny Bert glared at him. "Why didn't you say that before?"

His handlebar mustache twitched with a repressed smile. “You told me to keep my mouth shut.”

After a disgruntled *harrumph*, his spirited Belle turned back to the group. “Do we know who this guy is?”

“No clue,” Wanda said. “I only bumped into him once at the refreshment table.”

“I saw him one time upstairs in the ballroom,” Virgie said. “Come to think of it, Anastasia was up there, too. I don’t think I saw them together, but he seemed to be watching her.”

“You mean you got this old coot to go up two flights of stairs?” Granny Bert asked, looking at her old friend Hank.

“It’s not the first time I took those stairs up, you know,” he said with a twinkle in his old eyes. “Although you and I did prefer the back staircase. It was easier to spy on the party that way.”

Hank’s grandfather had been Juliet Blakely’s butler, and Bertha’s mother had been her cook. The two were her most trusted employees and the closest thing she had to family. While the two were at work, their children often came with them and had the run of the house. Most of the children’s antics were confined to the servant staircases and the secret passages running throughout the house; children simply couldn’t be seen when Juliet was entertaining. That didn’t mean, however, that her guests weren’t seen by the mischievous young spies.

When Juliet died and her will was read, they all expected for her to leave the house and the bulk of her estate to Hank’s grandfather. He had been more than a butler. He had acted as her business manager and so much more. It came as quite a surprise when she left most everything to the cook’s daughter. Juliet had always considered Bertha the daughter she never had, and once the girl grew into womanhood, the two had maintained a close relationship.

The surprise inheritance had driven a wedge between Bertha and Hank. It had taken a while, but the hard feelings between them mellowed and smoothed out over the years, keeping their life-long friendship intact.

"We had some good times in this old house," his friend agreed, a fond look softening her wrinkled face.

"It was worth the climb to see the ballroom back to its glory days, but I do believe that was my last time up," Hank admitted. He rubbed an offending knee. "I may not walk once these old legs get stove up."

"Has anyone seen Genny?" Sybil asked in concern. "How's she taking the news? I know she and Anastasia had that little run-in just a few days ago."

"She was one of the first interviewed," Granny Bert answered, "so that she could be with the girls. She and Cutter are staying the night here."

Sticker looked at his watch. "Looks like we all may be."

Granny Bert nodded. "I imagine we'll be some of the last to go in. They'll get all the others out of the way first, knowing we won't put up a ruckus like ol' Grouchy Pants Raymond."

"If we have to wait," Wanda sighed, "we may as well get comfortable. As soon as those folks on the sofa go in, I call dibs."

"I was thinking more like the kitchen," Granny Bert suggested. "We can wait in the breakfast nook, have as much coffee as we like, and keep Maddy company. I think that's where she's holed up. This has gotta be hard on her."

# 10

It was a long, tedious night. Madison sent her kids to bed, even though all three teens offered to help. She busied herself in the kitchen, trying to forget the moment she found Anastasia's body. And trying to forget that her best friend could very well become a person of interest, if not an outright suspect.

She welcomed Wanda's chatter, if only because it distracted her from all her worries. By the time Granny Bert and her friends were interviewed, it was the wee hours of the morn. Sticker and the Adamses went home, but the three single women and Derron claimed a bedroom for what remained of the 'night.'

Brash fell in bed for a couple of hours but was gone by the time Madison awoke. She went downstairs to find Wanda and Genny cooking breakfast. Sybil and Granny Bert each held a baby in their arms.

"Sorry. I must have overslept," Madison said.

"It's not late enough in the morning to call it 'over' sleeping," Sybil contradicted. "But three of us have an eighty-year habit of waking early, and that's hard to break. Genny, there, had these two precious alarm clocks to wake her." The old woman bounced Hope as she smiled down at the dark-haired angel.

"And Derron?"

"I'm sure he'll claim he needed his beauty sleep."

"As soon as he's up," Wanda turned from the oven to say, "I'll send him to the house to bring me some clothes. No way I'm pouring myself into that gown again!"

"Good thing Maddy and I have the same taste in clothes," Granny Bert said. The smile she gave her granddaughter could have been innocent, or could have been a veiled insult. Everyone chided Madison for wearing clothes that made her look older than her early forties.

At least it gave her grandmother and Miss Sybil something to wear.

Madison poured herself coffee and came to stand beside her best friend. "How did you sleep?"

Genny looked at her with red-rimmed eyes. The puffy bags beneath them seemed to prop them up. "I didn't."

"You okay?" Maddy asked quietly.

Her answer was blunt. "No."

Maddy squeezed her hand. "We'll talk later."

Genny sighed. "We may as well do it now. You know how quick gossip goes around in this town, and we may as well get the upper hand by telling the right story."

Hearing her, Granny Bert pretended offense. "Are you saying we gossip?"

"Uhm, maybe a little?"

"I prefer to call it sharing information, thank you very much."

"Then you ladies can share the right information when the other gossipers approach you with a juicy tidbit."

"Too late," Granny Bert said, motioning to her cell phone. "I've already had three calls and two texts. Word's out, and rumors are flying high."

As Genny and Wanda delivered breakfast to the table, Genny sighed. "How bad is it? And how many mentioned my name in their 'news'?"

"Of the five? Only four." She tried making her voice sound upbeat.

"I guess that's something." Genny shrugged. "Here, let me take a baby. I'll try putting them in their carriers. They should be ready for a little nap by now, and I really do need to go home soon. I'm almost out of formula."

"I see Cutter brought you clothes already." Madison nodded to the outfit she wore.

"No, this is the extra set I always carry with me." Genny finally smiled. "I never know when one of the girls will spit up on me, so I've learned to be prepared."

"Smart. Here, Granny," Madison said, bending over her grandmother. "I'll take Faith and get her all tucked in."

With the girls snuggled in their carriers nearby, the five women ate their breakfast.

"I notice you're not eating much," Madison said to her best friend.

"I don't have much of an appetite."

"So, where's that 'right information' we're supposed to share?" Granny Bert asked.

Genny pushed back her barely touched plate and shared her worries.

Miss Sybil was the first to comment. "So, you think that because there was a knife at the scene, they'll automatically blame you?"

"My knife is missing from this kitchen. I brought it with me, I dropped it right over there, and now it's nowhere to be seen."

"And you think someone took it and planted it as fake evidence?" Wanda clarified.

"I don't necessarily think it, I just worry that it's a

possibility."

"I don't believe in inviting trouble before it comes knocking on my door," Granny Bert said, "but say we agree that's a possibility. Who would want to frame you?"

"Myrna Lewis comes to mind. Not two days ago, she told Maddy and me that our reign was over, and we'd get our comeuppance soon."

"I agree it sounds like something she would do, but she wasn't even here last night."

"True. But she's not the only one who seems to have it out for me lately. Lawrence Norris is hardly a fan. He's done his best to make my life miserable, holding this ridiculous lawsuit over my head."

"Was he here?" Miss Virgie asked.

"Not that I saw. But I would have to see his face or hear his voice to recognize him."

Something tightened in Madison's gut. "You think he could have been the Phantom of the Opera, or the man in the full-face mask?" she asked.

Genny shrugged. "For all I know, he was Batman, or any of the men in partial masks. I honestly don't know the man well enough to recognize his walk or the set of his shoulders. I'd say he's average build, average weight, so there's not a lot to make him stand out."

"Batman, you say? Did Norris know Anastasia?" Granny Bert asked.

"I have no idea." The question made her reconsider her initial response. "I mean, I suppose not. Honestly, I don't know anything about the man except that's he's out to get me. I don't even know where he's from."

"Anyone else have reason to want to frame you?"

"Are we assuming this person killed her?"

"That's usually how it works," Granny Bert said. "Knock off your enemy, pin the blame on someone else, and get off scot-free."

"If that's the case, then the most logical person would be her business partner, don't you think? He could gain control of the company, collect any life insurance the business had on her, blame me, and get rid of the competition all at one time."

Wanda beamed with satisfaction. "Looks like we've done it again, girls! We've solved her murder!"

"I hate to burst your bubble, but it seldom works out like that, Miss Wanda," Madison cautioned. "I'm sure he would have already thought of that and come up with something less obvious."

"A hitman, you think?" she asked, rubbing her hands with an odd sense of glee.

Maddy looked horrified. "I certainly hope not! The last thing we need is a hitman in town!"

Wanda deflated like a balloon. "Oh. Yeah. I forgot that part."

"It still doesn't mean it couldn't happen," Madison admitted, "but let's consider other options." She turned back to her friend. "Genny? Anyone else?"

She looked hesitant to answer. "Well, there is one other person... But I really can't think of a reason she would want to kill Anastasia."

"Who is it?" Wanda demanded. "And don't count Myrna Lewis out! That woman is mean enough, and ornery enough, to do it just to spite you."

"I was thinking of someone else," Genny admitted, still hesitant to say the name.

"You're thinking Shilo Dawne, aren't you?" Madison guessed.

"I know I shouldn't." Genny wrung her hands worriedly. "We were once friends. At least, I thought we were. But ever since she came back to town, she's been... different. Maybe I'm being ridiculous, but I think she's trying to win Cutter back, even though she never had him to begin with. He said he thought of her more like a kid sister."

"Which has to smart. It was a blow to her ego, I'm sure. Maybe she thinks now that she's older and more successful, he'll see her differently. Which, of course, he won't."

"Agreed," Granny Bert said. "She doesn't stand a snowball's chance in hell of taking your man."

"Plus, I don't know why she would want to do Anastasia harm. She works for her," Sybil pointed out.

"Well, unless I have an unknown enemy out there, I can't think of anyone else who would want to frame me," Genny said. "My other known enemy, Barry Redmond, is still in prison. I'd like to think no one else hates me enough to kill an innocent person to get even with me."

"They probably had their own reasons to want her dead and knew you would be an easy scapegoat." Seeing her friend's fallen expression, Madison was quick to add, "*If* that's what happened."

"And I pray it's not," Genny muttered.

"I still don't understand something." Wanda poured syrup onto her third slice of French toast. "Why would you automatically be a suspect? Just because they found a knife, and just because she's your competition, doesn't mean you would want to kill her."

"I guess you didn't hear about the incident at the grocery store?"

"Oh, no, of course we heard it. But it didn't sound so bad, even when Myrna Lewis told it."

Genny puffed her cheeks with air and slowly rclcascd it. "I gucss I'vc just been under so much stress lately, I'm making mountains out of molehills. I was afraid everyone would think I had some huge vendetta against the woman. In truth, I'm a fan of her business model and all her accomplishments."

Sybil reached out to pat her hand. "Have a touch of

the baby blues, do you? It's nothing to be ashamed of, dear. It happens to the best of us."

Tears brimmed in Genny's blue eyes. "But I love my babies so much... I don't understand why I'm not bursting with joy! I mean, I am, of course. At least, I would be if I had the energy."

The experienced mothers offered words of encouragement and peppered her with advice, but their kind expressions of love made her cry.

"I hate crying!" she said, rubbing angrily at a tear. "It makes my face all red and splotchy!"

"The only cute criers in the world are babies like those two right there," Granny Bert informed her. "And if you can't cry among family, who can you cry in front of?"

"Thanks. You know you've always been like the grandmother I never had, and the rest of you are like my great-aunts."

Wanda looked delighted. "What a sweet thing to say."

"And don't you worry about cleaning the kitchen," Sybil said. "Whenever you're ready to take those sweet babies home, we'll take care of the mess here."

"Better yet, why don't you leave the girls here and go home to take a shower and freshen up?" Madison suggested. "Take a nap if you'd like. We can take care of the girls. And eventually, even my girls should be up and able to help."

"Oh, I couldn't do that..." Genny protested, even though she looked tempted by the idea.

"Why not? You and Cutter were planning to be here for our traditional New Year's meal. Don't worry about a thing. I'll put the peas on while you're gone."

It didn't take much persuading to get Genny to agree. She looked dead on her feet and obviously needed a few minutes to herself. Even without a nap, a hot shower would do her a world of good.

At the door, the blonde paused to look back at her babies and to offer a parting thought. “Since black-eyed peas are supposed to bring good luck in the New Year, make a double batch!”

Wanda and Sybil declined the invitation to partake in the traditional meal for New Year’s Day. When it came to the first day of the year, at least in the South, the menu always included salt bacon for health, cabbage for money, and black-eyed peas for luck.

“I already have my peas washed and soaking, dear, but thank you,” Sybil said.

“And all I want to do is go home and sleep!” Wanda declared. “I don’t even mind wearing my borrowed nightgown home.”

With the kitchen cleaned, their guests gone once Derron woke up, and the babies still sleeping, Madison made more coffee for her and her grandmother.

“What do you think, Granny?”

“I can see you’re worried about it. And to tell you the truth, so am I,” the old woman said. “I don’t think for one second that Genny could do such a thing—”

“Of course not!”

“—but I can see where someone else might.”

“I do, too,” Madison admitted. “For those who know her, they know it can’t be possible, but in theory, it makes a good hypothesis. Especially since she’s been going through a bout of depression lately.”

“Is she taking something for it?”

Madison squirmed in her seat. “I, uh, really couldn’t say.”

“I’ll take that as a yes. It’s our secret, of course. That’s why I didn’t ask in front of the others.”

“But she says they don’t help. If anything, she says they make things worse.”

Granny Bert twisted her mouth. “Maybe we’re overreacting. Maybe Brash has already found his suspect. Like I said earlier, I don't believe in inviting trouble before it comes knocking on my door."

As if summoned, Brash opened the door and strode wearily into the room.

One look at his face, and Madison's hopes crumbled.

"It didn't knock," she whispered. "It just barged right in."

# 11

Madison pushed from the table and greeted her husband with a kiss. "You look exhausted, sweetheart."

"Am," he said, as if using two words took too much effort.

"Here, have a seat, and I'll get you some coffee."

"I've already had so much coffee today, I may not sleep for a week."

"Water, then?"

"Thanks." He dropped into a chair and offered a weary greeting to the older woman at the table. "Hey, Granny Bert."

"You look plumb tuckered out, boy. Why don't you go up and take a nap?"

Noticing the two babies asleep in their baby carriers, he looked surprised. "Is Genny still here? I didn't see her car."

"No, we're keeping the girls while she went home for a shower and, hopefully, a nap of her own," his wife answered. "Would you like something to eat?"

"Thanks, but I ate at the station. Vina brought breakfast tacos for everyone."

"Of course she did. The woman's like the Energizer Bunny. She has to be as exhausted as everyone else."

"Yes, but she'll never admit it."

Madison brought his water and slid into the seat beside him. "So? I can tell by your expression that you have news, and that it's not good. You may as well get it over with."

"You're right. It isn't good."

"How did she die? Was she stabbed to death? And could I have missed that?"

"It's too soon to say whether or not she was stabbed to death. But there was definitely a knife in her chest, even if it were placed there after the fact. And what's worst, we've identified the knife."

"Please," Madison begged in a whisper. She placed her hand over her heart, as if that could still its crazy beat. "Please, don't say it."

"Not saying it doesn't make it any less true."

"It was *hers*?" Madison wailed.

"Yes. Her name is engraved in the handle."

"The knives the Morgans gave her when she graduated from culinary school! They're her favorite!"

"I doubt they will be anymore," Granny Bert muttered. She eyed her grandson-in-law shrewdly. "You're sure, Brash?"

"I saw it myself."

"This doesn't make sense!" Madison popped out of her seat to pace the floor. "Why would someone do this, Brash?"

"Kill Anastasia, or frame Genny for it?"

"Both!"

"Hard to say for sure. Greed and passion are the two most common reasons for murder. Sometimes the passion comes in the form of love, sometimes in hate."

"Did Anastasia have either? Lovers? Or haters?"

"I'm sure she did. It's much too early in the investigation to say."

"The girls and I were thinking," Granny Bert

started.

Brash put up his hand. “Don’t. Just... don’t. Don’t think about it, don’t talk about, don’t butt your noses into police business.” His sharp look encompassed them both. “You’re too close to this one. This is Genny we’re talking about.”

“If we’re too close, so are you!” Madison argued.

“You’re right. That’s why I’ve recused myself as the lead on this case. As the chief of police, I’ll remain in the loop, of course, but I can’t be seen as biased while collecting evidence.”

“Surely, you don’t intend to name Otis Perry as the lead! If you do, you might as well put Genny in jail now and throw away the key! The man hates her.”

Granny Bert murmured, “Good point. We forgot to add him to the list.”

“There *is* no list, Granny!” Brash practically yelled. It was the harshest tone he had ever used with her, even when she had pulled some of her most outlandish stunts. “There can’t be any lists. Not now, not ever. Not by any of you.”

“Well?” Madison demanded, still waiting for his answer to her question that wasn’t posed as a question. “You’re handing Genny’s fate over to *Perry*?”

“He has seniority and is a good officer, no matter how you feel about him personally. But, no, I have no intentions of doing so. I’ve named Abraham as the lead on this one.”

“Does she have experience gathering murder evidence?”

“She may look like a blond bombshell, but don’t be fooled. Abraham is as good an officer as any and a top-notch investigator, too. I met her when we were both working a murder investigation. I was acting as special investigator for River County, and she was a detective in the Navasota Police Department. We worked well together and caught our suspect right away."

"I'm sure you did 'work' well together," his wife sulked. "And a bombshell? Really, Brash?"

He looked impatient with the conversation. "I have nothing to hide, Maddy, and you know it. Misty and I had an on-and-off relationship, at best. Our schedules didn't allow time for anything more and frankly, we were both good with that. I know I was. And yes, most people refer to her as a bombshell. That has nothing to do with her abilities as a good cop. And I wouldn't choose her if she weren't the best person for the job."

"*You* would be the best person for the job. You know Genny couldn't possibly be guilty of this."

"I do," he agreed. "And I have every confidence that Officer Abraham will prove exactly that. Better yet, she'll find the person who did do this and get him or her off the streets."

Granny Bert interrupted their stare down. "What's next, Brash?"

"Next, we'll look through everyone's statements from last night and make certain there aren't any inconsistencies or red flags. We'll re-interview people as necessary."

"What about the people who were already gone? Like the men in full masks, for instance," Madison said. "You didn't interview them. If they left before her body was found, that should be your red flag right there."

"My parents left before then, too," he pointed out. "Doesn't make them suspicious."

"Not Andy and Lydia, of course. But none of those men revealed their identities when it was time to take masks off. Does anyone even know who they were?"

"We're working on that. It's not even been twelve hours yet, sweetheart. Give us a break."

"Just tell Ms. Bombshell the same thing. Give Genny a break."

"That's the whole point, sweetheart. I *can't* give Genny a break. We'll have to treat her the same way we'd treat any other suspect in a murder case."

"Sus—Suspect?"

Genny's voice broke through their heated exchange. They had been so busy arguing, they hadn't heard her open the door and come into the kitchen.

"I'm a *suspect*?" Her eyes welled with tears. She launched herself into Cutter's arms as he came in behind her.

"Not a suspect," Brash was quick to say. "A person of interest."

"You didn't say a person of interest, Brash." Cutter's eyes glittered like granite. His voice sounded as hard as any stone. "You said suspect."

One of the babies whimpered and stirred. Genny was too shell-shocked to even respond.

"I'll call Megan and Bethani down to take care of the girls," Madison said quickly, reaching for her phone. "I think you and Cutter need to have a seat."

"It's bad, isn't it, Brash?" Genny whispered. "That's why you called Cutter. You're going to arrest me, aren't you?"

"Of course not, Genny. But I agree with Maddy. Let's get our girls to take yours, and then we can all sit down and talk. Fair enough?"

Genny knew her knees wouldn't hold her, so she sank into a chair and asked her husband to bring the babies to her. "I need to hold our babies while I still can. Before—Before they put me in jail!"

"Genny, they'll do no such thing," Madison assured her. "You did nothing wrong. You aren't going to jail."

"Innocent people go to jail all the time, and we all know it!"

"Please, Gen, just calm down. Here's Faith. You don't want to startle her, do you? Show her that big smile she's used to."

Once the teenagers had arrived to take the babies, the five adults gathered around the table. Brash laid out the facts as he knew them.

"What you overheard," he concluded, "was me saying that, as a lawman, I have to look at everyone as a potential suspect. I can't show favoritism. The only way to conduct a fair and unbiased investigation is to consider the facts only. There's no room for emotions and personal feelings. That's why I am recusing myself as lead investigator."

"Perry?" Genny shrieked in horror. "You're going to let *Perry* decide my fate?"

"No, I'm letting Officer Abraham take the lead. She'll collect information in a fair and unbiased way and make a recommendation based solely on the facts."

"What if she recommends that you arrest Genny?" Cutter's jaw was set with defiance. "Are you going to charge her with murder?"

"I'm confident that it won't come to that."

"But if it does?" Cutter pressed.

Brash chose his words with care. "You're a first responder, Cutter," he finally said. "There are times when your job forces you to make tough decisions. Waste thousands of gallons of water on a fully engulfed home you have no hopes of saving, or let it burn so that you can use those resources to save the neighbor's house. Risk your crew's life to go back in for a family's pet, or pull back and thank God you saved the people inside. Harden your mind to the fact that you're pulling your friend's lifeless body from a mangled car. I have to make tough decisions the same way as you do. I don't always like them, but I have to do what's best, what's right, and what's fair."

Cutter wasn't in any state of mind to be rational. He visibly recoiled, pulling back in his chair. "How could taking Genny away from our babies be fair? You know she didn't murder that woman! How is that right? How could that be for the best?" The more he talked, the more upset he became. Cutter scraped his chair back and stood, glaring down at his friend. "Best for who, Brash? Best for Genny? Best for our family? Or best for your career?"

Maddy gasped at his brazen accusation. Even Genny was surprised by the insult. "Cutter," she hissed, "sit down. You know you don't mean that!"

He sat as she requested, but he didn't back down from his claim. All the while, his eyes burned into Brash's. "Do I? Do I really? Because right now, it sure looks that way!"

Brash cleared his throat, trying hard to keep his temper in check. "May I remind you that nothing has happened yet? No formal suspects have been named. No one has been arrested. The investigation is still in its earliest stages."

"But *if* it progresses in the wrong direction, and *if* your oh-so-fair officer recommends that you charge Genny with murder," Cutter pressed, "what are you going to do then?"

Again, his friend spoke with care. He knew everyone at the table held their breaths, waiting for his answer.

"*Then* I'll make the tough decisions," he replied. "Will I risk turning my best friends against me by making a decision based on evidence rather than emotion, carry out my duties as required by law, and allow her defense lawyer and the American justice system to defend Genny's innocence once and for all? Or do I ignore my vow to uphold the law even as it applies to me, risk undue scrutiny by the press and DA's office for showing favoritism—"

"See?" Cutter broke in, yelling at his friend. "You're

thinking about saving your own neck!"

"I'm thinking about saving Genny's!" Brash shouted back.

The room went still. The harsh reality of Brash's outburst rendered them all silent. Even Cutter.

Brash released a long, weary sigh. His head drooped forward, and he forced himself to calm down, take deep breaths, and speak in an even voice.

"Look. Let's say no one else is a viable suspect, and I refuse to implicate my friend. Even if the DA doesn't press charges now, there's no statute of limitation on murder. You know how relentless the media can be. Politicians can be ruthless in their climb to the top. It could be ten, fifteen, even twenty years from now, but there will always be some hotshot reporter, some ladder-climbing ADA, who decides to re-open the investigation on a newsworthy cold case. What do you think they'll do when they get even a whiff of impropriety in this case? They'll automatically assume Genny was guilty, and that I withheld evidence. They'll build a case around rumor, suspicion, and the illusion that something shady went down."

Brash's dark eyes implored them to understand. "Even if I refused to press charges, should it come to that—even if I quit my job to keep from doing so—I doubt my successor would hold the same convictions. I would be taking a stand, but I would also lose what little control I have over the situation. At least with me in the background, I can see what's happening in the case and watch its progress. I can direct my officers to explore *all* possibilities, not just the most obvious ones."

Madison's voice was small and hurt as she said, "So, you'd just let them arrest an innocent person? A person who's my oldest and dearest friend and the only sister I've ever known?"

"No one's getting arrested yet, Maddy!" Having reached the end of his patience, Brash slapped the top of the table with his palm. "Everyone here is jumping to conclusions, the same way the public will do when they get wind of the knife." His knee popped as he pushed to his feet. "Let. Us. Do. Our. Job. Let us do a full investigation and find the person responsible for Anastasia Rowland's murder. Trust us to be professionals. Trust *me.* Is that asking too much?"

Without waiting for an answer, Brash strode from the room.

# 12

Their New Year Day celebration didn't go as planned. Genny and Cutter decided to leave and spend a quiet day at home with their babies. Granny Bert helped Madison finish cooking but opted to take a to-go plate home with her. After a long shower, Brash returned to the station. When Maddy asked if they could talk about what had happened earlier, he said it would have to wait. That left Madison and the kids to eat, but no one had much of an appetite.

Members of the drama club had agreed to clean up after the party but in light of last night's events, Madison wouldn't hold them to it. She was relieved when the drama instructor and two other faculty members volunteered to help. Without notice, Lydia deCordova showed up to help and in no time, had coordinated a small army to come in to lift, move, and clean. They had the house mostly in order by evening.

Best of all, Brash's mom knew to ask only family members and close friends guaranteed not to ask a lot of nosy questions. One look at Madison's face told them all they needed to know about the status of the investigation.

By the time Brash came home that evening,

Madison knew he was too tired to talk. Anything they said now would end in an argument, and another argument with her husband was the last thing she wanted. He warmed up a plate of New Year's luck, took another shower, and fell into bed. He was asleep before Madison could clean the kitchen and climb the stairs to their bedroom.

The next morning, Genny knew it was crucial that she show up at the restaurant. Anything else would be seen as cowardly, if not a silent admission of guilt.

"Hey, boss lady," Thelma greeted her. "We weren't sure you'd be here this morning."

"Why not? I'm here every morning, unless the girls are sick."

"I just meant... well, you know. No one would blame you if you stayed home."

"She's right. We can handle things here," Ann assured their boss.

"I appreciate it, ladies. But we all know that people are taking bets on whether or not I'll show my face in town after recent events. Half the town already has me tried and convicted."

"Not half the town," Dierra protested. "Maybe a fourth," she admitted, "but not half. Most people love you, Miss Genny."

"Thank you, sweetie. And thank you ladies for looking out for me. But I'll be fine. Honestly, I will. What I need is to get to work, show people I have nothing to hide and nothing to be ashamed of, and maybe things will go back to normal." Even as she said the words, they sounded hollow upon her tongue.

"That's the spirit!" Ann said.

Trenessa Long came bustling through the door,

speaking over her shoulder as she hung her coat on the nearby hooks. "Okay, girls, we've got the café on our own today. We're going to plaster smiles on our faces, speak in upbeat voices, and take nothing off our customer's smart mouths! We have to rally for Genny's s—" She whirled around and saw the woman she referred to standing before her. "G—G—Genny!" she stammered. "I wasn't expecting you this morning."

"Obviously. But like I told the girls, I'm always here in the mornings. Today's no different."

"Uhm, no. No, of course not."

Genny grew impatient. "Look, why don't we just say it and get it over with? Get it off all our chests, so we can get on with our day. Yes, Anastasia Rowland was murdered on New Year's Eve. She was our rival, and our business suffered because of her, but I never wished the woman any harm. I would *never* have hurt her! And in case you heard the ridiculous lie Shilo Dawne is spreading about me attacking her, that is a lie. She is making a fool of herself fawning over my husband, but I have nothing to feel insecure about. I would certainly never attack her. All of this is just too ridiculous to take seriously, and yet I must. I'll be blamed for both, but I had nothing to do with either incident."

"Of course not! We never thought you did!" Thelma said.

"I didn't mean to imply guilt," Trenessa apologized. "But I think it's prudent that we approach this with an upbeat attitude."

"I think we should approach it as the solemn occasion that it is," Genny countered, "and express our heartfelt condolences on behalf of her family, friends, and employees. As for Shilo Dawne's accusation, we shouldn't stoop so slow as to even acknowledge it." Genny fastened her apron around her waist. "Now, with that out of the way, it's time to get to work. If I know this nosy little town of ours, we'll be extra busy. Everyone will show up, hoping to get a confession from me or to see some mysterious blood trail behind me."

"Hey," Thelma said on a shrug, "if it fills seats..."

Genny's prediction not only came true, but there was a waiting line trailing out the front door and down the sidewalk. *Fresh Starts* was naturally closed out of respect for its owner, but this went beyond the new eatery's seating capacity. This was curiosity, plain and simple. Outright nosiness.

Genny didn't dare hide in the kitchen. She waited tables the same as she always did and brought the subject up before the busybodies could. "It's such a shame what happened to Anastasia Rowland, don't you think? We're donating all of today's tips to her staff, in hopes of offsetting any loss in pay they may face. So don't be afraid to drop an extra dollar or two on the table. It all goes to a worthy cause. Now, what can I get for you?"

By the time the breakfast crowd left, the noonday crowd had arrived. On the second turn-around, trouble came through the door in one round bundle of misery and mankind.

"See? See," Myrna Lewis told her companions, "I *told* you she did it! *She* killed Anastasia! She did it to get business back. And it seems to be working, until they lock her up and throw her in prison."

Myrna smirked when she saw Genny's stricken face.

It had been a long day already, and Genny was exhausted. Her feet hurt. Her back ached. And she missed her babies something fierce. She had little patience for any of the customers she heard whispering behind her back today, and none at all for the obnoxious woman standing across the room, directly challenging her.

She was done with being nice.

Genny held up her hand, motioning for Myrna to stop where she was. Without bothering to have the conversation in private, she spoke so all could hear. It made their gossiping and speculation so much easier this way.

"Stop right there, Myrna." Her voice was clear and distinct. "We reserve the right to refuse service to anyone, and I refuse to serve you. A woman has died. Show some respect and, for once in your life, act like a halfway decent human being. No one will put up with your petty attitude and accusations today."

"You—You can't do that!" the red-faced woman sputtered. "You're obligated to serve your customers, and I'm a customer."

"Not a welcomed one, and no, I'm not. Please leave."

"I'll do no such thing! I demand to be seated."

Genny crossed her arms across her chest and gave her a stony look. "And I refuse to seat you."

"I'll make you!"

"Why?" Genny countered. "All you do is complain. About the food. About the service. About the prices. If you're so unhappy eating here, why do you bother? And why today, of all days? Shouldn't you be at home, grieving for your friend?"

"You imply she wasn't my friend, but she was!" Myrna insisted emphatically. "She was a dear, dear friend, and I am *devastated* by her death."

"Then go home and grieve for her. If my dear, dear friend died, I would be too distraught to go out for lunch."

"She didn't just die. *You* murdered her!" She pointed a pudgy finger at Genny. "You!"

Genny knew she should have kept her mouth shut, but Myrna had pushed her too far. "Are you sure you want to eat here, then? Aren't you afraid I might poison you?"

Myrna gave an exaggerated gasp, worthy of any drama club scene. Genny almost asked if she had considered joining Troupe Over the Hill. But Myrna's outraged comments were nothing to laugh about.

"Did you hear her?" she demanded of the room. "Everyone in here heard her threaten me, right? She said she was going to poison me!"

"I said no such thing, you foolish woman!" Genny hissed. She moved closer, hoping to herd her out the door. "Now leave, before I call the police and have you thrown out."

"They'd do it, too, because you have them in your back pocket," the woman hurled with hate. "Everyone knows the investigation will be biased with Brash deCordova running it. My poor friend won't get any justice at all! Maybe someone should call in the Texas Rangers and let them take over."

From somewhere in the back, a man yelled, "It'll probably take a whole unit of them just to haul your fat ass out of here!"

Everyone chuckled, making Myrna that much angrier. She wagged her finger again. "Just you wait, Genesis Baker Montgomery. You won't be laughing when you're standing behind bars, separated from those babies of yours!"

Genny's hands clenched at her side, itching to plant themselves in Myrna's fat, sneering face. It took everything she had not to launch into the woman, but her resolve was fading fast.

Thelma saw Genny's hand begin to move. She hurried forward, putting her hands on her boss' arms from behind. She hoped it looked like a show of support rather than an attempt to avoid a fiasco, because, in truth, it was exactly that. She had to stop her boss from doing something they would all regret.

"Miss Genny, don't listen to that old toad. She's mean and hateful, and everyone knows it. She's leaving anyway. Right?" Thelma stared at Myrna, daring her to argue.

Myrna, of course, argued.

"I'm doing no such thing! I demand service."

Feet shuffled within the restaurant, and soon four able-bodied men placed themselves in front of the portly woman. A fifth and sixth man soon joined them.

"Miss Genny asked you to leave," one of them said.

"But we ain't askin'," another said. "We're escorting you out."

Myrna puffed up like the toad Thelma called her. "First, she refuses to serve me. Then she threatens to poison me! Now she's throwing me out?"

"She ain't throwing you out, *we* are!"

The men crowded around the door in front of Myrna, forcing her to retreat. She screamed protests all the way to her car, throwing in a few obscenities for variety.

Inside, Genny quaked with suppressed rage. It was tempered with horror at what she had almost done. She almost struck a customer, even if that customer was Myrna and had very well deserved it. It was the very thing Shilo Dawne had accused her of doing, the thing she had believed she wasn't capable of. Until now.

Genny barely heard those who cheered and offered a round of applause. *Good riddance,* they all agreed.

She whispered a weak thank you to the men and quickly fled from the room.

Her employees insisted she go home, assuring her they could handle the rest of the crowd. Before she left, they huddled around her in support. Their kindness made her cry even harder.

The tears followed her home. Megan was there with

the girls and was surprised to see her home so early.

"Is everything—oh, Aunt Genny!" she said, seeing the tears streaming down Genny's face. "What's wrong?"

"Everything!" Genny flung herself on the couch and buried her face in a pillow.

"Do you want me to call Cutter?"

She shook her head, lifting it from the pillow enough to say, "No, don't bother him at work."

"You're sure?" the auburn-haired teen asked.

"Maybe you should," she decided. As Megan turned away, Genny changed her mind again. "No, don't. I'm okay. Really, I am."

Without promising anything, Megan turned away and discreetly texted Cutter. Genny hadn't even asked about the girls. That meant something was terribly wrong.

# 13

Brash tramped into Madison's office, his face dark as thunder.

"*What* was your friend thinking?" he demanded.

Madison looked up from her computer in surprise. Her eyes immediately went to Derron's empty desk. He said he had errands to run, which usually meant another shopping spree or a trip to the hair salon. One time, he came back with a particularly colorful result, and Brash had complained he caused a fender-bender in town because everyone was gawking at him.

"What has Derron done now?" she asked. "Whatever it was, it's not my fault."

"Not Derron. Genny!"

"Genny? Is she okay? What happened?"

"That's exactly what I want to know! What in the world got into her? What was she thinking?"

"I honestly don't know what you're talking about. I haven't talked to Genny since midmorning. I knew it would be a tough day for her, but they were slammed at the restaurant. She was too busy to talk."

"Myrna Lewis stormed down to the station, wanting to press charges against Genny for threatening to kill her."

"I know we all fantasize about it, but...."

"This is no joking matter, Madison! Genny has enough going against her without adding more. How do you think it looks, having someone else accuse her of attempted murder?"

"Someone *else*?" Madison picked up his use of words. "Is Misty Abraham actually accusing her of killing Anastasia?"

"I didn't say that. But you know there are plenty of people who are, and it doesn't help if someone adds a complaint of attempted murder."

"How, exactly, did Genny supposedly try killing Myrna?"

"Myrna says she threatened to poison her."

"First of all, a threat is different than an actual attempt."

"That's exactly what I told Myrna, but thank you, Granny Bert, for explaining the law to me."

Madison ignored his sarcasm. "Second, Myrna *says*. How do you know she isn't making the whole thing up?"

"She dragged in two witnesses with her. Both claimed they heard Genny make the threat."

"And you *believe* them?"

"It doesn't matter what I believe. I don't make arrests based on other people's demands, but I am obliged to look into the matter and take their concerns seriously."

"No one takes Myrna Lewis seriously. Not two months ago, she claimed she got food poisoning from eating there. Nothing came of it. I doubt they'll start listening to her now."

"Death threats are always serious, Madison, no matter who makes them."

"Have you talked to Genny about this? Or to other witnesses?"

"Genny went home after the incident. Her phone goes straight to voicemail. Megan told me she came home so distraught, Cutter gave her something to calm her down and sent her to bed. Meg's staying until the girls are down for the night."

"What about other witnesses?"

"Most of them that I talked to said she didn't actually threaten Myrna." He relayed the happenings as they were told to him but remained focused on Genny's response. "But what was Genny thinking? Doesn't she know making a scene right now, any scene, is only going to make things worse? She's not helping her cause, Madison, throwing out statements that can be perceived as threats!"

She knew he was upset with her. He only called her by her full name when he was mad. She stood from behind her desk and came around to stand in front of him, arms crossed over her chest.

"Make things worse, how, exactly?" Madison asked, narrowing her eyes. "I thought you said your oh-so-professional officer would investigate the case based solely on the evidence. Complaints about a different matter shouldn't come into play when investigating Anastasia's death."

"You're right, they shouldn't. But they can establish a pattern of behavior and offer a glimpse of the suspect's frame of mind at the time."

"Are you even listening to yourself? This is Genny we're talking about! You honestly think she has a pattern of murderous behavior?"

"Of course not. I'm simply pointing out that she should be more careful of what she says and what she does, especially at a time like this."

"A time like what?" Madison pressed. "Say it, Brash. A time like what?"

"A time when she's under close scrutiny."

"And why would that be?" she asked, tapping her toe in aggravated impatience.

"Why are you pushing me on this, Madison? You want me to say it? Fine! I'll say it!" Brash's dark eyes snapped with his own ire. "At a time when she's seen as a potential suspect in a murder investigation!"

"A suspect?" Despite pushing him on the matter, she was somehow surprised to hear him say it.

"What did you expect, Madison?" He sounded impatient. "The two of them were business rivals. They had some sort of altercation at the grocery store just two days before the murder. Genny's knife was found at the scene. You had to know she would be a suspect."

"But hearing you say it..."

"I don't like it any more than you do, but it's still a fact. Genny is a potential suspect in this murder."

Madison felt numb. "You know about the grocery store incident," she mumbled.

"I told you, Abraham is a good investigator. She also picked up on the fact that Genny has been on edge lately and acting out of character. I haven't noticed it myself, but I'm sure you have. Do you know what's she talking about?"

She didn't quite meet his eyes. "It's taking Genny a little time to adjust to all the changes in their lives."

"Like what the old wives tales call the baby blues?"

Madison bristled at his cavalier attitude. "It's called postpartum depression, and it's a very real thing. Almost twenty percent of all new mothers suffer from some form of PPD, so don't you dare act like it's an old wives tale! Even Shannon told mc she had it after having Megan. Did you not think it was real then, either?"

"Honestly, I was too busy being a jerk and blaming her for ending my football career to even notice," Brash admitted.

"You didn't notice your wife crying more than normal?" she said sharply.

"She always cried. Before, during, and after pregnancy. I figured it was something I had done."

Madison rolled her eyes. "You have no idea what hormones can do to a woman's body. *And* to her mind."

"Yeah? What's it doing to Genny's mind?"

She avoided eye contact and a direct answer. "I—I don't know what you mean."

"You can't always protect her, you know. If other people have noticed, Genny must be pretty bad off."

"All I can say is that Genny is having a particularly hard time right now, but she's working her way through it."

"'Working her way' as in medication? Therapy? Altercations at the grocery store?"

"What are you implying!"

"I'm not implying anything. But those are questions Abraham is sure to ask, and the answers may play a role in the investigation."

"Meaning what? How is that even relevant?"

Brash looked at her incredulously. "How can acting out of character play into allegations of physical assault, threats of murder, and the act of murder, itself? *Really*, Madison? You really have to ask that question?"

"Genny's depressed, not murderous!"

"Is she getting help for it?"

Madison was terrible at lying to her husband. "I—I really can't say."

"That could help her out in court, but not in having charges pressed against her."

Panic surged through her. "Meaning what?"

"If her symptoms are bad enough that she needs medical intervention, it would be reasonable to assume that she is, indeed, 'acting out of character.' Depending on the medication, it could also alter her behavior and her critical thinking. The argument could be made that the medicine had an adverse effect on her."

"I think that's exactly what it did," Madison murmured.

"By all sakes, don't let anyone hear you say that!"

"Why not? I would think a reasonable explanation for her behavior would be helpful."

"It would. For the DA. It would offer the perfect scenario for murder."

"M—Murder?" she squeaked. "You could charge her for murder because of the medication she's taking?"

"If it made her more aggressive or made her think and behave irrationally, yes. Again, a good defense attorney could use the same argument that the medication was at fault, not Genny herself, but by then, charges would be filed, and she would be arrested."

Madison stared at him in shock. The gravity of the situation had finally sunk in, and she was devastated. How could Genny—sweet, loving, kind-hearted Genny—be accused of murder? It was unthinkable.

She propped her bottom onto the edge of her desk, heedless of the papers she knocked aside. She was afraid her knees wouldn't support her much longer.

"Sooner or later," Brash pointed out, "Abraham is going to find out."

"Let it be later. She won't hear it from me!"

Brash rubbed the back of his neck, working out the tension that had steadily gathered there. "This is what I knew would happen," he grumbled. His voice lacked venom. He sounded more defeated than anything. "I knew I would be put in this position. Basically, if I don't tell her what I know, I'll be withholding evidence."

"You can't tell, Brash! Genny told me in confidence. The only reason I told you is because I can't lie to you, even when I want to."

He arched his brow in his signature look. It was half-frown/half-arched brow. Depending on the situation, it was interpreted as cynical, skeptical, slightly amused, or flat-out intimidating. "When you *want* to lie to me?" he questioned.

She waved off his comment. "Not about this. About things like the scrape down the side of the Expedition, or how much I paid for something."

"What scrape on the Expedition?" Brash frowned.

Madison wrung her hands. "Does it really matter right now? My best friend is in trouble!"

"If she pulls another stupid stunt like this, she will be. She'll be in a lot of trouble, and I may not be able to get her out of it."

"Brash, we have to do *something*. This is Genny we're talking about."

He turned away to pace, then turned back again. All the while, he massaged his neck.

"It's more like what we're *not* going to do," he said decisively. "We're not going to say a word about this to anyone. Not about her postpartum depression, not her medication, not anything. And not to anyone. Let Abraham discover it in her own time. By then, it may not matter."

"What—What do you mean?"

"Shilo Dawne is sticking to her claim that Genny assaulted her. I know, I know," he said, staving off the argument he saw forming on her lips. "It's not true, but it's her word against Genny's. There's rumors that Shilo Dawne may press charges. Coupled with Myra's claims, and the fact that Genny's knife was found at the scene, circumstantial evidence against her is stacking up fast."

Tears pooled in Madison's eyes. "I'm scared, Brash," she whispered.

Softening, Brash pulled her to him and held her close against his chest. "I am, too, sweetheart," he admitted. "I am, too."

As soon as Brash left for work the next morning, Madison called her grandmother.

"If it's not too early, I think I'll swing by for a cup of coffee."

"You know I've already finished a pot by now," Granny Bert assured her. "But I'll be glad to put on another."

"Maybe Miss Virgie would like to join us?"

She heard the excited uptick in her grandmother's voice. "You're working on something, aren't you? Should I call Wanda and Sybil, too?"

"Not just yet. I'll be there in about ten minutes."

"If it takes you ten minutes to get here, you must be walking."

"No, but I thought clothes might be nice. See you then."

Miss Virgie arrived only a few minutes after Madison. The older woman carried a plate of assorted breads and sweets with her, no doubt remnants of her overzealous love for holiday baking.

"I made bacon to offset the sweet," Granny Bert said, sliding a small platter onto the middle of the table.

Over their impromptu breakfast, Granny Bert asked what Madison wanted to talk about.

"I'm worried about Genny and this investigation. Brash didn't come out and say it, but I think she may be their prime suspect at this point."

"At this point," Granny Bert stressed. "It's only been a day and a half. Way too soon to jump to conclusions."

"We can't ignore the fact that Genny's knife was sticking out of Anastasia's dead body."

"Have they determined what time she died? And

what she actually died of?" Miss Virgie asked.

"If they have, I don't know about it. And probably won't, for that matter."

"I guess this new hoopla about Myrna doesn't help, either."

There was no need in wondering if they had heard. Her grandmother was like some all-knowing, all-seeing, all-hearing superpower. Nothing happened in The Sisters that escaped her attention.

"I'm sure it made matters worse. Shilo Dawne's accusations from the ball are unconfirmed, since no one actually heard or saw anything happen. But apparently, everyone in the restaurant heard what took place yesterday. Even if it didn't happen the way Myrna claimed, Genny did goad her and said things she shouldn't have said."

"In her defense," Granny Bert said, "she was dealing with Myrna. That woman could make a nun lose her temper. Her religion, too!"

"I don't think anyone would argue with you, but that doesn't help Genny."

"So, what will?" Miss Virgie wanted to know. "What can we do to help her?"

"I know Brash told us to stay away from this," Madison began.

"Which, he knew we wouldn't," her grandmother butted in.

"Of course not. And I know Miss Blond Bombshell is head of the case and will check things out on her own, but it won't hurt for us to launch our own quiet little investigation." She looked innocently at the ceiling, musing aloud as she drummed her fingers. "If only someone had officially hired me to prove Genny's innocence. That way, I would be obligated to check things out on my client's behalf."

"Consider yourself hired!" Granny Bert said.

"Virgie, you'll have to do the honors on this one. Brash told me to stay out of it, but you weren't in on the lecture."

"Done!" Virgie slapped her hand on the table like an auctioneer's gavel. "Tell me what I owe."

"Ten dollars should cover it," Madison decided.

Granny Bert nodded with approval. "Is that why it's just the three of us and not our loose-lip friends?"

"Miss Sybil can be discreet," Madison said, "but she's too sweet for her own good. She can't keep a secret from Wanda. For now, I think it's best we come up with a plan without them."

"What do you have in mind?" Miss Virgie asked.

"There has to be more suspects than just Genny, Doyle Nieto being one of them. What do we know about the man?"

"I know he's not the man in the full venetian mask," Granny Bert said.

"How do you know that?"

"When he doesn't commute back to Houston, he stays at the Bumble Bee. The man I danced with had no idea the Bumble Bee was an inn."

Madison jotted down notes in a spiral notebook. "That's a start, anyway. What else do we know about him?"

"I forgot all about this till now, but we saw him and Anastasia at *Montelongo's* on half-price margarita night. It looked like they were arguing. I caught a few words here and there. Anastasia looked mad enough to plumb *eat* a bumblebee. She called somebody an idiot. Probably him, from the look on his face. I know she told him, in no uncertain terms, not to push her."

"Hmm. Worth noting, but it could have been about anything. A new menu item, maybe. Hardly something worth killing her over."

"With all the hullabaloo, I didn't tell you this part,

either. Sticker went out to help Sybil get Wanda into the car—remember, it was half-price margaritas, and Wanda took advantage of the bargain— and he saw something strange happen outside. Nieto barged out of the restaurant, and that Norris character was there. They had words, and Nieto pushed him."

The news took Madison by surprise. "So, Nieto knows Norris?"

"Sure sounds like it. Sticker said it looked like Norris was hanging around, waiting for him to come out. That doesn't sound like an accidental run-in to me."

"Not at all." Madison scribbled in her notebook. "This is good. It gives us something to work with."

"How?" Virgie asked. "What are we supposed to do with that?"

"I'm not sure yet, but it's more than we had."

Granny Bert nodded in agreement. "Didn't Genny ask you to check out that nasty Norris man when he first threatened her with a lawsuit?"

"Yes, but honestly, I didn't do as much as I could have. The masquerade party was thrown into my lap, there was so much to do with Christmas, and then Cutter hired a lawyer to represent them. I admit I let it slide."

"But if I know you, you didn't delete any of the files you made. Pull 'em up on your computer and see if there's anything in there that's useful."

"I'll get Derron on that," she said. She stopped to shoot off a text to her employee.

"You think he came in to work so early?" Miss Virgie snickered. "I bet Wanda hasn't even cooked him breakfast yet."

Madison frowned. "She shouldn't spoil him so. Then he comes to the office and expects me to fix him coffee. Sometimes lunch!"

"You should burn a couple of meals—I know you can do it— and maybe he'll quit asking."

"Hey! In my defense," she reminded her grandmother, "I was fifteen at the time, and my new boyfriend was calling. Besides, it was time you got a new skillet."

"I may have something," Virgie offered, breaking into their trip down a scorched memory lane. "Not much, but every little bit helps. The day after that power glitch in town, Shilo Dawne called the fire department to *Fresh Starts*. She claimed they smelled gas. A week or two before that, she said she smelled smoke. The point is, Hank's cousin works there. She says no one else noticed the smells, just Shilo Dawne. Both times, she trailed Cutter out to the truck and fawned all over him. Both times, she blamed someone else for panicking and made herself out to be the hero when Anastasia asked about it. But this last time, Peg said the boss lady was none too happy about it. She called Shilo Dawne into her office and closed the door."

"You're saying Shilo Dawne may have held a grudge against her boss?"

"I told you it wasn't much, but it's possible."

"True. So, I'll add Shilo Dawne as a potential suspect, alongside Doyle Nieto. Anyone else?"

"Myrna Lewis," Granny Bert said.

"Why? Did she have some sort of argument with Anastasia? I thought she considered herself a bosom buddy to the woman."

"She did. But she also thought she had a stake in running the place, since she owned the building. Besides," Granny Bert admitted, "I'd just love to pin the murder on the old broad and get rid of her for the next twenty-five to forty years."

"I hate to break it to you, old friend, but we won't be around that long," Virgie said.

"I'm thinking of our grandchildren and their children."

"Thanks for looking out for us, Granny, but we can't blame her for something she didn't do."

"*Maybe* didn't do. She could have. Put her name on that list, just in case."

"Even with her name on it, it's still not much of a list," Virgie said, motioning to all the empty lines on the page.

"It's a work in progress. We'll add more as things develop," Madison decided.

Granny Bert harrumphed. "Let's just hope they develop before the Blond Bombshell decides she has enough on Genny and makes an arrest."

# 14

"I know she's your friend," Misty Abraham said to her superior, "but I'm building a real case against Genesis Montgomery. So far, she's shaping up to be our prime suspect."

It was hardly the sort of thing Brash wanted to hear first thing in the morning. He leaned back in his chair, studying the officers gathered around his desk.

"Friendship can't play into this, or any, investigation." His voice was firm. "In this office, we deal with facts. Facts that can be substantiated with eyewitness reports, time sequence, physical evidence, and opportunity to commit the crime. Even motives mean nothing without the facts to back them up."

"I'm working on gathering those facts, but I feel confident I can get them."

"We also don't deal with feelings, rumors, or hearsay. Facts only."

"Give me a few days, and I'll have them."

"A few days? Our victim has been dead for just over thirty-two hours. Doc Leonard puts the time of death right at midnight. We haven't even identified everyone who attended the party, much less interviewed them. This investigation is just getting started. We won't be naming a suspect until we have *all* the facts gathered." Brash's dark eyes bore into hers until she was forced to look away.

Brash turned his attention to Otis Perry. "Have you flagged anyone who needs to come in for additional statements?"

"Quite a few, actually," the older man answered as he flipped through his notes. "I asked Vina to set up interview times. There were several inconsistencies. We need to ask more questions and verify that information."

Nodding, Brash moved on to Schimanski. "Have you been able to identify the guests wearing full masks?"

"I'm aware of three men and one woman," the officer replied. "Phantom of the Opera, Batman, and one man in what was described as wearing a full venetian mask. The unknown woman wore a veil over her eye mask. From what I hear, none took off their masks when it was time to do so. No one remembers for certain when any of them left. And no one can identify any of them."

"Keep at it. I've gone over the footage from our security camera, but that was the one camera that wasn't working."

"Coincidence?" Abraham asked, jumping on the possible lead. "Who installed your system? Did they have reason to hold a grudge against our victim or reason to want her dead?"

"*By the Yard*, a professional company out of Bryan-College Station that the Home Again team initiated. They installed the system, and I highly doubt any of the techs had reason to dislike, much less kill, our victim. The truth is, Christmas bulbs interfered with most of the cameras along that side of the house. What wasn't blocked by the bulbs themselves was distorted by their glow."

"Why on earth would a professional lighting company do such a thing?"

"Because Maddy and I authorized it," Brash informed her. "A fuse went out, probably as a result of that ice storm just before the ball, and we needed a quick fix. They came out and rerouted a few wires and strings of lights. It will be fixed by next year, but it was a temporary solution for what's left of this holiday season."

"Did Genesis Baker know about it?"

"I can't be for certain, but I doubt it. She and Cutter came over on Christmas Day, before the storm, and she didn't come again until the day of the masquerade ball. She wouldn't know about the blocked field of vision unless she viewed the live feed."

"And could she have?" the officer pressed.

"I doubt it. Remember, Home Again was making a television show that had nationwide coverage. In exchange for sponsors providing their goods and services for free, the show highlighted each sponsor in a different episode. The security system is top of the line and high tech, designed to wow the audience and sell more systems. Hidden panels slide out to reveal multiple live screens, but we only open the panels when there's an alarm or reason to survey the grounds."

"Where are the panels? Did she have access to any of those areas?"

"Theoretically," Brash acknowledged, "every person who comes to the house has access to the panels. Now, moving on." Bringing up the next item on the agenda, he signaled the topic was closed.

When the meeting ended, Misty Abraham hung back, but Brash asked Otis to stay, instead. The female officer clearly wasn't pleased but said nothing as she closed the door behind her.

"It goes without saying," Brash told the man before him, "but I'm going to say it, anyway. When questioning witnesses, do not lead them. If they have something to say, they will do so without you putting any notions and names into their heads. I recused myself from this case because of my relationship to one of the possible suspects. You have a history with that same person, but with an entirely different perspective. I didn't name you as lead for that reason, along with the fact that Abraham has more experience in murder cases." He paused for effect. "I need you on this case, Otis, but not if your personal bias interferes with the case. Are we clear on that?"

Perry gave a perfunctory nod. "Yes, sir."

"Good. I'm glad we're on the same page. Facts, only."

He should have known Misty wouldn't give up so easily. The door had barely clicked shut before she knocked.

"Yes?" he asked when she was inside. He noticed she closed the door behind her.

"Are you unhappy with my performance on this case, sir?" she asked in a formal tone.

"Not at all. I think you're doing an excellent job."

She dropped the formality. "Then what was all of that about?"

"All of what?"

"Admonishing me in front of the others."

"I wasn't admonishing you. I was giving you instruction."

"From where I sat, it didn't sound like instruction. It sounded like ridicule."

"It wasn't meant as such. I was pointing out that it's much too early to name any one person as a suspect, much less the primary. Until all the facts are gathered or until we have a confession, there are only persons of interest."

"Don't you want to hear what I have so far?"

Brash didn't answer at once. He finally nodded. "I do. But I don't want to hear what you have on Genny Montgomery. I want to hear what you have on the business partner, Doyle Nieto. I want to hear what you have on Batman, the man she was seen dancing with for much of the night. I want to hear what you have on the last person to have seen her in the house. And on anyone who may have seen her go outside. I want to hear what you have on any of her prior relationships, business or personal, that went south. I want to hear what you are collecting on other persons of interest."

"You heard Perry and Schimanski. They're working on gathering most of that."

"You can't complete a puzzle, Officer Abraham, until you have all the pieces. I'll wait to hear what you have until then."

"Yes, Chief," she murmured. Her manner was stiff as she left the room.

Before Brash could open and read any of his emails for the day, Vina appeared at his door. "I don't know what you said to Abraham," she speculated, "but I wish I had worn my cotton uniform today. She had steam coming out of her ears. Could've taken the wrinkles right out of it and saved me the trouble of ironing."

Brash arched his brow as only he could do. "You would have ironed it again anyway, and we both know it."

"True. But I didn't interrupt you to discuss my ironing habits. I come bearing news. Mayor Posey wants to see you."

"Tell him to make an appointment."

"He did. He'll be here in thirty minutes."

"I came down to get a full report," Mayor John Posey announced a half hour later. "What's happening in the murder investigation?"

"It's still early in the investigation, John. Too early to have a clear picture on where we stand."

"There was a dead body on your lawn! What's not clear about that?"

"Quite a bit, actually. We still don't have a conclusive cause of death—"

"She had a knife stuck in her chest, for God's sake! How much clearer could it be?"

"According to the witness who discovered the body, the knife may have been placed there postmortem."

The mayor recoiled. "What kind of sick soul would stab a dead body?"

"That's one of the things that's still unclear."

"You're running out of time to clear them up, too."

"It's been less than thirty-six hours, for Heaven's sake. A thorough investigation takes time."

"Reggie Carr is already demanding that you step down. He says you're too close to the case. The murder took place at your house. Word has it that your wife's best friend is the prime suspect."

"There have been no suspects named at this time. Naturally, I recused myself from the investigation, as the murder took place at my home. Officer Abraham is taking lead, and I won't be collecting or processing any of the evidence. I will act in an overseeing capacity only, making certain my officers follow procedure and the rule of the law."

"He's not calling for you to step down as the lead. He's calling for your resignation from the force. He says no one in this office can conduct a fair and impartial investigation as long as you're in charge."

Brash leaned back heavily in his chair. "Mayor Posey, we live in a small community. Everybody knows everybody else. Everyone is connected in some way or another, either by blood, friendship, or community. Virtually every case we've ever handled in this department involved someone we knew, and it will always be that way. No matter what our connection is to any of the parties, it does not dictate the way we do our job. We follow the law, we uphold peace and justice, and we do so without bias."

Some of the starch left the mayor's posture. He slumped a bit in the chair, settling in more comfortably. John Posey had taken over mayorship when Bertha Cessna retired four years ago. He was a local, born and raised in Juliet, and presided over his domain with a style similar to hers. Be a good neighbor, mind the law and the Ten Commandments, and take pride in your community. Yet lately, as newcomers moved in and tested the limits of his philosophy, he had to be more forceful.

Until recently, most city ordinances were considered more of a suggestion than a law. There was still an obscure ordinance in the books stating that horse and wagons must be tethered at the back of all city buildings and weren't allowed on main thoroughfares. Juliet Blakely had written the code herself, back when she created the town in 1918. Nowadays, horses were an integral part of their parades and proudly pranced right down Main Street. No one bothered checking codes or ordinances for compliance.

The city folks from Dallas and Houston, those newcomers pushing their way into their peaceful little community, claimed to want a simpler, less complicated life. Yet the first time something didn't go their way, they yelled for stricter laws and more ordinances. They brought their rules and regulations with them and pushed for growth and progress. Basically, they tried to turn the little community into a mini replica of the cities they had vacated.

"Durn city folks," John Posey muttered. "I told him as much, but he's a hot head, that one. It's going to be a long two years with Reginald Carr on the council."

"You can tell Carr I won't be stepping down. If he wants me out, he'll have to personally push me out the door."

"You do know Joel Werner was behind his campaign for councilman." The mayor gave Brash a pointed look. With Myrna Lewis' help, Werner had tried taking Brash's job less than two years ago. His efforts were fruitless, but it didn't mean he wasn't still trying. "Not many people like either man, but money talks. Werner paid for that ridiculous commercial Carr made, plus the signs he plastered all over town. If you want my opinion, Werner is trying to buy influence on the council so that he can get himself appointed to your job."

"If the entire council feels he can do a better job than me, so be it. I won't compromise the integrity of this department for the sake of my own career."

"We all know that, Brash. No one can stand Reggie Carr, but we're forced to get along with him. Still, I gotta tell the council something. This is murder we're talking about. And it took place in our police chief's own yard! Carr and Werner are squawking about this being the second murder at one of your parties." He held up his hand to rebut his own statement. "I know, I know. Your wedding reception wasn't held at the Big House, but it still involved you. I don't have to tell you how bad that looks."

"I've never once seen a murder that looked pretty."

"No, but those two are already stirring up trouble."

"It's been less than two days!" Brash said with impatience. "Besides, you and Carr were both there. Did either of you see the murder take place?"

"Of course not! That old mansion was packed."

"Exactly. At the very least, give us time to identify all the guests present. We can't name a potential suspect if we don't know everyone who was there. Our suspect had to have access, and they had to have opportunity."

"What about motive? Who had motive to kill her?"

"That's one of the things my officers are working on," Brash assured him. "If you need specific details, you'll need to speak with Officer Abraham."

"Fair enough," the mayor said. "I'll remind Carr you need time to conduct a thorough investigation. But I can only stall him for so long. Then we'll all, myself included, want answers."

"We all do, John. We all do."

# 15

"Derron, did you read over the file on Lawrence Norris? What did you find?"

Madison asked the question as she warmed her hands by the fireplace. After a warm-up for New Year's Eve and New Year's Day, the weather had turned cold again. She was still chilled from her visit to Granny Bert's.

"Since you didn't give me much notice," the man pouted, shooting her a disapproving look, "I had to speed read, but in all honesty, there wasn't much to go through."

"I know I probably disturbed your leisurely breakfast, but you do work here," she reminded him dryly.

"You keep saying that, but my paycheck begs to differ, dollface."

"Your paycheck reflects what little time you actually spend working!"

"I have a very efficient system established. I do everything you ask of me, in less time than it would take someone else. Look at it this way. I'm saving you money." He batted eyelashes that may or may not have been enhanced by mascara and flashed his brightest smile.

Madison knew he was right. She also knew he was the best assistant anyone could ever ask for and that he kept her business running smoothly. Putting up with his antics and his eclectic personality was a small price to pay for loyalty and efficiency.

"Just tell me what you did find," she said with impatience as she crossed the room to her desk.

"I know I found my coffee cup empty," he grumbled under his breath.

"I have the same problem. You can fill them both after you tell me what you found."

He rolled his eyes the same way her teenagers did. "Fine," he huffed. Turning back to his computer screen, he read off the paltry list.

"Norris grew up in Houston and now lives one town over in Pasadena, which everyone knows is just a part of Houston. He's divorced with no children and apparently no girlfriend. Spends most of his time working and advancing his career."

"Where? Who's his employer?"

"It says he's an acquisition manager for *Greater Lone Star Developing, Inc.* They specialize in luxury condos, high-end resorts, and unique shopping experiences." Derron wagged his manicured eyebrows. "Sounds delightful. Just the sort of places I adore!"

"Hmm. That's odd."

"That I find such places delightful?" He looked offended. "You know I have highly curated tastes."

Madison glanced at his outfit for the day. His salmon-colored cashmere turtleneck cost more than her entire wardrobe. His full-length coat, now hanging nearby, was trimmed in mink. Derron didn't work here for the money. Between inheritances from his money-pinching mother and the late soap queen Caress Ellingsworth, plus his own savvy investment skills, he could afford whatever luxuries he desired.

"Not that. I was thinking about Lawrence Norris. He claimed he was in The Sisters on business but what kind? He dropped by for lunch at *New Beginnings* because of its excellent reputation. Which, of course, he is now trying to ruin due to his own clumsiness."

"Remind me. What happened to inspire his wrath?"

"Dierra said he was in a hurry the whole time he was there and very demanding. A terrible customer, she said. A kid at another table spilled their drink, and Thelma went for a mop to clean it up. Before she could get back, he jumped up from his table and started for the front. Apparently, he wasn't watching his surroundings, stepped in the drink, and fell."

"*That's* what he's suing over?"

"He hasn't officially filed a lawsuit yet, but he says it threw his hip out of joint and caused undue stress and public humiliation."

"Clumsiness usually is humiliating. Or," Derron grinned with another bat of his long eyelashes, "so I hear. I wouldn't personally know about those things."

"Not everyone has your poise and grace. Or your humility."

Ignoring her sarcasm, his eyes returned to the screen. "Back to Lawrence Norris. This isn't the first lawsuit he's been involved in. He sued—where did that go? Oh, yes, the now defunct *Lamoge* restaurant in Humble. They settled out of court with an undisclosed agreement. The restaurant went out of business shortly thereafter."

"What's in the location now?"

"It doesn't say in our notes. I'd have to look that up."

"Okay, do that. What else was in our initial files?"

"Just his educational and professional history. He attended Rice University, where he double majored in business and architectural design. His first jobs include a local construction company, a brief stint with a law firm, managing books for a restaurant, and working in the loan department of a bank before he was hired as a consultant for a new shopping mall in Baytown. From there, he went to work for the development firm."

"That's quite a resume. He's done a little bit of everything, hasn't he?"

"Sounds like it. Construction, loans, law, accounting, consulting, and now acquisitions."

"Maybe he's a jack of all trades, master of none?" Madison suggested.

"It's possible. Or maybe he had his eye on the prize all along and was learning the different aspects of business takeovers."

"That's what *Greater Lone Star Developing* does? They buy existing spaces?"

Derron tapped on his keyboard. "Yes, along with buying undeveloped land. From the looks of their website, I'd say they're a diversified company. Where there's a dollar to be made, they make it happen."

"It says that?"

"I did. Feel free to use the slogan if we should ever get a gig with an advertising agency. Just have them make the check out to Derron Mullins."

"I don't suppose you see a connection on there between Lawrence Norris and Doyle Nieto, do you?"

"Should I?"

"I'm not sure. Granny Bert said Sticker saw the two of them having what looked like a heated conversation outside *Montelongo's* last week. Nieto ended up shoving him."

"Maybe Norris wasn't looking where he was going and bumped into him? We've already established that he's clumsy and doesn't pay attention to his surroundings."

"Sticker said Norris was hanging around, like he

was waiting for Nieto to come out."

"Maybe there was a previous bump-in," Derron suggested. "From what you say, the man doesn't give up easily. When did he slip at Genny's?"

"October, I think. Maybe early November. It's been a while."

"Hold a grudge, much?"

Madison made no comment as she logged into her own computer. "You keep digging into Norris' past. I'm curious as to what business he had here in The Sisters. I think I'll find out more about Mr. Nieto."

Twenty minutes later, Madison gave a low whistle. "Wow. This guy is everywhere."

"What guy, and where is he? Is he cute?" Derron asked as he handed her the coffee she had requested earlier.

"I swear, you have the attention span of a three-year-old," she grumbled. "Doyle Nieto, that's who! He owns, or has an interest in, a dozen or so restaurants scattered all over the general Houston metro area. He and Anastasia have two locations together beside this one. The other two are in The Woodlands and the Galleria Mall."

"What is he doing here in little po-dunk Juliet, Texas?"

Madison narrowed her eyes. "Good question."

That afternoon, Madison checked in on Genny.

"Hey, sweetie," she said as she hugged her friend. "How are you doing?"

"I've been better."

"No offense, but you've looked better, too."

Genny's hair was tangled with uncombed waves, her bare face was red and splotchy from crying, bags pouched beneath her eyes, and she was still in her pajamas. They were a favored pair from Cutter spouting 'I'm so hot, I come with my own firefighter.'

At the moment, she looked lukewarm, at best.

"You're nothing if not honest," Genny sighed. "Come on in. The girls are napping."

The house, too, was a mess and so unlike her friend.

"Gen? Are you sure you're okay?"

"Honestly? No. No, I'm not!" She plopped down on the couch and buried her face in her hands.

Madison shucked her coat and took the seat beside her friend. "I understand. That's why so many people are concerned about you, and why one particularly worried individual has hired *In a Pinch* to launch a private investigation."

Genny looked up with a wry frown. "You can't hire yourself, Maddy."

"This was a paying customer."

"Granny Bert," she said with a knowing nod.

"Not Granny Bert. And not Cutter, either. Someone outside the family."

"Really?" A look of hope crossed Genny's face.

"Really. So, on behalf of my client, I'm here to ask questions." Madison took out her notebook and straightened into a professional pose.

"Go ahead. But I'm not sure what I can tell you because I have no idea how any of this could happen!"

"For starters, tell me about the cut on your hand."

Genny looked down at her still-bandaged hand, turning it over a couple of times. "I saw that the food trays were empty," she recalled, "so I was in the kitchen, pulling together one last offering. It was close to midnight, and Cutter suggested we celebrate right there, just the two of us. Now I realize he was trying to spare me from Shilo Dawne's ridiculous lie, but at the time, I thought it was romantic. Anyway, he offered to take the tray in for me, and I started cleaning up. The knife slipped as I started toward the sink, and it cut me as it fell."

"Did Cutter help you bandage it?"

"No. I told him it wasn't bad and to go on with the tray while I bandaged my hand. I knew you kept some supplies above the laundry room sink."

"Did anyone see you go in there?"

"I doubt it. The kitchen was empty, and the door into the hallway was closed."

"How long were you gone?"

"I don't know. Five minutes, maybe?" she guessed. "I had trouble wrapping it with only one hand. By then, it was bleeding pretty good."

"I thought you told Cutter it wasn't deep."

Her look was sheepish. "You know him. He's a worrywart."

"True. What happened after you came back in?"

"I finished cleaning up my mess. But... my knife wasn't on the floor. I thought someone came in, saw it laying there, and put it in the sink. There were some other dishes in the sink, so I didn't think anything about it. I just put the cutting board and stuff on top of it. I didn't want to get my bandage wet and about that time, someone from the clean-up crew came in, so I let them do it," she said with a shrug.

"When did you notice the knife was missing?"

"While they washed and dried, I collected the things I brought with me and put them in my storage tubs. The knife wasn't among them, and most of the cutlery was done. I was planning to go through everything one more time when Cutter came in. He didn't want everyone to hear, so he dragged me into the laundry room and broke the news that Anastasia had been murdered, and there was a knife found at the scene."

"Do you think it's possible someone came in while

you were bandaging your hand, took the knife, and used it to kill Anastasia?"

"It's the only thing that makes sense, but even *that* doesn't make sense!" Genny ran her fingers through her hair, explaining its tangled mess. "How could they get from the kitchen to the opposite side of the house in just a few minutes? The house was packed! With the firework display, I'm sure working their way through the lawn was like a maze. Besides, how could they possibly know Anastasia was there, in the one spot of the house that's blocked from the cameras? Even if it's the only possible explanation, it just doesn't make sense."

"I see what you mean," Madison admitted.

"Wait. You said they used the knife to kill Anastasia. So, they've completed the autopsy and determined that was the cause of death?" Her pale face turned even whiter.

"No, I meant theoretically. Besides, you know Doc at the funeral home acts as our ME. He usually determines the cause of death unless an official autopsy is ordered. To my knowledge, he's made no definitive statement. I think that means there's no cut and dried answer, if you'll pardon the pun."

"What if he decides she *was* stabbed to death?" Genny wailed.

"What if he doesn't?" Madison challenged. "Genny, you can't let this take over your life. You have to pull yourself together and get back to work. People will talk if you don't."

"They'll talk even if I do."

"What's that Miranda Lambert song say? Go paint your lips, fix your makeup, hide your crazy, and act like a lady. Hold your head up, Genny. You did nothing wrong. Start acting like it."

"You're starting to sound an awfully lot like your

grandmother," Genny muttered. "About as bossy, too."

"She did a pretty good job raising us, didn't she?" From the time Madison's parents dumped her on her grandparents' steps, she and Genny had been the best of friends. Faced with a strained relationship at home, Genny spent more time at the Cessna household than she did her own.

"Okay, okay," Genny relented. "I'll go to work tomorrow."

"Good. Now, tell me about Myrna and how you 'threatened' to poison her?" Air quotes emphasized the word.

Genny rolled her eyes. "You know how melodramatic Myrna can be. I was in no mood for her and her spiteful ways, so I stopped her at the door and asked her to leave. She demanded I let her in and serve her. I asked her why. All she ever does is complain. And I told her that if she and Anastasia were as close as she claimed, she should be home mourning her friend instead of gallivanting about town."

"Now who sounds like Granny Bert?"

"Anyway, she pointed her fat little finger at me and said I was the one who killed Anastasia. I should have kept my mouth closed, but I couldn't help it. I asked her again why she wanted to eat here. I mean, if I were indeed a murderer, wouldn't she be afraid I might poison her?"

Madison fought a smile at Genny's vivid recap. "And then?"

"Then she gasped like some soap screen diva and claimed I had threatened to kill her. By then, everyone in the restaurant had turned to listen. Luckily for me, most of them were on my side and let her know it. Joe Don Peavy and a bunch of other guys marched up to the door and all but threw her out. Unfortunately, they didn't have any duct tape for her mouth. She accused me of having the police department in my back pocket. And she made some horrible comment about when I was behind bars and separated from my babies. I swear, I was *this* close" —her fingers were so close, they almost touched— "to punching her in the face. I think I would have if Thelma hadn't stepped in."

"I'm so glad you didn't. She definitely would have pressed charges, then."

"She deserved it, saying such a despicable thing!"

"Absolutely, but you know you only fueled the flames for more gossip. If, for some reason, Myrna does come back in, promise me you won't do anything rash."

"You mean, like, actually poison her? Because I'm tempted!"

"Genny, you can *not* be overheard saying that. Promise me you'll keep any such thoughts to yourself. You need to be extremely careful of what you say and do in public."

Genny cut her eyes toward her friend. "Does this warning come from your client or from your husband?"

"From a very concerned police chief who is trying very hard to walk the fine line between being loyal to you and being loyal to his oath." Madison put her hand on Genny's leg. "Gen, I know things were strained between all of us on New Year's Day. You have no idea how difficult this is for Brash. But he's trying. He really is."

Genny didn't quite meet her eyes. "I know that. And I don't want this to affect our relationship. But even if I can understand, I'm not sure Cutter can," she admitted. "He's in all-out 'defend-my-wife-with-life-and-limb' mode."

"Naturally. And for the record, Brash knows you didn't do this. But you know he can't be seen as prejudiced, or it could taint everything. He has to stand back and let the evidence prove that someone else committed the crime. You can't imagine how frustrating it is for him, not being actively involved in this investigation."

"My head knows that. Doesn't mean my heart agrees."

"Believe me, I understand. And to be honest, I feel the same way. That scene with Myrna just about sent him over the top, and he stormed in, fussing at me about it. We had a big fight."

"Oh, Maddy! The last thing I want to do is come between you and Brash." Genny gripped her friend's hand in sincerity.

"Like you, I understand his predicament. Doesn't mean I like it." She squeezed back. "But we'll get through it, the same way you will." With a decidedly brighter smile, Madison added, "And just because Brash can't be involved in the investigation doesn't mean I can't. Unofficially, of course. But there's no law against snooping, and I happen to have access to some very prolific snoopers."

For the first time since Madison had arrived, Genny managed a small chuckle. "That you do, my friend. That you do."

# 16

Genny opened the restaurant the next morning, arriving before any of her workers. She needed the place to herself in order to find the comfort and inspiration *New Beginnings* had always afforded her.

She had used the funds she inherited from the Morgans to start the business. The elderly couple had taken her under their wing when she first moved to Boston, where they used their influence to get the up-and-coming chef a position with a very prestigious restaurant there. Genny had been miserable there, hating the petty competition among chefs and the drama that went with it. The Morgans encouraged her to quit and become not only their private chef, but the manager of all their affairs. They were the loving, supportive parents she had craved growing up, and she had been devastated by their deaths.

The Morgans had believed in her and encouraged her to pursue her dreams, so Genny moved back to her hometown, purchased one of the town's vacant old buildings, and launched her dream of owning a restaurant. She transformed the empty, drafty shell into a warm, cozy space full of mouth-watering aromas and the sound of friends and family gathering over a meal. Food, she believed, was the universal symbol of love and caring.

*New Beginnings* wasn't only her dream, it was a tribute to the Morgans and their unwavering faith in her abilities. It had given her new focus and helped her manage the grief of losing them. And it was there that she had met Cutter, the one true love of her life.

Walking into the restored space had always given her a sense of pride, knowing what she had created. Working with her hands—kneading made-from-scratch dough for her pastries, stirring up a special sauce for an entree— brought her a sense of peace and satisfaction. Until she became a wife and mother, it was the best feeling in the world, and the thing that gave her the most joy.

These days, Genny found the lines between her professional joys and her domestic joys blurring. Worse than blurring, the two seemed to bump into one another, both vying for her attention. She had yet to find the right balance between them. This madness called postpartum depression wasn't helping.

Nor was this new disaster with Anastasia. What if she were charged with murder?

Fighting off a wave of panic, Genny pulled her cannisters, bowls, and measuring cups in around her. These were her armor, fending off inner demons and wrapping her in a cocoon of safety. If she could get her head in the right place and her balance back on track, she could face anything.

Soon, the magic of baking overtook her worries. Kneading the pliable dough, working it into the shape and consistency she wanted, watching it rise and go into the oven, and knowing it would come out golden and delicious gave her the peace and resolve she sought. If the dough could be stretched and pulled, punched and poked, and still emerge from the fire as an even better version of itself, then so could she.

For months now, someone had been targeting her business, trying to sully her hard-earned reputation and turn clientele against her. Anonymous sources had turned her in to the health department on numerous occasions. Then came Lawrence Norris and his threats of a frivolous lawsuit. Close on the heels of his so-called accident had been the arrival of *Fresh Starts*. Now, it appeared she was being framed for the murder of Anastasia Rowland.

Genny didn't know if the latest situation was related or not. Perhaps her dropped knife had simply been a convenient weapon for a crime of passion. But something in her gut told her it was somehow tied to the downward spiral she had been trapped in recently, and if she didn't do something soon, she might just crash.

If her staff was surprised to see her there that morning, they hid it behind genuine smiles of affection. And her timing couldn't have been better as customers poured into the restaurant. *Fresh Starts* had reopened that morning, but the real buzz was at *New Beginnings*. Townspeople speculated on whether or not Genny would show up. They came to see for themselves, crowding into the café like old times.

As the noonday crowd dwindled down, Genny sneaked home to check on the girls. She promised the staff she'd be back in time for their dinner guests. Normally she didn't work the full day, but if she wanted to be seen, it may as well be for the entire day.

She missed the arrival of Dierra's mystery man. Since she had mentioned doing an article on her boss, Dierra hoped he would come in again to meet Genny. But for now, she had him to herself. Lucky for her, she was on her lunch break and had time to talk. She was delighted when he asked to join her at her table.

"This place is amazing!" he said with enthusiasm. He looked around, taking note of the soaring ceiling and the blended elements of old and new, industrial and antique, functionality and charm.

"You should have seen it before Miss Genny bought it," Dierra lauded. "It was practically in ruins. She gutted the entire thing and started over."

"Three floors?" he inquired.

"Yes, but the third floor isn't fully refurbished."

"That's fine," he murmured, still absorbed in the exposed brick walls and the stained and sealed concrete floor.

"I guess she redid the plumbing? Electrical?" he asked.

"She redid *everything,*" Dierra told him. "Gutted it and started from scratch."

"Impressive."

"Just wait until you taste her food!"

"Then why aren't you eating yours?" he teased.

"I—I was waiting for yours to come out," she admitted shyly. "I thought we could have lunch together."

"That would be nice."

Warmed by his smile, she dared to admit, "I'm glad you came. I wasn't sure if you were still in town."

"There was a complication that took longer than expected."

"Sorry," she said. A shy smile belied the statement. "Ah, here's your food now."

At the back of room, two older couples finished their meal. Granny Bert and Sticker had invited the Adamses to join them for a late lunch.

"After that scene with Myrna, it's good to see Genny back in the saddle," Sticker said. "That's what you gotta do. You get bucked from your horse, you get right back in there and ride."

"No one in their right mind would believe Myrna over Genny," Virgie said.

"It ain't just Myrna," the old cowboy complained. "Now there's this nonsense from the Nedbalek girl and, on top of that, rumors that Genny was involved in the Rowland woman's death. That's a pretty hard buck. Gotta hurt coming out of the saddle like that."

"Has Cutter said anything more about Anastasia Rowland's death?" Virgie asked.

"Nope. Just that Genny's all tore up about it."

"By the way." Virgie tried hard to sound casual. "Bertha says you saw that partner of hers and the Norris guy in a heated conversation the other night."

"Looked that way to me, 'specially when Nieto shoved him."

"Do you know what they were arguing about?"

"Didn't hear it, just saw it. I had my hands full stuffing your friend into Sybil's car."

"I should have gone out," Granny Bert snickered, "just to watch the show."

"Say," Hank remarked, his eyes roving about the restaurant. "There's that fella I told you about, Virgie. The one who came up out of the blue and wanted to buy a piece of our place."

"Where?" his wife asked.

"Over yonder, talking to DeeDee."

His wife slapped at his arm. "For the hundredth time, her name is Dierra."

"Okay, Dierra. It's him, all the same."

"Do you know him, Bertha?"

Granny Bert peered over her shoulder and shrugged. "I reckon it's her new boyfriend."

Hank made a sound of disgust. "He told me he was from Houston."

"Silly man," Virgie said. "They can live in different towns and still be an item."

"What's this about buying some of your land?" Granny Bert wanted to know. "I didn't know it was for sale."

"T'aint. Told him so, too."

"What'd he say to that?" Sticker asked.

"Upped his price, but I said it wasn't for sale. Period."

"Looks like he's still trying to woo you," Virgie mumbled. "Don't look now, but here he comes."

The young man approached their table with a broad smile and an outstretched hand. "Mr. Adams, what a pleasure to see you again."

"Same. This here is my wife Virgie and our friends Sticker Pierce and Bertha Cessna. Sorry, but I don't recall your name right now."

"Kelvin Quagmire, sir. It's a pleasure to meet you all."

After a few minutes of chitchat, Kelvin said he had only come to say hello and would let them get back to their meal.

"Done with lunch," Hank said, "but there's always room for one of Genny's desserts."

"Then I'll be sure to order one when I'm done with my meal. Good day to all of you."

When he was gone, Virgie acknowledged, "He seemed nice enough. But we still aren't selling to him."

When Granny Bert watched him walk away, Sticker chided, "He's too young for you, Belle."

"It's not that, you old coot. But something about him is awfully familiar..."

"Maybe you've seen him in here before," Virgie suggested.

"You heard him say it was his first time here."

"Maybe you've seen him in town with Dierra?"

"Maybe." She sounded doubtful as she turned back around to face her friends. "What were we talking about before he came over? Oh, yes. Nieto's altercation with that snake Norris."

"Not much more to say," Sticker told her. "That's it. Saw them talking, he pushed the guy, and they both stalked off."

"And you didn't catch *anything* that was said?"

Sticker twirled his white mustache in thought. "Maybe I caught a word or two. Seems like one of them said something about money. The other said the word threat. Like, are you threatening me? That's all I heard."

"Keep thinking on it. Maybe you'll remember more. You didn't say any of this the first time I asked."

"I told you about seeing Ms. Rowland talking to the Phantom of the Opera at the party, didn't I? That looked like a heated exchange, too."

"You didn't by chance hear any of that conversation, did you?"

"I could hardly hear you, even when we were dancing together. That place was hoppin' like a June bug on hot pavement."

"Did we ever figure out who that was?" Virgie asked.

"No clue," Granny Bert answered.

"If Belle doesn't know," Sticker asserted, "then no one does."

"True," Virgie asked. "But Hank here told me something I didn't know until that night. I didn't realize Joel Werner was behind Reggie Carr's bid for the council."

"He's no doubt still gunning for Brash's job," Granny Bert complained. "Probably figures if he can buy enough seats on the council, they'll fire Brash and give him the position."

"Where'd he get all his money, anyway? He's been in law enforcement most of his life, and nothing high level. Not a lot of money there," Hank said.

"Unless you're involved in something shady," Granny Bert harrumphed. "And I hear there's plenty of shade hanging over him. I think they're still investigating that supposed suicide of a rancher in Walker County. Werner was tangled up in that somehow. Botched the evidence, if I recall."

"Sounds about right. And Carr is just the sort to fall in with him. Didn't he scam his insurance company when some of their gifts were stolen during the Christmas Crimes?"

"Sure did. Claimed they had purchased all sorts of high-end stuff, when Maddy said everything in their house was more of the garage sale variety."

"We don't need men like him on the council, that's for sure!" Hank proclaimed. "Now, about that dessert... where did Sierra get off to?"

"Dierra, Hank. *D*ierra. And she wasn't our waitress. Thelma was," his wife corrected him.

Even the dashing Kelvin Quagmire had gone before the foursome finished their leisurely meal, complete with scrumptious desserts and more coffee. With only one table still occupying a spot during the afternoon lull, Thelma took her break and invited Dierra to sit with her.

"So? Tell me all about your handsome lunch companion! Did he ask you out?"

"Not exactly," the younger woman admitted. "But he did say he'd come back in again soon."

"Okay, okay. Nothing wrong with taking it slow."

"Maybe Miss Genny will be here then, and he can interview her."

Thelma frowned. "About that."

"Yeah, you're right. His interview with Anastasia may not run now. It might look bad on Miss Genny if she capitalized on the situation."

"That's true enough, but that wasn't what I was

talking about."

"Really? Then what did you mean?"

"Didn't you say he freelanced articles and did a food blog? Did he talk much about his job today? Or the food?"

Dierra propped her chin up with a cupped palm, clearly pouting. "Not really. He seemed more interested in the building than he did the food. He spent most of our conversation on the intricacies of the brickwork, the clever placement of air ducts, and how much natural light would pour into the space if the wooden shutters were removed. But you know Miss Genny uses them in the summer when the heat comes in through the glass, and sometimes in the winter, if it's bitter cold outside. Honestly, he spent more time looking at his surroundings than he did me! I'm not sure he even paid much attention to his food."

"Sounds like he's a fan of old architecture."

"Borderline fanatic, if you ask me," Dierra complained.

Thelma pushed the food around on her plate. "How well did you say you knew this fella?"

"Hardly at all. We met at the Christmas Parade and hit it off. We found a bench and had hot chocolate together. We ended up talking for a couple of hours. Why?"

"Well, maybe it's nothing. Maybe he has a couple of jobs. A lot of folks do these days, just to make ends meet. But Hank Adams mentioned that he had approached him about buying a piece of his property."

Dierra was surprised. "Kelvin did?"

"That's what he said."

"Maybe he decided he liked the area well enough to move here." Her voice held a hopeful note. "He did say he had friends here."

"I don't think it was personal. Hank said he left a

business card."

"If he's in business for himself as a freelance reporter, that makes sense."

"He couldn't remember the name of the realty firm he was with, but he said it was some group out of Houston. Sure sounds like a real estate agent to me."

"If that's so, why wouldn't he just tell me?"

"Maybe he wanted to impress you and thought being a reporter sounded more interesting? If he knew you worked at a restaurant, maybe he threw in the bit about doing a story on Anastasia just to sound important."

Dierra twisted her lips. "I didn't peg him for a salesman. Then again, he was obsessed with this building. Thinking about it, he did sound sort of like someone trying to sell, or maybe buy, a piece of property."

"Then what about his offer to Hank? What's so all-fired hot about The Sisters real estate market all of a sudden?"

"Beats me." Dierra shrugged. "Oops, gotta go. Table fifteen is ready to check out."

# 17

Blake came home looking for his mother.

Her fingers busy on the computer keyboard, Madison didn't take time to text him back. She used the intercom to say, "In my office, sweetie."

A few minutes later, her son ambled into her office, munching on a snack.

"What's up?" she asked without looking up from her screen.

When Blake remained silent, she glanced up to see him wearing an uncertain expression. It wasn't a common look on her normally confident son.

"Blake? Honey, is something wrong?"

"I have something for you, but I'm not sure I should give it to you."

"They mail report cards to the house, you know."

"It's not that."

"A speeding ticket?"

"Not that, either."

With work to do, Madison grew impatient. "This isn't forty questions, Blake. Just show me."

He handed over a computer-generated list.

Madison puckered her brow. "What is this? All I see are numbers with names beside them."

"It's the list of all the tickets sold for the ball. The teacher, uh, doesn't know I made a copy."

The pucker deepened. "Will you get in trouble for this?"

"I don't *think* so," the teen said, but his tone was uncertain. "I mean, the information was there for all of us to see. Everyone had the same number of tickets to sell. We had to know who sold all their tickets, who to collect them from if they didn't, that sort of thing. Before the ball, it was posted on the wall at school."

"And now?"

"On his desk," he admitted. "I don't think it's a big deal but, just in case, maybe you shouldn't mention this to anyone at school."

"I won't. And thanks. This may prove to be helpful."

"I hope so. Everyone is saying how Aunt Genny might be arrested. I know she couldn't have done this, but it doesn't keep people from talking."

"People will always talk. The juicier the news, the faster it spreads."

"You sound like Granny Bert."

Madison smiled. "I've been getting that a lot lately."

"Cool. So, anyway, just hope it helps."

"I do, too, sweetie. Thanks again."

Madison perused the list after Blake was gone. Not surprisingly, the first tickets had been sold to the parents of drama club members. Close friends and other family members were next, along with a few business owners and local politicians from around the county. When the venue was changed to the Big House, the list became more diversified. Many of the older citizens around the community splurged on the cost of the tickets, no doubt eager to see the grand ballroom one last time.

Even though the mansion was packed that night, Madison remembered seeing most of the people on the list. There were a couple of names there, however, that surprised her.

*Lawrence Norris dared step foot in my house? If I had recognized him, I would have thrown him out!* Inwardly, she fumed.

*And Doyle Nieto? I don't recall seeing him there.*

Her phone rang, showing Miss Virgie on the display.

After initial greetings, the older woman explained the reason for her call. "I found out a few things of interest today that might help."

"I'm all ears."

"Wanda called me and said Arlene Kopetsky invited her to have lunch at *Fresh Starts*. She almost didn't go out of loyalty to Genny, but she wanted to hear what was being said in enemy territory. Her words, not mine. Anyway, they were sitting behind Sharese Werner and Mona Carr."

"Sounds about right," Madison mumbled. "Their husbands seem to be in cahoots, trying to boot mine out of his job."

"Kinda makes you queasy in the stomach, don't it? Anyway, Wanda could hear most of what they said, especially since Arlene was late meeting her there. They were talking about some big project that would set this town on its ears."

"Besides having a crooked Joel Werner as police chief? That would definitely set us on our ears!"

"Sharese said it's bigger than getting her husband appointed chief, which confirms that's their plan. They get Carr on the council and push for Brash's removal, making room for Werner. This business with Genny only fuels their argument against him. They say Brash has too many connections to the community and makes exceptions for his friends and family."

"Better for friends and family," Madison groused,

"than for the almighty dollar, like Werner has been accused of. Multiple times, in several different departments, no less."

"But Brash doesn't do that!"

"No, no. Of course not," Madison said, quick to defend her husband. "He treats everyone the same, no matter who they are. I was just being cynical about Joel Werner."

"You don't suppose... No, I guess that's too outlandish, even for lowly worms like the two of them." Virgie dismissed her own thoughts before voicing them aloud.

"You may as well say it. We can vote on how ridiculous it is."

"I was just thinking. It sounds like someone is trying to frame Genny for murder. We know she couldn't possibly have done it but having her best friend's husband investigating the matter does throw shade on things. It would give them plausible reason to ask Brash to step down."

"I don't find that ridiculous. If it were anyone but Brash, I might tend to agree."

"But doesn't it strike you as odd that it happened now? Right after Carr gets elected and, according to their wives, just before something all hush-hush is about to happen?"

"Yeah, what about that? What sort of hush-hush thing?"

"Well, now, I suppose that's why it's all hush-hush. Not even Bertha knows anything about it."

"Ohh-kay." Madison pulled out the word. Only the best-kept secrets escaped her grandmother, and usually those weren't safe, either. "Wait. Are you suggesting Joel Werner and Reggie Carr could have had something to do with the murder, just to frame Genny?"

"I know. Outlandish." A beat later, Virgie sounded less sure. "Isn't it?"

Madison didn't answer right away. "I'd like to think so. Surely, no one would be that desperate to get a job. I have no idea what this hush-hush thing is that's supposed to happen, but it can't be big enough for murder."

"I know. I told you it was way out there."

"On the other hand," Madison continued, "Werner is somehow tangled up in a suspicious death in Walker County. Something about how a rancher—according to his investigation— committed suicide. Now they've overturned the ruling and are calling it murder. He had already lost one job due to sloppy investigating. It could have been the same in this case, but I hear they haven't ruled out tampering with evidence. If he could do that, you have to wonder what else he might do. Still," she admitted, "outright murder is a stretch."

"Maybe it wasn't outright. Doesn't mean he wasn't somehow involved."

"I guess that's something we should keep in mind," Madison said, jotting it down in her notebook.

"That's not all. We had a late lunch with Bertha and Sticker today—at *New Beginnings*, of course— and ran into Kelvin Quagmire there. When he left, he met Doyle Nieto on the sidewalk. They stopped to talk and kept pointing at *New Beginnings*, like they were talking about it. That might be something, too."

"Who's Kelvin Quagmire? I don't know anyone by that name."

"Oh, right. A couple of weeks before Christmas," Virgie explained, "this guy comes out to the place and asks Hank, right out of the blue, if he can buy part of our land."

"The caves, by chance?" Just the thought of the drug lab their son and grandson had secretly operated there made her shiver.

"Those? We sold that whole corner to Alan Wynn as soon as the police released it. We didn't want the memories associated with it. No, plumb around on the other side. He wanted to buy at least seventy-five acres."

"What did Mr. Hank say?"

"He turned him down, of course. Had a few choice words to say about him, too, but at least he was polite when we saw the young man at the restaurant. But I wonder what this Quagmire has to do with Doyle Nieto, and why they were pointing at Genny's restaurant. You could tell they were looking at the outside of the building, not through the windows."

"I have no idea. Was he wanting to buy your land for himself? Maybe he wants to move here and build a house."

"Said he was a real estate agent."

"Do you remember what agency he was with?"

"He left a card, but Hank can't find it."

"If he does, let me know, please."

"Will do. It may be nothing, but it felt like something. They looked awfully intent."

"Okay. Thanks, Miss Virgie."

"One more thing. He must know Dierra Sanders because he came in during her break and ate with her."

"I'll check it out. Thanks."

Returning to her computer, Madison typed in the name Kelvin Quagmire. The image of a nice-looking man popped up, along with a bio. According to what she read, he was a real estate agent with *Greater Lone Star Developing, Incorporated.*

"Hold everything, boys and girls," Madison said aloud, reaching for her notebook. "I think that's the same company as... yes! It is. It's the same one where Lawrence Norris is an acquisitions manager. That's either one very strange coincidence, or something bigger is going on here."

Madison found a new page in her notebook. Computers were great for research, but sometimes she needed to map out her thoughts on pen and paper.

"The question is," she said, still talking aloud, "what connection does Doyle Nieto have to this Quagmire guy and Lawrence Norris? Assuming both of them are here on company business, is that what brought Nieto and Anastasia here? Did this Lone Star outfit find them the building? Knowing Myrna Lewis," Madison grumbled, "*she* contacted *them*. She could make money and ruin Genny, all in one fell swoop. Maybe Granny Bert was right about adding her to the suspect list, after all."

Brash's angry voice boomed from the doorway. "*What* suspect list?"

"Brash!" she said in surprise. "I, uh, I didn't know you were standing there."

"Obviously." He crossed his arms over his chest, his biceps straining against the confines of his shirt.

"I didn't expect you in so early." Trying not to look guilty, she slammed her notebook closed. "You said you had no idea what time you'd be home."

"I have to go back. I came in for something to eat and a fresh shirt."

"I'll fix you a bite while you're changing," she offered.

"I just lost my appetite. And don't try to change the subject, Madison!" he stormed. "What suspect list? As far as you are concerned, there is no suspect list. Didn't I explicitly tell you to stay out of this?"

"You did."

"So why are you making a suspect list? Why are you scribbling in your notebook? This is none of your business."

"Excuse me? None of my business?" She came out

of her chair with hazel eyes spitting fire. "This is my best friend we're talking about. That makes it my business! And you can't stop me from worrying about her, any more than you can stop me from wondering who could have done this. Because it sure wasn't her!"

"I know that, Madison." His tone carried impatience. "But you can't butt in on this one. I told you to stay out of it."

"Tell me one thing, Brash. If Laura were a suspect in a murder investigation, would you just sit back and let people accuse your sister of something she didn't do? Genny may not be blood kin, but she's my sister, nonetheless."

Brash made no reply. His flared nostrils and flexing muscles spoke for him.

"You know it's true, Brash!" she insisted. "Just because I'm making a list doesn't necessarily mean I'm investigating the case."

"So, you *are* investigating!" His tone was part accusatory, part victorious.

"I never said that."

"And you never said you weren't. Tell me the truth, Madison. You claimed you couldn't lie to me, so I'm asking you a direct question. Are you, or are you not, investigating this case?"

Not quite meeting his eyes, she offered the only defense she had. "I—I have a client. Someone hired me to prove Genny's innocence. The same way Lucy Nguyen hired me to clear her son's name," she reminded him, "after *you* arrested him for murder. One he didn't commit, I might add!"

"And the evidence cleared him, the same way the evidence will clear Genny."

"Evidence *I* discovered!"

"You were almost killed in the process, in case you've forgotten. And you didn't have to take this case!

Genny hasn't even been arrested yet."

"But she will be, unless someone stands up for her." She put up a hand to stop his argument. "And before you remind me that you can't, I understand that. I don't like it, but I know it's for the best. But I'm not held to the same standards you are, so I'm the most logical one for the job."

"But you're held to the law, Madison, and interfering with a police investigation is against the law!"

"I'm not interfering. I'm just... looking into a few things."

"Same thing, and you know it!" he bellowed.

Madison matched his defiant stance. "Fine. I admitted I can't lie to you, so let's see if you can say the same. I'm going to ask you a question, and I want an honest answer."

"You know I can't talk to you about official business."

"I'm not asking you to. I have a different question. Can you look me in the eye and tell me that Misty Abraham *doesn't* see Genny as the prime suspect in this case? No dancing around the bush, saying no formal charges have been made yet. Just yes or no."

A muscle worked in his jaw. "No," he bit out. "I cannot tell you that."

"No, you can't divulge that sort of confidential information, or no, you can't say she's not the most likely suspect at this time?"

"Both."

"So, you admit Misty is focusing on Genny. Correct?"

He looked none too happy about confirming her claims. "Correct."

"And that," Madison said, her tone both sad yet victorious, "is why I took the case. Genny needs someone in her corner. She's always been there for me, and I swore I would always be there for her, too. It's as simple as that."

"There's nothing simple about this, Madison. Nothing." On that, Brash whirled around and walked away.

She heard the alarm bing a few minutes later as he stormed out the kitchen door and headed back to the police department.

# 18

Without Anastasia there to thwart her, Shilo Dawne did a little snooping around her late boss' desk. If anyone saw her and questioned her motives, she had a valid excuse: she was the business manager for *Fresh Starts,* after all.

Those entries in the books still bothered her. Some of the figures and notations didn't match up. She often wondered if her boss kept a separate set of books, and this might be her chance to find out. It was too late to hold anything over Anastasia's head, but knowledge was power. A girl never knew when she might need to pull an ace out of her pocket.

Anastasia kept an appointment book on her desk, and it was filled with appointments and reminders for the rest of the month. Shilo Dawne didn't look further than January. This afternoon, for instance, her late boss was scheduled for a Zoom meeting. It didn't specify with whom. There was simply a star drawn beside it.

She also had an appointment to have her teeth whitened—*I knew that bright smile wasn't natural*—and an upcoming meeting about catering a political rally in the spring. The same appointment was on Shilo

Dawne's calendar, as she was included in the budget details. There were notes jotted down on several of the squares, reminders to call suppliers and business associates, to send her regrets for missing an upcoming fundraiser in Houston, to keep a particular afternoon open for "K," and to coordinate a meeting between Doyle, herself, and her financial adviser in the city. To Shilo Dawne's consternation, she saw a reminder to set up a meeting with Cutter M.

"Over my dead body!" Shilo Dawne huffed beneath her breath. After a second thought, she mused, "Or, in this case, yours."

When snooping through her calendar didn't reveal any shadowy secrets other than plans to steal Shilo Dawne's man, she moved on to the desk drawers. *Dang it, they're all locked!*

There was a file folder on top of the desk, buried beneath the local newspaper, two from neighboring towns, and a to-go menu from *New Beginnings*. It seemed her late boss was sizing up the competition, which she agreed was a financially smart thing to do. Shilo Dawne flipped the folder open, surprised to see an aerial shot of the Brazos Valley. Another brought River County into focus. There were computer-generated lines crisscrossing the area, including one that sliced through the outer edge of Juliet. Different colors distinguished each of the lines, none of which made sense to the woman holding the black and white glossy print.

Beneath the aerial shot were copies of multiple surveys, all of local properties. The names of the owners were buried within the mumbo-jumbo of physical descriptions, which Shilo Dawne didn't take time to read.

She tried logging into Anastasia's computer, but it was password protected.

Finding nothing more, Shilo Dawne gave up. For now.

She returned to her desk, contemplating her next move. She had come too far now to have things go wrong. Admittedly, her initial plan hadn't included Anastasia's death, but it did work in her favor. All she had to do was take advantage of the new opportunities opened up to her.

Shilo Dawne hadn't always been so self-centered. Sometimes, she could barely remember the girl she had once been. Even when she did remember, most times she chose to forget. But on rare occasion, usually late at night when she was curled up on her couch, alone and lonely, she missed the old her.

That Shilo Dawne had been naive and innocent, full of romantic dreams and simplistic hopes for the future. She had found pleasure in farm-girl pleasures like riding barrels in ranch rodeo competitions, raising steers for the River County Show, making homemade crafts and even her own clothes, and working at the local café while she saved for college.

That money, coupled with prize money she earned from selling her steers or winning rodeo jackpots, paid for her education. When those funds ran out before she completed her studies, her parents were in no financial condition to pay the rest. They encouraged her to sit out for a year and earn enough to go back. They urged her not to take out a student loan, warning her it would plunge her into debt before her career could take off. But she hadn't listened. She had taken out two different loans, earned her degree, and planned for a bright, successful career. She would make enough money to live in a cute little apartment in Houston, make payments on her loans and a new car, and still have enough for a shopping spree in trendy boutiques and the Galleria Mall.

In reality, the only position she could find was a boring job in the accounting firm of a local real estate company. She shared a cramped apartment with a girl she barely knew nor liked. If she simply *had* to buy something new, she shopped at thrift stores and Wal-Mart. She was still driving her old car from high school, and her college loans were falling into default.

Still nursing the heartache of losing Cutter—she conveniently ignored the fact that she had never had him to begin with—Shilo Dawne let a smooth-talking Romeo sway her with hopes of marriage and a solid future. When his current wife, a small detail he had failed to mention, threw a wrench into the works, Shilo Dawne felt a frosty blast of bitterness move into her heart.

She was done with dreaming. Done with romantic fantasies. Done with men.

The only exception were the men at work. The men who could further her career. The men she could use, the same way they used her.

The new Shilo Dawne clawed her way to a better position in the firm, heedless to the people she stepped on along the way. It was a competition, the same way the county show and ranch rodeo had been, and her only goal was to win.

When she met *him*, she discovered he was as hungry to win as she was. They made a good pair, both focused on advancing their careers and making enough money to buy their own new concept of happiness. It wasn't a romantic relationship. It was all about using the other to achieve the same, yet separate, goal.

Her phone rang, and she saw her mother's name on the screen.

*I don't have time for this right now.* Ever since her father had died unexpectedly—another example that loving someone only brought heartache—her mother had become exceptionally needy. Shilo Dawne accepted her mother's offer to move back into her old bedroom, not so much to keep her mom company, but to keep from paying rent somewhere else.

After the fourth ring, she answered impatiently. "Yes?"

"I'm sorry to bother you, honey, but I need your advice on something."

"I don't care what color you paint your bedroom, Mom." Re-doing the master bedroom had become her mother's latest obsession and the topic of many conversations. "Dad wouldn't let you paint it lavender, but you're free to do what you want now. Paint it whatever color makes you happy."

"It's not about painting the bedroom. Which I've decided to paint pale green, by the way," she added as an aside. "A man approached me about selling some of our place, and I want to know if it's a good offer."

"What man?"

"I can't remember his name, but he left a card. What I want to know is if it's a fair offer. And if selling it is the right thing to do. You know how much your dad loved this ranch."

"How much was the offer?"

She rattled off a number.

"I think you should hold out for more," Shilo Dawne advised.

"But you think I should sell?" Her mother sounded nervous. Unsure.

"What else are you— what is that god-awful racket?" Shilo Dawne broke off to ask in irritation.

"I asked Cutter Montgomery to come out and repair the horse pen. Normally, your father would take care of it, but..."

"You know what?" The younger woman had a sudden change of heart. "We can discuss it in person.

I'll be right there."

With a fresh coat of lipstick and a sassy swing to her hips, Shilo Dawne approached the man working on the iron-railed fence around a bare patch of land. The corral was the makeshift arena where she had practiced barrel racing throughout her school days. Those days hadn't been so long ago, but it felt like a lifetime had passed since then.

"How's it coming?" she asked over the clatter of his welding machine.

Cutter looked up through the tinted shield of his helmet. "Good," he answered. "Better stand back if you don't want the sparks hitting your clothes."

"These old things?" she said, posing in just the right position to show off her snug-fitting jeans and the new sweater she wore. She had left her coat in the car, knowing the turtleneck showed off her figure.

When he would have dropped the shield back in place, she put her hand on his arm and asked, "Can we talk?"

"I need to finish this, Shilo Dawne. I promised your mom I'd be able to finish in eight hours."

"Please? It's about my mom."

With a reluctant expression, Cutter removed his welding helmet. Despite the cold temperature, sweat curled his dark-blond hair, making it hug his handsome face. As he turned away to kill the motor, she admired the muscles stretching and splaying across his back.

"What is it, Shilo Dawne?" He didn't even pretend to have patience for the interruption.

"Can we sit down for a minute? I brought a thermos of coffee." She motioned to the crude two-tiered set of benches that served as the grandstands.

He only agreed because coffee sounded great right about now.

She had decided to take a more subtle approach in gaining his favor. She kept the thermos between them as she handed him his cup, her fingers brushing his in the process.

Cutter pretended not to notice.

"I'm worried about my mom, Cutter," Shilo Dawne said. "I moved back home to keep an eye on her and to help around the ranch, but there's only so much I can do. She insists on keeping her finances to herself. I mean, I'm a trained accountant. Finances and keeping businesses solvent are my specialties."

"Your mom's hardly an old woman, Shilo Dawne. She's still capable of making her own decisions."

"You may think so, being married to an older woman and all, but I can see changes is her. Her memory isn't what it used to be. Just yesterday, she forgot whether or not she had mailed the electric payment. I told her to let me put it on autopay, but she wouldn't hear of it."

"That sounds perfectly normal. Especially since she's still grieving your father's death and adjusting to all the changes in her life this past year."

"The same way you are, I suppose," Shilo Dawne said. She kept her eyes cast downward to her coffee cup, hoping to look sincere. "I know it can't be easy, still practically a newlywed and suddenly having two babies in the house. Hardly the honeymoon period you expected, I would imagine."

"No," he admitted. "It's even better."

"And now to think you could be making another adjustment... Cutter," she said, looking up at him with a worried wrinkle in her forehead, "please know if there's anything—anything— I can do to help you, I will. I could babysit or bring dinner over or-or anything, especially if... well, you know."

"No, Shilo Dawne, I don't know." His voice was cold. "Why don't you spell it out for me?"

"I—I just meant... I'm worried about Genny, is all. I heard that the police had incriminating evidence against her. She couldn't have done it, of course. Not Genny. But people go to prison all the time on circumst—"

"Genny is *not* going to prison! She hasn't even been arrested. As far as I know, no one's been named a formal suspect yet."

Shilo Dawne pressed a hand to her chest, right between the 'v' of her breasts. "Oh, good. I've been so worried!"

"Cut the act, Shilo Dawne. We both know that's not true."

"It is! Honestly, Cutter, you take me all wrong. I was so hurt the other night, I didn't have a chance to tell you how mistaken you've been. And—And I didn't want to wound your pride." She looked up at him through lowered lashes, appearing to be embarrassed. "You have the mistaken impression that I've been flirting with you, trying to get you back. In—"

"You never had me, Shilo Dawne," he broke in again. "We were nothing but friends."

"Still, you think I've been *flaunting* myself at you, I think you called it. I suppose it's been good for your self-esteem. But the truth is..." She looked up at him, as if bracing him for a harsh truth. "The truth is, Cutter, I'm involved with another man."

Her words surprised him, but he didn't let it show. He wondered, briefly, if he had been right that night she was caught out in the ice storm. Had she been on a secret rendezvous with a married man? She referred to her new relationship as 'involved with another man' rather than calling him her boyfriend. Not that he cared. Quite the contrary, Cutter was glad she had found someone. He had never been the man for her.

"I'm happy for you, Shilo Dawne."

"So, you believe me when I say you had the situation all wrong? I was simply glad to see an old friend. I realized how much I missed my hometown and all the people from my past."

"It's been like three years, if that," he frowned.

"Does that matter? I can still miss my old friends!"'

"You're right, you're right." He pretended to believe her. "Thanks for the hot coffee, Shilo Dawne. It hit the spot, but I should get back to work."

"So, you'll call me if you need anything?" A hint of suggestion slipped into her voice, but her wide eyes looked innocent enough. "I mean it, Cutter. Literally, *anything.*"

"Yeah, thanks. I'll share that with Genny." Cutter stood, missing the flare of anger that flashed in her eyes.

Slipping his helmet back on, he muttered thickly, not caring if she heard, "Worried about her momma, my foot. She only mentioned her once, before starting in on Genny and offering to help me with anything. And she meant *anything.*" He spat on the ground before firing up the roaring machine.

Even it didn't drown out the desperate, pathetic sound of Shilo Dawne's offer as it echoed in his ears.

# 19

"Girl, you're carrying those suitcases around with you again," Granny Bert told Madison.

"If you mean these bags beneath my eyes, Brash and I had another big argument last night, and he stormed out. I have no idea what time he finally got in, and he was already gone this morning when I got up."

"Maybe avoiding each other is the best way to avoid an argument right now."

Madison glared at her grandmother, who apparently thought she offered a valid point. "Not helping."

"I didn't come by to give marital advice, anyway. I came for an update."

"At this point, I still have more questions than answers."

"Maybe I can help with that. Virgie told me she called you yesterday and told you about her off-the-wall theory. Sorta makes sense, doesn't it, in a sick, twisted sort of way?"

"I'm still not so sure," Madison said. "It is a little off the wall."

"So are Werner and Carr. Anyway, I called your cousin George again, the one who's a deputy in Walker

County. He said the case involving the rancher is still under full investigation, and Werner has been called back in two times for additional questioning."

"That doesn't make him guilty, Granny. Just means he might shed light on the case."

"Which he helped in, and which he may have messed up. My old friend Bentley with the DA's office said it could have been sloppy work or could have been a deliberate cover-up. He hinted that charges against Joel Werner still aren't out of the question."

"Even so, it doesn't mean he's guilty of killing Anastasia."

"They don't think he's guilty of outright killing that rancher, either, just that he was somehow involved. Could be the same case here."

"Okay, I'll give you that much. Maybe he knows something," Madison admitted. "But could he really be so desperate for Brash's job that he would go along with killing an innocent person? Not to mention framing Genny, who did nothing wrong but drop her knife and leave it on the floor for five minutes while she bandaged her cut?"

"He tried to capitalize on Nigel Barrett's death when Brash's football buddy was accused of the murder. Said Brash couldn't be impartial."

"That sort of backfired when Brash put handcuffs on Tony and arrested him."

"But Werner kept trying. He made out Brash to look like a playboy and a member of the good ol' boy law enforcement club."

"He did do that," she agreed, "but this..."

"And do you remember who egged him on? Myrna Lewis, that's who! The two of them were in cahoots then, and I'm telling you, they're in cahoots now!"

"I told you, Granny, that just because we want Myrna to be guilty doesn't mean she is."

"Give me time, girl. I can connect the dots."

"That's the thing," Madison said worriedly. "I think we're running out of time. I hear people are getting antsy and want someone, anyone, to be named as a suspect and charged with murder. It makes people feel safer, somehow, even if the wrong person is arrested. And from what I understand, Reggie Carr is leading the pack."

"With Werner and Myrna right behind him," her grandmother pointed out purposefully. "Am I right? Huh? Am I right?"

"You're right. About pushing for an arrest, anyway."

"Not just any arrest. Genny's arrest."

Ready to change the subject, Madison asked, "Miss Virgie said something about a hush-hush project that's in the works. Something big according to Arlene Kopetsky, who said she overheard Mona Carr and Sharese Werner talking. Do you know anything about that?"

"Not a blasted thing," Granny Bert snorted. She sounded fully disgusted. "I've asked around, but no one seems to know a thing. I have to wonder if it's just a rumor Werner started to throw people off his tracks."

"Or maybe, for once, someone has been able to keep a juicy bit of news from the almighty Bertha Cessna."

"You think?" The older woman looked rattled by the very thought. Then she shrugged it off with a chuckle. "Nah, that can't be it."

"Either way, it doesn't help us with Anastasia's murder, and how and why Genny is being framed."

"I think she's a convenient scapegoat. Everyone knows she and Anastasia were in competition. Most of the town has heard about the grocery store incident by now. If you needed to pin Anastasia's murder on someone, can you think of anyone more convenient than your best friend?"

Madison frowned. “I see your point.”

“So, the why is easy. It’s the 'how’ that presents a conundrum.”

“That bothers me, too. How did someone get from the kitchen to the other side of the mansion in such a short time? Think about how big this house is and how packed it was that night. Even the lawn was crowded at that time, with people waiting for the big light show. I can’t figure out how they managed it.”

“Even if it was premeditated, they couldn’t have known Genny would drop that knife.”

“That part had to have been an accident,” Madison agreed. “A convenient stroke of luck on their part.”

“A disaster on Genny’s.”

Their conversation was interrupted by a new voice.

“Good morning, ladies!” Derron said as he breezed into the room.

“It’s hardly morning,” his boss said, looking at her watch.

“I beg to differ. It’s three minutes until noon. So, technically, morning.”

“Technically, three hours later than you’re required to be here.”

“You’ll forget all about that when you see the lunch I brought.”

He pulled a huge container from the bag he carried and flashed a glimpse of the fried rice inside.

“You’re cheating. That’s Lucy Nguyen’s rice, and you know it. You met her, probably on the sidewalk, and offered to carry it in for her!” Madison accused.

Ever since Madison had helped clear her son’s name for murder, the Vietnamese woman insisted on showing her gratitude. For her, the best expression came via food, so at random times, she brought food for Madison and her family.

“Maybe,” Derron agreed. “But I saved her the walk,

and that should count for something. Besides," he announced triumphantly, "I have something else."

"Egg rolls, I hope?" Granny Bert asked.

"Those, too, but I meant information-wise. I uncovered information you're sure to find interesting."

"Let's hear it, then," Madison said.

"Really? Can't we eat first?"

Rolling her eyes, Madison nodded toward the coffee station. "I just put some paper goods left from the party in that box over there. There should be plates and utensils. After you fix us all a plate, you can share your discovery."

"Fine, then," the man huffed.

After getting each of them a bottled water and filling three plates, he handed the two women their lunch.

"Happy?" he asked sweetly.

"Very," Madison replied. "What's the news?"

Derron's desk was across the room, but he rolled his chair over to hers, using the surface as his table. "Remember how I told you this wasn't the first lawsuit Lawrence Norris was involved in?"

Madison nodded. "He sued another restaurant, I believe you said, in Humble. It later closed down."

"And you asked me to find out what took its place."

"That's right."

"It's now the location—wait for it— for *Seasonings!*"

Her response was lackluster, at best. "Is that supposed to mean something?"

"Of course!" Derron took a bite of the fried rice and practically swooned. "So good," he said with reverence, eyes closed. The perfect blend of ingredients captured his full attention. "Lucy should consider opening a restaurant, herself."

"Derron! What is *Seasonings*?"

"Oh, right," he said, ignoring his boss' exasperated shake of the head. "*Seasonings* was the first of what became a very successful chain of Houston-area restaurants, owned by none other than Doyle Nieto."

"Hmm. That is interesting," she agreed.

"You said Nieto owned a dozen other businesses in the greater Houston area. You didn't tell me one of those was in Pasadena, the town where Norris now lives!" There was a hint of accusation in his voice.

"Pasadena is basically Houston," she reminded him. "Doesn't necessarily mean anything."

"True. But how about this? When Norris worked in banking, one of the loans he pushed through ended in default. He even helped repossess the property a year later. Guess what stands in the location now?"

"I'm going to guess another *Seasonings*?"

"Close. The name is *Clementine's Kitchen*, but it's owned by Doyle Nieto."

"Again, interesting. Very interesting, in fact," Madison told him.

"I thought you'd think so," he said smugly.

"What are you saying?" Granny Bert asked. "Nieto is getting this Norris fellow to scout properties for him, and Norris goes about securing them in any way possible?"

"That's one way of putting it," Derron sniffed. He was miffed that Granny Bert cut to the chase, therefore stealing his thunder in the process. He planned to say it much more dramatically, using this new discovery to barter for the afternoon off.

"You may be on to something, Derron," Madison said. For the first time, she felt a spark of hope start to kindle. "Where are the rest of Nieto's restaurants?"

"You were looking that up," he whined. "But I know there's a *Seasonings* in downtown Houston and another in Baytown. Of course, the two restaurants he co-owned with Anastasia are in The Woodlands and The Galleria."

"Find out who sold him those properties, and the history behind each." Swallowing a bite of rice, she recalled their previous conversation. "Didn't you say Norris had some connection to Baytown?"

"Seems like it. A mall or something."

"Find out what that something is. And anything else you can dig up."

"I'll get on that, first thing in the morning," Derron promised.

"Right now," she corrected. "As soon as you finish eating."

"About this afternoon..."

"You'll be right here in this office, getting me that information."

"But dollface," he whined.

"But nothing." She used her mom voice on him. "You drag in here late, and now you want to leave early. Whatever it is you want to do this afternoon can wait. This can't."

Acting more like a teenager than a grown man, Derron huffed loudly and rolled his eyes. "Yes, madam."

"Now *that*," Madison grinned, munching on an egg roll, "is more like it."

"Give me a scotch on the rocks," Kelvin Quagmire told the bartender that evening. Loosening the knot of his tie, he amended, "Make it a double."

With drink in hand, Quagmire spotted an empty table in the far corner of the hotel's bar. He slid into the bench seat, his briefcase hitting the tabletop with a thud. He was tired and discouraged and more than fed-up with this entire project. *Greater Lone Star Developing* didn't pay him enough for this!

So far today, he had been cussed out, fussed at, and threatened with a shotgun. The crusty old landowner told him he was trespassing on private property, and he had every right to shoot varmints threatening his livelihood. The man held the gun pointed to the ground, but Kelvin wasn't about to test his sincerity. He spun out on a trail of dust, spewing rocks as his tires slid across the gravel.

Kelvin had negotiated plenty of deals in his career, but none of the projects had been as difficult as this one. None of the landowners were interested in selling. He wasn't above going the extra mile to further his career, but this time, even unconventional methods couldn't secure enough property to reach his goal. Not with this many stubborn sellers to deal with.

He welcomed the warmth of the scotch as it spread through his tensed muscles and settled in his limbs. He needed this.

He also needed a hot shower, a warm woman, and a massage. Not necessarily in that order.

Instead, he got a phone call.

Seeing the name crawl across the screen, the scotch felt suddenly sour on his empty stomach. He motioned for the bar's hostess as he took the call.

"Hello?"

"Did you get the contracts?" the man on the other end of the line asked.

Kelvin grunted. No greeting, no idle chit-chat. Just straightforward demands, as always.

"I'm working on them."

"What the hell is the holdup?"

"A bunch of stubborn hicks, that's what!" His temper flared at the other man's attitude. He didn't bother covering the phone when the hostess appeared. "Chicken wings, with a side of fries. Extra barbecue sauce."

"If eating is all you do," the man on the phone complained, "I can see why you're behind schedule."

"I'm falling behind because this isn't like acquiring property in the city, where people see dollar signs and are eager to sell. These country folks aren't all that interested in money. They keep telling me stories about how their great-great-granddaddy came here in a covered wagon." He put an exaggerated drawl into his words. "Or how the almighty Sam Houston himself once had supper right there on the place, over yonder beneath that shade tree where the old cabin used to stand. That's what they call it. The place. Not the ranch or the farm. Not the property. It's *the place*. And their fields have the crazy names, too." Quagmire continued to complain. "The elm field, or the old Tucker patch, or the Granny patch. These people are too sentimental about their land to sell to an outsider."

"Quit your grousing and just get the job done."

"It's not that easy, and you know it."

"What I know is that we have a deadline to meet, and if we don't meet it, this whole deal will blow up in our faces!"

"We need a local," Quagmire said. "Someone who the old-timers trust. What about that Lewis woman?"

"Myrna Lewis? You met the woman when you negotiated the lease. Believe me, no one in this town likes her, much less trusts her."

"Well, apparently, they don't like me, either."

"You're saying you've lost your charm? I thought that was what the expensive outfits and haircut were all about."

"These country folk don't care about that. I'd be more likely to win them over by wearing a pair of overalls and a straw hat, but that's not going to happen. And why are you so worried about me? That thing with *New Beginnings* has cost us enough time."

"Unless the other acquisitions come through, that one won't matter anyway. Just hold up your end of the bargain and get it done. Now."

Quagmire took a deep gulp of his scotch, feeling the alcohol burn his throat the same way the man's orders ignited his blood. Who did this joker think he was, telling him how to do his job?

"Is that a threat?" he demanded.

"Take it any way you want," the man said.

Without comment, Quagmire stabbed the *end* button and let his head fall against the seat's high back. How had such a carefully orchestrated plan gone so far astray?

As painful as it was to bear, Anastasia's death should have offered one less obstacle to deal with. Instead, it only complicated matters. Now the locals were too busy focusing on gossip and speculation to give him the time of day. Worse, the few people who had bothered listening to him before the holidays had already forgotten about his proposal. They were more focused on drama to think of their own financial futures.

He couldn't wait to get out of the Brazos Valley. Out of the crazy community known as The Sisters. Even the towns came with a long, convoluted backstory. And as nice as this College Station hotel was, he couldn't wait to get out of it, either.

Give him the rat race of Houston, any day.

# 20

"Chief? Can I come in?"

Brash had been avoiding Misty Abraham for the last two days, but his luck had run out. He couldn't even use the excuse of being on the phone. She had seen him hang up. And he had just come in from the cold, so saying he was late for an appointment probably wouldn't work, either.

He could have said he was busy and told her to come back later, but that wasn't his style. He told his officers he was always accessible, and he meant it. He wouldn't change that policy now.

With no options left, he told her to come in.

Misty Abraham closed the door behind her. "Have a minute?"

"A few."

"This won't take long." She sat a folder down on the desk in front of him. "With your permission, I'd like to make an arrest in the Anastasia Rowland murder, sir."

Brash hid his surprise behind a stern stare. "On what grounds, Abraham?"

"I have an eyewitness."

"To the murder?" he asked in a sharp voice.

Until that moment, her manner had been sharp, on-point, and completely professional. At his question, a hint of vulnerability slipped into her armor of formality.

"Not exactly," she admitted.

"How is an eyewitness an eyewitness, then, if they didn't actually see the murder take place?"

"They didn't witness the murder, sir. But they can dispute the falsehood of the key suspect's flimsy alibi."

"I wasn't aware we had a key suspect, Abraham."

"With all due respect, Chief deCordova, you made me the lead in this case. I invoked that authority to rank suspects in the order that evidence suggested. Thus, I have a key suspect. Sir." She added the last as a show of respect, not a request for approval.

"I see. And who might that suspect be?"

He knew how she would answer, even before she said, "Genesis Montgomery."

"And how did you come to this conclusion, Abraham?"

"She had motive, means, and opportunity. And now, thanks to our witness, she has no alibi."

"Walk me through this."

At that, the officer dropped her cool, professional demeanor. She saw his manner as condescending. "Oh, come on, Brash! Do I have to spell it out for you?" she asked impatiently.

"As a matter of fact, you do."

"It's all there in the file, but fine. I'll spell it out for you." She motioned to the chair beside her. "May I?"

"Of course. You know you're always welcome in here."

She seemed momentarily flustered by his answer, but she recovered quickly enough.

"My reasoning," she said in a matter-of-fact tone. She held up one finger.

"Genny Montgomery had motive to kill Anastasia

Rowland. Anastasia moved in on her established niche here in town, assuming a name similar to hers and stealing a healthy portion of her customers. I wasn't able to obtain financial records, but it's a known fact that *New Beginnings* has suffered because of the competition. The vacant parking spots outside and the empty tables inside attest to that fact."

Brash gave her his infamous smirk. "Even a rookie ADA would point out that during the holidays, restaurants often experience a lag in sales. As do most places when a new option comes into town. When the new wears off and routines go back to normal, those same businesses retain their loyal customers. You have to bring something better than that to the table."

She held up a second finger. "Prior altercations and disturbing conditions. Less than a week before the murder, Genny Montgomery made a scene in the grocery store, demanding that Ms. Rowland move her car. She made a veiled threat to the victim. Plus—"

Brash held up a hand to interrupt, "Did she make a threat to Anastasia's body, or to her car?"

"Her car. But—"

"Again, gotta do better than that. No DA would pursue murder charges on something as flimsy as what you've told me so far."

"There's more. As I mentioned, there are disturbing conditions that have come to light. Genny Montgomery has been under tremendous stress the past several months. As a new mother, she is suffering from postpartum depression. We all know that stress and depression play a key factor in behavioral changes. Add to that the use of a drug that has known adverse effects and—"

Again, Brash interrupted her. "Hold up. How did you obtain this information? Did you have a search warrant to obtain her doctor's records?"

"I didn't need it. The doctor's office confirmed the reason for her next appointment. The pharmacist confirmed the medicine she's taking."

"Both confirmations were highly inappropriate and against HIPPA rules. At best, all you can prove is that her doctor prescribed the medication, not that she took it."

"It may not matter. Almost everyone has noticed a change in Genny, me included. I eat there regularly and have noticed she isn't her usual bright, happy self. I've seen her be sharp, even with customers. And of course, there's the recent threat she made to Myrna Lewis." Misty Abraham implored him with her eyes. "Even if she's your friend, you can't continue to overlook her erratic and hostile behavior!"

"Hostile?"

"How else would you describe her threat to Myrna Lewis?"

"Unsubstantiated."

"The entire café heard her!"

"Yes, and their accounts vary drastically from the statement Myrna gave in this office. But go on," he encouraged. "You have my attention."

Up went the third finger. "Means. Genny is the owner of the exact knife discovered in our victim's body. Even without her fingerprints, it has her name engraved on the side. There's no denying the knife belonged to her."

"Agreed. What *is* unclear is whether or not this particular knife was the cause of death. Doc suspects she was initially stabbed with a jagged-edged knife. That would explain the damage to skin tissues and the amount of blood present. Even Doc said he couldn't make a call with any absolute certainty," Brash pointed out.

"All the more reason to request an autopsy."

"Convince the DA of that."

Misty Abraham popped up a fourth finger. "Genny Montgomery had opportunity to commit this crime. She claimed to have dropped the knife, cut herself, and went to dress the wound in the other room. I have an eyewitness that says Genny lied. She didn't drop the knife. She left the room with it in her hand."

"Is this a reliable witness?"

"I believe so, or else I wouldn't have bothered you with this."

"Who's your witness?"

"A local. Shilo Dawne Nedbalek. She's an accountant for—"

"I know who she is. Are you saying she was in the kitchen with Genny?"

"No. She says she was in the butler's pantry, where she hid after Genny assaulted her. I spoke with witnesses who confirm that she had the imprint of a hand on her face, and her dress was torn when she came from the kitchen in tears. Their testimony and exact wording is in the report."

"Did they happen to mention the time of this alleged assault?"

"I don't recall, but if they did, it's in the report."

"Because I have an eyewitness who knows for a fact that Shilo Dawne was crying to a small audience of sympathizers before the clock struck midnight. Another witness says she saw Cutter Montgomery come through the butler pantry a few minutes after midnight. She didn't realize the woman was Shilo Dawne but said there was a woman seated in a chair with people around her. He spoke a few words to the woman and broke up the crowd. The witness says that the woman, obviously Shilo Dawne, left the dining room through the hallway, not the butler's pantry as she claimed."

"Can you give me their names, so I can reach out to them for a statement?"

"No need. One of those witnesses is sitting in front of you."

"You?" she asked in surprise.

"There's no mouse in my pocket," Brash replied. "I saw the ruckus just before the clock struck midnight but waited before checking it out."

"And why was that?"

"For one thing, the true chaos was about to begin. You were there. You saw the crowd and how zealously they greeted the New Year."

"And the second reason?"

He answered with unabashed honesty. "I wanted to start the New Year off right, kissing my wife."

The officer averted her gaze, unable to meet the blunt truth in his dark eyes. As much as she tried denying her feelings for him, they seemed determined to linger.

"And the other witness?"

"The woman I was kissing. Maddy didn't realize it was Shilo Dawne, but she was certain that Cutter came in from the butler's pantry and that Shilo Dawne left out through the hall."

"That doesn't mean she didn't go back after the crowd dispersed."

"That's true," Brash granted. "But it seems to me that she left out a few of the details when she gave her 'eyewitness' report. And you do realize her statement could very well be seen as an effort to get even with Genny, the same way she made the false claim that Genny assaulted her."

"How do you know Genny didn't assault her?" his officer challenged.

Brash's expression was dark. "I recused myself from this investigation because I didn't want to put a murder case in jeopardy with my own personal views and opinions. I won't do the same for a libel case. In the matter of this so-called assault, I will tell you that Shilo Dawne is jealous of Genny's marriage to Cutter. She's been in love with him since she was a kid, and that was one of the reasons she moved away. Everyone in town was aware of that, long before you ever came here. You may want to keep that in mind when relying on her as a viable eyewitness in a murder investigation."

"I see," she said, her lips pressed thin. It took her a deep breath before rebounding, her formal demeanor back in place. "At any rate, the cut on Genny Montgomery's hand could easily be viewed as a defensive wound. The victim may have tried to defend herself, and her attacker cut in the process."

"Good point. Were the victim's fingerprints found on the knife?"

"I'm... not sure."

"Then find out. What about the other potential suspects I asked you about? Did anyone see Ms. Rowland go outside? Have we identified all the people in the masks yet? Have we searched for a second knife used in the attack?"

"Not yet, sir."

"Then we still don't have all our puzzle pieces, do we?"

"In light of an eyewitness who provided reasonable doubt as to the validity of Ms. Montgomery's alibi, I felt we had all the pertinent pieces in place."

"You never know which are the pertinent pieces until you have them all collected, Abraham. Detective Work 101."

"Yes, sir."

"In this department, we don't cave to pressure from the outside," he reminded her.

"I understand."

Some of the edge left his voice. "It's not just you. We all need to be reminded of that fact from time to time. The public is always eager to see someone behind bars, but they don't understand that if we jump to a hasty conclusion and arrest the wrong person, we're leaving a murderer free to roam the streets. No one wants that. I'll be sure to bring that point up in tomorrow's briefing. Maybe we'll have collected a few more puzzle pieces by then."

"I'll get started on those now, sir."

Misty Abraham left his office, still clutching her armor of formality around her wounded pride.

Madison was in her office, trying to find more that linked Doyle Nieto to Lawrence Norris, when her cell rang.

"Madison?"

"Yes?" She frowned at the hoarse whisper on the other end of the phone line. "Vina, is that you? Why are you whispering?"

"Because no one can hear me say this," the older woman hissed. "I've never done this in all my many years with the department, and if anyone asks, I'll deny I'm doing it now."

"Ohh—kay," Madison agreed. Then, "Doing what, exactly?"

"Giving up a tip."

"Are you at the station?" No matter how juicy the tip, she didn't want Vina to lose her job. The station would be in shambles without her.

"Yes, but I'm outside in my car."

"Then why are you whispering?"

"Because I don't like the sound of my own voice ratting out another officer. I feel less guilty this way."

"Sure, sure. Whatever makes you more comfortable." A brief worry went through her mind. Had Brash done something foolish? Had he actually arrested Genny? "Wh—What officer?"

"Two, actually. Two of the three officers investigating this murder have their sights set on Genny as the prime suspect, and they're ignoring pertinent information."

"I know Perry has it in for Genny. He has since we were in high school. But, is—is the other one Misty Abraham?" She knew it was so, but she hated to hear her worst fears substantiated. Abraham had the lead in this case.

"Yes. Brash is stalling her the best he can, but she's determined to jump the gun and arrest Genny."

"Brash is stalling her?"

Even whispered, Madison heard the censure in Vina's voice. "You doubt him? Brash is loyal to his profession, but he's also loyal to his family and friends. Don't ever forget that, young lady."

"Yes, ma'am. I won't, I promise. Not anymore."

"But that's not the tip."

"What is?"

"There were probably two knives used in the attack."

"Seriously?" Madison gasped.

"Doc thinks one had a serrated edge. It did the most damage, so the butcher knife probably isn't what killed her. Probably. He said he can't be certain."

"That's something, right?" Madison asked with weak hope.

"Now to do something with it, before it gets swept under the rug."

"Have they identified the masked men yet?"

"Schimanski is in charge of that. There was also one unidentified woman."

"Oh? I don't remember her."

"Silver eye mask, pale blue veil over that. It matched her gown."

Madison searched her memory banks. "Maybe," she said.

"Have you checked your surveillance tapes?"

"Digital. Brash turned the files over to the team."

"No back-up files?"

"Vina! You're a genius! I forgot all about those! They're stored on my computer."

"Worth a look."

"Thank you, Vina. Thank you. I hope you don't get in trouble for any of this."

"I hope not, either. But I just can't see sweet Genny being accused of something she didn't do."

"It's not just that. Thank you for reminding me what a wonderful man I'm married to."

"I love that boy almost as much as you do," the older woman whispered roughly. "But if asked, I'll deny ever saying that, too."

Madison laughed her first genuine laugh in days. "It's our secret. Thanks, Vina. Now go eat a cough drop and rest your throat!"

# 21

Madison pulled up the surveillance tapes stored on her computer. It was a safety feature that came with the top tier of the software Home Again provided. Should a camera or any of its footage be lost, erased, or stolen, a copy was automatically downloaded onto the primary account holder's computer. Since she and Brash weren't married when the system was installed, she was the primary.

It would be a long, tedious search, but worth it if it paid off.

She chose the camera facing the front door and fast-forwarded until she came to images of her and Brash greeting guests. About seventy-five couples in, she saw the woman in the pale blue dress. She came on the arm of a man dressed in a dark blue suit with a tie and mask matching her dress. The mask covered most of his face, but something about him was familiar.

Madison kept watching the tape, now watching for someone else. While she and Brash manned the door, she was fairly certain Lawrence Norris never came through. She had only seen the man once in person, but she had looked at his image enough over the last few days to ingrain him upon her memory. None of the guests fit his size or frame, from what she could determine. *Possibly* the guy in the Dracula-style cape, but doubtful.

She didn't think she recognized Doyle Nieto among the guests, either, but both men had purchased tickets. It was possible they passed the tickets on to someone else. Doyle, for instance, could have purchased his for one of their employees. Each ticket included a guest, so it would have made a nice bonus for the lucky recipient.

Somehow, she couldn't imagine Lawrence Norris being as generous.

She switched her view to the camera nearest the path where she stumbled across Anastasia's body, stumble being the operative word. No matter how hard she examined it, those pesky Christmas bulbs were in the way! The best she could do was look for people coming and going somewhere along the path. None appeared headed into the shadows.

She backed up the tape to several minutes before midnight. She saw Anastasia come out the front door at 11:41. She stopped to talk to someone, a couple in matching dark pants and capes. With their masks off, Madison knew it was no one she recognized, so possibly one of Anastasia's employees who came with her from another location? Or someone from Riverton? Since she didn't know the couple, and they were headed in the opposite direction, she let the footage roll.

Anastasia moved along the path, picking up her trailing gown to keep it from brushing the grass. A lot of good that would do her in the long run, but she had no way of knowing the doom that laid ahead.

Just thinking about it sent a shiver through Madison's shoulders.

Anastasia kept turning her head to either side, possibly seeking someone or trying to avoid them. Once, she looked back over her shoulder. After that, she appeared to pick up her pace. She disappeared into the shadows around the house, to where the camera's view was obscured by the bright, fuzzy light of Christmas bulbs.

She and Brash should have never authorized the *By the Yard* tech to reroute that string of lights! Yet, like Anastasia, they had no way of knowing what doom laid ahead.

Just as she hit the fast-forward button, she noticed another woman hovering near the main porch, somewhere between the front door and the shadowy corner. Only the front door camera played back color footage. The rest was in black and white, so it was impossible to know what color gown she wore, but Madison recognized the filmy veil over her face.

The woman in pale blue. The one no one had identified as of yet.

She just seemed to stand there, doing nothing in particular. Every so often, she glanced down at her watch or perhaps into the shadows. It was difficult to tell at this angle.

Madison hit the fast-forward button, looking for anyone who ran from the shadowy corner. No one ran. Only a few people moved along the path. Most moved to or from the lawn, where Damian's light show was now in full swing. The twinkling lights and majestic sparks made viewing the tape more difficult. Madison saw the shadowy figure of a man come from the corner of the house, but it was hard to see him well.

Had he paused in front of the woman with the veil? She still stood there in the same spot. Perhaps she had arrived early and been waiting for the light show to begin. And perhaps he hadn't paused, so much as waited for the path to clear. Madison played the scene at least a dozen times. It *looked* like he paused. It *looked* like he may have even passed something to the woman. But it was only a fleeting moment and too indistinct for her to make a definitive judgment, even when she zoomed in.

Madison backed the tape up a few minutes, concentrating on the woman. At 12:02, she pulled a cell phone from her pocket and tapped on the screen, presumably sending or reading a text. One thing was for certain. After the text, she watched the shadows intently.

Madison let the tape play, seeing the same crowd gravitate toward the light show. Saw the man pause/possibly pause in front of the woman. Saw her stand there for only a moment longer before moving toward the front door. Saw Brash run across the lawn toward the shadowy corner, followed a few minutes later by Cutter. Saw Misty Abraham racing after them, her bosom threatening to bounce free of the binding dress.

Curiosity nibbling at her mind, Madison switched to another camera view. This one covered the foot gate at the front of the property and angled toward the front door. Instead of rejoining the party inside, the veiled woman hurried down the cobbled front walk, crossed through the gate, and disappeared beyond view. The veil hid her features from the camera.

"Well, that didn't tell me much. Not enough, anyway."

Madison jotted down the few facts gleaned from watching the tapes. Her eyes protested from the strain of staring at the screen for so long, so it seemed like a good time to take a break. She needed to stretch her legs, grab a bite to eat, and lay out something for dinner tonight.

The break did her good. Back at her desk, Madison felt energized enough to resume her search on the computer. She was still looking for something more to link Nieto and Norris together. Somehow, Kelvin Quagmire and *Greater Lone Star Developing, Inc.* factored into the equation, and something told her it all added up to a motive for Anastasia's demise.

Derron hadn't come in that morning, citing a dental appointment. She doubted that was the case, but then again, the man did take his stunning white smile quite seriously. At least he sent his file containing the new information he had gathered.

The new information included more on Lawrence Norris' career. Derron notated that the mall Norris had consulted on in Baytown was the same mall where Nieto now had a *Seasonings* restaurant. As acquisitions manager with GLSD, Norris had secured the properties needed to house a new country club and elite private village outside of Huntsville, all centered around a fabulous eighteen-hole golf course. He also negotiated deals for a spur off Interstate 45 that led to the new property, and for an apartment complex to the south of there. The complex was just across the Walker County line near Willis.

"Sounds like Norris is mostly into major projects, so I'm not sure what his business is here in River County, especially around The Sisters." Madison talked out her reasoning, if only to herself. "This Kelvin Quagmire character, on the other hand, seems to tackle smaller projects. He's inquired about Hank's property and was interested in Genny's building. Unofficially, I heard he was the one to secure the old dry cleaner's for *Fresh Starts*. He has connections to Norris, seeing as they both work for the same company, but he also has connections to Nieto." She toggled her head back and forth, trying to see a broader picture. "Found the building for him and Anastasia, was seen with him outside of Genny's... Hmm. Not much. Maybe if I see his listings, both current and past, they might shed some light on the matter."

She went back a few years before finding anything of interest. "Hmm. A vacant spot in The Woodlands Mall, previously occupied by a restaurant. Let's see who... It's now *Tang*, a trendy eatery according to this, owned by *Anato, Inc.*"

A quick search told her that *Anato, Inc.* also owned *Fresh Starts* and The Galleria's *Texas Italiano*.

"*Ana*, Anastasia, and *to*, long o, for Nieto," she reasoned. "*Anato*. Makes sense."

Among his older listings were the former *Lamoge*, now Nieto's *Seasonings* in Humble, and another property in Galveston where Anastasia owned a restaurant.

"What a busy man," Madison said. "And obviously the go-to for both Nieto and Anastasia. If I were to guess, I'd say he finds a property, Norris finds a way to make it go under, and then Quagmire comes back and sells it to two of his best customers. Quite a little racket they have going. But... is it enough to commit murder? And why kill Anastasia, when GLSD is obviously making money off her?" She twisted her lips in thought. "It presents quite the conundrum, as Granny Bert called it."

"Maybe," she decided aloud, "I should find out more about this GLSD. Who's behind *Greater Lone Star*, I wonder. Do they know what their people are doing? Maybe they don't care, as long as it makes them a profit and keeps shareholders happy."

It took longer than she anticipated to find the answers to her questions. The corporation was owned by several other corporations, as well as a few individuals. She recognized the names of several people who were prominent business leaders around the state. Even a politician was listed as a major shareholder.

She was surprised to see *Anato, Inc.* as one of the majority shareholders in the corporation.

"Wow. Any way you go, they make a cut. That's either genius, or borderline unethical."

Madison didn't bother with the names of other, lesser shareholders. None held a large enough share to buy a vote in the appointment of the corporate board of directors.

She skimmed over the names and pictures of current board members. Her eyes snagged on one name in particular.

"You've got to be kidding me!" she said. "That can't be right."

She glanced up at the picture above the name.

"Yep, it's right," she confirmed to herself. "Wow. Just, wow."

The alarm binged with an alert. Her phone app showed Brash's arrival home.

She hurriedly minimized her computer screen and shut the trusty notebook. She didn't need another confrontation with her husband, particularly after the chiding she had received from Vina. Not waiting for him to seek her out, she stood and straightened her blouse. She would meet him in the neutral territory of the kitchen.

"Maddy?" Brash spoke through the intercom after removing his coat and hanging it nearby.

She replied in person. "I'm right here."

He whirled around in surprise. "Hey. I didn't see you there."

"Just came in." She wagged her eyebrows, grinning. "I used the hidden passage. It's the fastest route from my office."

His reply came with the humored version of his infamous smirk. "I wondered why you decided to clean that out."

"I only use it on occasion," she admitted. "Like when I'm trying to beat Blake to the kitchen, or when I need to welcome my husband home after a hard day's work."

"I've had plenty of those lately." His muttered grunt gave way to a tentative smile. This recent tension between them was so foreign, it was like treading unknown waters. But her light attitude gave hope things were returning to normal.

"Maddy," he began, taking a step forward.

She had done the same, saying his name at the same time.

"Ladies first," he insisted, moving a few more steps in.

Her words came in a rush. "I need to apologize to you, Brash. This whole thing with Genny is so crazy, I think it's made me a little crazy, too. I guess I never stopped to consider it must be doing the same to you, knowing she's innocent but being unable to prove it."

"Funny thing is," he said, stepping close enough to touch his hand to her cheek, "I came to apologize to you. I'm sorry, sweetheart, for taking some of my frustration out on you. The truth is, I don't blame you for butting in. It may be the only thing that clears her of this. But," he said, slipping his hand around the back of her neck as he came ever closer, "I didn't come home to discuss the case. I came home to do this."

After his kiss, their world settled back on its axis. It was exactly what they both needed to feel centered again.

"I'm sorry, sweetheart," he whispered.

Arms wrapped around his neck, Madison coaxed another kiss from him. "I am, too, my love."

Pulling slightly apart, Brash cupped her face again, dropped a kiss on her nose, and released his hold on her. “Think a man could get a decent cup of coffee around this place?”

“One cup of coffee coming up.” She hugged him again before letting go.

Brash dropped onto a stool at the bar as she made a cup for each of them. He munched on an apple he found in the fruit basket.

“Are you done for the day, or do you have to go back in?” Maddy asked as she settled beside him.

“I’m quitting for the day, whether I’m done or not. I’ve been picking up the slack while the other three officers concentrate on the investigation, but I’m not as young as I used to be. These long hours are getting to me,” he admitted.

“You poor old man,” she teased, leaning over to kiss his cheek. “Ancient before you turn forty-five.”

“Following up a football career with a job in law enforcement takes its toll.”

“It’s a pity, isn’t it, that the public values your game career over the one that really matters? Too bad lawmen aren’t hailed as the heroes they truly are. Instead, people worship celebrities and athletes, and forget the sacrifices made by the people who keep them safe.”

Brash blew out a weary breath of resignation. “It’s the weight of the badge, sweetheart.”

They sipped on their coffee in silence until she brought up something he had said during his apology. “It’s bad, isn’t it, Brash?” she whispered. Fear made her voice wobble. “Genny could be arrested for murder.”

“As impossible as it sounds, yes. I’m afraid she could be. Abraham is building quite a case against her.”

“How, Brash? How can she build a case around something Genny didn’t do?”

"Circumstantial evidence, babe. Circumstantial evidence."

"Like what?"

"You know I can't give you the particulars. But Abraham came in my office earlier, and she had some pretty strong arguments. They still need fleshing out, but she has the makings of a solid collar. Motive, means, and opportunity. She also knows Genny is suffering from PPD. Put it all together, it does look incriminating."

"Brash, we both know Genny couldn't possibly have done this, PPD or not. She's no killer."

"I agree. I do. But I had to recuse myself. It was in Genny's best interests, no matter whether she and Cutter realize that or not."

"I think they know it, but they're so hurt and confused right now—so stunned that such a thing could be happening in their life! They don't know what to think."

"I just hope that when this is all over, they can forgive me."

Maddy rubbed his back to show her faith and support. "I'm sure they will, sweetheart. They know you're a good man, a good lawman, and a good friend."

"Thanks, babe. I needed to hear that."

After accepting his peck on the lips, Maddy asked, "What about other suspects? Surely Genny isn't the only one with a motive to want Anastasia out of the picture. And anyone at the party had the opportunity to kill her."

"Schimanski is trying to nail down all the attendees, and Perry is pulling all the information together."

"That's not very comforting. Perry has always had it in for Genny and me. Genny, especially."

"I've warned him to leave his personal feelings out of this, but we all know it's easier said than done."

Madison ran her hand along his back again. "Why don't you go take a shower and get out of this uniform? How does King Ranch Chicken sound for supper?"

Appreciation lifted one corner of his weary smile. "You know it's my favorite."

# 22

Madison called a staff meeting the next morning. It included Derron, who was her only paid employee, plus Granny Bert and Virgie Adams, two members of her so-called 'Senior Division of *In a Pinch,'* aka her geriatric crew.

"I have a plan," she told them, "but I'm going to need help pulling it off."

"I'm in," Granny Bert said, not bothering to hear the details.

"I need to warn you. It's iffy. Borderline crazy."

"Sounds like our specialty, doesn't it, Bertha?" Virgie nudged her oldest friend with her elbow, cackling in delighted anticipation.

Not to be left out, Derron raised a dainty hand. "If they're in, I'm in. What's the plan?"

Madison laid it out for them. They spent the better part of an hour hashing out details and planning who would do what.

"That reminds me," Virgie said. "We were in town yesterday when Dolly Mac Crowder and Jimbo Hadley had that fender-bender. We took a backstreet and guess who we saw in the parking lot behind *Fresh Starts*? Shilo Dawne and that fella that Dierra's sweet on, the same one who approached Hank about buying a piece of our place. That Calvin somebody."

"Kelvin Quagmire?" Madison asked in surprise.

"That's the one. Kelvin, not Calvin. Now I'm as bad as Hank, saying Sierra instead of Dierra." She shook her gray head in amazement.

"Kelvin Quagmire knows Shilo Dawne?" Madison was puzzled. "That's... not so crazy, now that I think about it. He scouted out the location for *Fresh Starts,* where she's the business manager."

"And she's a local girl," Granny Bert pointed out, "who had connections here. Quite handy for someone hoping to move in on Genny's territory."

"True. Okay, let's find a way to work him into the plan."

"I guess I could tell him Hank and I have reconsidered his offer," Virgie suggested, "and want more information. We could say we want to run it by you. For all he knows, you have experience in real estate."

"That may work," Madison said. "Okay, let's do that." She looked at the three people gathered around her desk. "Everyone has their assignment. Are we ready to do this?"

Granny Bert rubbed her hands together with savor. "Let me at 'em!"

"I'm in," Virgie agreed.

"Sure, dollface." Derron gave her his winning smile. "You can add a nice little bonus to my paycheck in appreciation for going above and beyond."

Hank had finally found the business card from the real estate agent. It matched the telephone number

Madison had given his wife. "Is this the agent from *Greater Lone Star Developments* I'm talking to?" Virgie asked.

"Yes, this is Kelvin Quagmire."

"This here is Virgie Adams. You came out to talk to my husband about some land. We met a few days later at the restaurant." She threw in an extra drawl for good measure, playing the part of a country bumpkin. "Let me see. I believe that was Thursday. No, that's not right. Thursday I had to go a specialist over in Bryan. I've been having the worst trouble with a bunion on my—"

Kelvin Quagmire interrupted her with an overly energetic, "Oh yes, of course, I remember you, Mrs. Adams! What can I do for you?"

"Well, now, I reckon my husband may have been a little hasty in turning down your offer to buy a piece of our place. I reminded him we ain't getting no younger, and we could use that money to take that cruise we've been saving for. Are you still interested?"

His enthusiasm was now real. "Of course!"

"Good, good. We ain't decided yet, mind you, but I'd like to hear what you have to say."

"I could come out this afternoon. I'm in the area."

"This afternoon works out swell, but if you don't mind, we'd like to meet somewhere else."

"We can meet for dinner. My treat."

"I had somewhere else in mind. You see, we have a good friend we'd like to sit in on the conversation. Being as Hank and I don't understand all those facts and figures and things like deeds and such," she out-and-out lied, "we'd like for her to advise us on matters. Translate all those big words, and such."

"I'm sure that won't be a problem. She's welcome to join us."

"Well, you see, that's the rub. She's a

businesswoman and has a tight schedule. She could meet with us today at her office at two forty-five. Does that work for you? If not, it will be at least a week before she can squeeze us in."

"Two forty-five sounds fine. What's the address? I'll meet you there."

"Her office is in her home. The big white house on the corner of Second and Main in Juliet."

"W—Wasn't that where...?"

"Yes, that's where the New Year's Eve party was, and that poor lady was killed. But don't worry, they cleaned up all the blood and such. If you're a bit queasy in the stomach, we'll open the gates up plumb over on the other side of the house. Just drive right up, and we'll take you in through the kitchen. You'll never even see the markers still out there on the grass."

On the other end of the line, Kelvin Quagmire's face blanched. The thought of his beautiful Anastasia just lying there, her blood seeping into the ground beneath her, definitely made him queasy.

But Anastasia was dead, and he still had a job to do. "The kitchen door sounds fine, Mrs. Adams. I'll see you at two forty-five."

From her office, Madison dialed the second number on their list. "Shilo Dawne? This is Madison." She put a smile in her voice as she clarified, "Madison deCordova. How are you today?"

"I'm fine," the younger woman said. There was a hint of caution in her voice. She couldn't remember Madison ever calling before.

"Before I forget to tell you, that was a lovely dress you wore to the party last week."

"Thank you. So was yours."

"The reason for my call, Shilo Dawne, is that... well, I recently discovered something I'd like to speak with you about. In private."

"I suppose you could come by my office at *Fresh Starts*. Afternoons work best for me."

"Good. I was thinking this afternoon, around three or so. But I think it would be best if we spoke here, to ensure privacy."

"What—What exactly is this about?"

"As I said, it concerns something I recently discovered. I wanted to hear your side before I speak with Officer Abraham. She's the one heading up the investigation around Anastasia's murder."

"I—My side? What are you—"

"I don't want to discuss it over the phone. Brash has recused himself from the case, as I'm sure you know. He shouldn't come home early, but just in case, would you mind parking across the street at the library? I don't want him to know about this."

"Uhm, yeah, sure."

"You know what? Let's make it about ten till. I know he won't be home by then."

"O—Okay," Shilo Dawne said.

Madison hung up the phone with a frown. The younger woman definitely sounded afraid. She hadn't thought Shilo Dawne was involved, but maybe she was wrong. Maybe the waitress turned business manager was more involved than she suspected.

"Hello, Mr. Nieto, this is Derron Mullins. I'm Madison deCordova's assistant. I believe we have something of yours you may have lost at the New Year's Eve Masquerade Ball last week. I'm calling to set up an appointment for you to come by and pick it up this afternoon."

"Can't be mine," Doyle Nieto argued. "I wasn't there."

"You weren't? Oh, dear." Derron sounded distressed. "You never think these things will happen to you, and then, *bam*! Just like that, you're a victim of identity theft."

"What are you talking about?" The other man sounded irritated.

"We found a credit card in your name when we were cleaning up after the party. I'm sorry it's taken so long to call you, especially considering the card must have been stolen. I'll just turn it over to the police and—"

"No need to do that. They're busy enough without bothering them with this."

"But if you weren't at the party..."

"What party did you say?"

"The masquerade party at the home of Brash and Madison deCordova, better known as the Big House."

"Oh, yes, yes. I thought you said a different name. What time did you want me to come by?"

"I didn't, but three works well for me. Please don't arrive before then, as we'll be in meetings and can't come to the door. Oh, and please bring your driver's license or passport with you to confirm your identity. I wouldn't feel right releasing it without proof of ownership."

"Fine, fine."

"If you arrive promptly at three, I'll open the drive-through gate via remote. Just take the walkway around to the front, and I'll meet you."

Derron marked one name off his list and moved to another.

"Mr. Norris? This is Derron Mullins. I'm Madison deCordova's assistant. I believe we have something of yours you may have lost at the New Year's Eve Masquerade Ball she and her husband hosted last week. I'm calling to set up an appointment for you to come by and pick it up. Does three fifteen this afternoon work for you?"

"I wasn't at the ball," Lawrence Norris answered shortly.

"You weren't? Wow, then how did... The thing is, sir, we found a credit card in your name while cleaning up. Since you weren't in attendance that night, you may want to check activity on all your cards and bank accounts to guard against fraud. I'll just turn this card over to the police, and they can—"

"No, no," Norris said quickly. "Don't do that. What time did you say?"

"Three fifteen. Come to the front door, and I'll return your card. Oh, and sir?"

"Yes?"

"Could you please bring your driver's license or passport with you to confirm your identity? One can never be too careful these days, you know. You can park along the street and come through the foot gate to the front door."

"Mr. Carr?"

"Yeah, this is Reggie Carr. If you're selling something—"

"Just the opposite. This is Bertha Cessna. And I may want to buy something. You're on the city council, right?"

"That's right, Mrs. Cessna. But I'm pretty sure you already knew that. You seem to know everything that goes on in this town."

"Darn tootin', I do! And I also know about this big project you're working on."

"What—What project?"

"Oh, come on. A smart cookie like you knows exactly what I'm talking about. Did you hear the part I said about buying something? That's what I want to do. I want to buy in on this project."

"Mrs. Cessna, I think you're confused. There's no big project."

"You tryin' to tell me that you and Joel Werner aren't partnering up on the biggest deal to ever hit River County? I may not like the man, but I know he's smart enough to get in on a sweet deal like this. I thought you were, too."

"I don't really know Mr. Werner, outside of council meetings and all."

Reggie Carr was many things, but a convincing liar wasn't one of them.

"Rumor has it that he backed you for a seat on the council. And once I heard about this, I knew why. He needs you to help push it through. Given my standing in the community, I can help with that. But I want in."

"There's nothing to be 'in' on," he continued to protest. "Besides, if there was a project, and that's only an *if*, how did you hear about it?"

"I know it's all hush-hush and all, but like you said, nothing happens in this town that I don't know about. So, are you interested in my support, or what?"

"I don't—"

"I'll tell you what. Let's meet in person. Heck, you can bring Joel Werner with you, if he'll promise to act like a human being." After Werner's first failed campaign to root Brash out a job, Granny Bert had made her feelings toward him perfectly clear. It was too late now to pretend otherwise, so she decided to play on that fact. "We'll meet, discuss the project, and I can write you a check on the spot. If you need more than a hundred grand, I'll need a few days to clear up the funds."

"Hun—Hundred thousand?" Carr squeaked.

"Like I say," she quickly added, "I can give you more, but that should prove I'm serious, don't you think? How's three-twenty sound to you?"

"I can be there by three twenty-five. I can't say for sure about Werner."

"Let's make it three-thirty on the dot. If you need more money, I may be able to call the bank before they close. Oh, and I'm afraid we can't meet here at my house. I had a pipe break this morning, and there's water all over the place. We'll have to meet at my granddaughter's office."

"Which granddaughter?" he asked sharply.

"Maddy, but don't worry. She and Brash took their son to check out a college campus today. Even if their daughter comes home, we'll have that whole side of the Big House to ourselves. Park in the *In a Pinch* parking space, and we'll use her office. There's plenty of room in there to go over all the paperwork."

When he hesitated, Granny Bert dangled the bait again. "Remember, I'm in for a minimum of a hundred grand."

She could hear his greedy gulp. "See you promptly at three-thirty."

Hanging up, Granny Bert's hand triumphantly shot into the air. "Suck-er!"

# 23

Virgie waved Kelvin Quagmire into the driveway. The automatic gates were used primarily by family and close friends. The drive led to the old carriage house and the side entrance of the house. There was also a walkway around to the front of the mansion, so she motioned him to the kitchen door.

"Thank you for coming, young man," she said.

"Thank you for having me."

Once he was inside, and she had taken his coat, Virgie looked apologetic. "I'm afraid Hank's not here yet. He had a cow having a calf, and he may have to pull it."

"Pull it?"

"Yeah, sometimes calves need a little help coming out, especially if it's a heifer's first calf or if it's out of a big bull. Sometimes they get stuck halfway out, and you have to pull it the rest of the way."

The real estate agent from the city looked at her in horror. "P—Pull it? Don't you call a vet and let him do a C-section, or something?"

"Ranchers do the *something,* unless it's an emergency and you're in danger of losing the mama. If you can't pull it by hand, a block and chain usually do the trick. Say, you feeling okay? You look a might green around the gills."

"I, uh, could use some water."

"Coming right up. If Hank ain't here soon, we'll go into Maddy's office and get started without him."

"Shilo Dawne. Thanks for coming," Madison said. "Let me take your coat."

"This won't take long, will it?" the dark-haired woman asked.

"I suppose that depends on you. How about some coffee?"

"No more caffeine for me, thanks." Her hands shook just a bit as she handed Madison her coat.

"Water?"

"That sounds good."

Madison retrieved a bottle from the refrigerator tastefully hidden behind a panel. In a room full of built-ins and secrets spaces, the appliance was almost invisible.

"I asked you to come today for two reasons, Shilo Dawne," Madison said, glancing at the clock to check the time. "First, I want to ask you about the supposed assault that took place in the kitchen."

Shilo Dawne looked startled. "Assault?"

"Surely you remember accusing Genny of attacking you. You said she slapped you in the face and tore your dress."

"Oh, that. Well, uh, in light of... everything else that happened that night, I suppose I forgot all about it."

"Our insurance agent needs to know if you plan to file charges."

"Insurance? What does insurance have to do with this?"

"We have a homeowner's policy that protects us from libel and personal injury lawsuits. We contacted our agent, just to be on the safe side."

"I have no intentions of suing you, Miss Maddy. What happened was strictly between Genny and me."

"Well, that's a relief. Our agent mentioned something about insurance fraud, and I almost went to pieces. I've been so worried."

Shilo Dawne's voice rose. "Insurance fraud?" She hadn't considered that in her plan to win Cutter back. Should she have, or was Madison reaching for straws?

"It's nothing to be concerned about. Not if you aren't pressing charges against Genny."

Straws. It was a ruse so that she would drop charges against everyone's beloved blonde. Shilo Dawne pressed her lips together in displeasure. "Is this why you called me over here?"

"Only in part. The other reason is because of something that has recently come to my attention."

Having regained her confidence, she used her best tone of indifference. "And that is?"

"Your... relationship... with Kelvin Quagmire."

"I beg your pardon?"

"Kelvin Quagmire, a real estate agent with *Greater Lone Star Development, Inc.* You do know him, correct?"

"I don't *know* him, know him. Anastasia introduced us when he showed her the *Fresh Starts* building."

"You're a local girl. I heard you were the one to find the building for him, so that he could arrange a deal with Anastasia Rowland and Doyle Nieto."

"Wherever did you hear such a thing?" She laughed off the idea without denying it.

Madison showed her palms and grinned. "What can I say? My grandmother knows everything that happens around here."

With her lie exposed, the younger woman took the offensive. “I did nothing wrong! I knew the old dry cleaners stood empty, so I suggested it would make a good location for a business. There’s no crime in that.”

“So, you do know Quagmire.”

“I hardly see how that would be reason to call the police, as you threatened over the phone.”

“I didn’t threaten, Shilo Dawne. I said I wanted to hear your side of the story before I spoke with Officer Abraham.”

“Because he and I are friends? I can assure you, Officer Abraham won’t care.”

“She will when I tell her the rest.”

Some of Shilo Dawne’s bravado fled. “The... rest?”

“I know what you did.”

All the color leaked from her face. “You—You couldn’t possibly... How? How did you—”

Before she could finish, the interior door opened, and Miss Virgie came through, speaking over her shoulder. “That Hank,” she complained. “Always late. We’ll just get started without him.”

Kelvin Quagmire stepped through the doorway with a smile, ready to win Madison over with his charm and good looks.

The smile died on his face when he saw the other woman seated in front of the desk.

“Sh—Shilo Dawne. What are you doing here?” he asked.

“What are *you* doing here?” she countered.

“I came here to speak with—” He turned to look at Virgie in dismay. “This was all a ruse?”

“Hank doesn’t even know you’re here,” the older woman scoffed. “He wouldn’t have let you through the door. Now, have a seat, and let’s get down to business.”

“I hardly see...”

“Hush up,” Granny Bert advised, “and you will.”

"Where—where did you come from?" He looked at the older woman in confusion. He hadn't seen her when he first came in.

Recovering from her own startle, Shilo Dawne eyed the secret passage behind Madison's desk, the one Granny Bert had just stepped from. Having visited the mansion once before with Genny, she knew about its existence.

Madison cleared her throat and took the conversation from there.

"Mr. Quagmire, I'm Madison deCordova, and this is my grandmother Bertha Cessna. You know Mrs. Adams and Miss Nedbalek."

He gave Shilo Dawne a stilted nod. "Nice to see you again, Miss Nedbalek. It's been a while."

Madison borrowed her husband's signature raised eyebrow. "Really? Because Shilo Dawne was just telling me what the two of you have done."

Kelvin Quagmire sent the brunette a dark glare. She, in turn, denied vehemently, "I didn't tell her a thing! Honest!"

In truth, Madison didn't know much of what had transpired between the two. This was mostly a fishing expedition, a handy little tactic she had learned as the mother of mischievous twins. By accusing them of a vague *something*, they might just reveal a true transgression.

Coming to his feet, Kelvin glared at Shilo Dawne. "I knew I couldn't trust you!"

At three o'clock on the dot, Derron opened the swinging gate to allow another vehicle through. This one stopped several yards from the other parked vehicles, nearest to the walk leading to the front door.

"Mr. Nieto," he greeted the businessman before he could knock. "I don't believe we've had the pleasure. Derron Mullins."

"Doyle Nieto," he returned needlessly.

"If you'll come right this way, I'll get that card for you." Derron led him to the right, into the sitting room formally known as the ladies' parlor. When building the house, Juliet Randolph Blakely had been all about formalities. "Have a seat."

"Not necessary. I won't be here that long."

"Did you bring the other documentation? One can't be too careful these days, you know. I certainly wouldn't want to turn the card over to someone only claiming to be Doyle Nieto."

"I brought it." He pulled his driver's license from his wallet, complaining, "I still don't know how this happened, or even what card is missing."

"Hmm, give me a sec, and I'll tell you. Yes, this certainly looks like you in the photo. Let me get that card now, and you can be on your way. I know you must be a busy man."

"Yes, I am."

Derron opened the antique secretary desk residing alongside the wall. "It must be exciting, owning so many restaurants. I don't know how you keep them all straight!"

"Good management is key. I have some of the best employees in the world working for me."

"Maddy—Mrs. deCordova— often says the same thing about me," he said with unabashed egotism. "I'm sure they know how much you appreciate them."

This was taking longer than expected. "Is there a problem?" Nieto asked, easily looking over the petite man's shoulder as he rummaged through the desk. Derron had a perfectly sculpted body, complete with washboard abs most men could only hope for. His petite, rather feminine size was another matter.

"No, no, I'm sure it's in here. I distinctly remember putting it right here."

"It must have fallen."

Derron made a show of looking beneath papers and on the lower shelf. "Tell me," he said, as if trying to distract from his own lax standards. "Who were you at the ball? I was the knight in full armor."

"Yeah, I think I saw you."

"And you were?"

Nieto hesitated before saying. "Phantom of the Opera."

"Ah, that was a good one. Very professional looking. Where did you get your costume?" Derron sorted through another cubbyhole for good measure.

"Look, are you going to give me my card, or what? Like you said, I'm a busy guy, especially with my business partner dying recently. We have to keep the café open, so it's up to me to take up the slack."

"I was so sorry to hear about Anastasia. I didn't know her well, but she seemed to be a lovely woman. She and I shared the same flair for fashion and the finer things in life."

"Yeah, I think she had a sweater like that," Doyle Nieto said, nodding toward Derron's pearl gray mohair. He held out his hand. "My card?"

"Ah, I remember now!" Derron said, whirling around. "I put it in the safe for safekeeping. I suppose that's why they call it a safe, isn't it?" he mused.

"It appears that way. Where's the safe?"

"In the office. Just let me make sure the door's not locked. Sometimes Maddy has a client and locks the door for privacy."

Derron pranced to the door, rocking his mohair sweater over skinny jeans.

"Oh, you're in luck. The door's unlocked. Let's go

get that card."

Doyle Nieto growled, "It's about time," as they walked into the adjoining room.

Seeing the others there, he came up short.

"Miss Nedbalek, what are you doing here? Why aren't you at work?" he demanded. His eyes then fell on the still-standing Kelvin Quagmire. "Quagmire? What's this all about?"

Behind them, Derron squealed in delight, "Oooh, Batman!"

"*This* is Batman?" Granny Bert asked. "How can you be so sure? He kept his mask on the whole night."

Derron's eyes roamed over Kelvin Quagmire. "Believe me, sista. *This* is Batman. I'd know that body anywhere."

Doyle Nieto had had enough. "Stop this foolishness!" he demanded. "Quagmire, you didn't answer my question. Neither did you, Miss Nedbalek. What is the meaning of this?"

The doorbell rang. "Oops," Derron said. "Hold that thought until our next guest arrives."

Ignoring his statement, Nieto glared at the others. "I'm waiting for an explanation."

"You—You heard the little man. He wants us to wait until he gets back." Obviously, Kelvin Quagmire was hoping to buy himself time to come up with a plausible excuse.

"Could I offer you a beverage while we wait?" Madison broke in. "And a seat?"

"That won't be necessary. I don't know what's going on here, but I don't intend to stay and find out! Quagmire, Nedbalek, you're coming with me."

"Not so fast, Mr. Nieto. I think you'll want to hear what I have to say. And here's our other guest now."

Derron ushered a confused Lawrence Norris into the room. Seeing the assembly of people before him, he started to bolt.

Derron stopped him by locking the door and setting the alarm. "If you'll just indulge us for a moment, we'll get to the bottom of this in no time."

"You can't hold us hostage in here!" Norris protested.

"Would you prefer I call the police?" Madison asked, hand poised over the desk phone.

"I would prefer you tell me what is going on!"

"I second that!" Nieto agreed.

"Derron, pull up a chair for our guests."

"I'll stand," Norris said stubbornly.

"I insist," Madison said with a smooth smile, her hand moving to the receiver again. "Mr. Quagmire, take a seat."

Once they were all seated, Doyle Nieto said, "We've done as you asked. Now, what is this all about?"

"Good question. That's exactly what I'd like to know. Who wants to go first?"

No one spoke up.

"Ooh, can I go?" Derron asked, waving his dainty hand in the air.

"Certainly," his boss invited.

"Well, I think that these four have a nice little racket going. Our divine Mr. Batman finds a piece of property, occupied or otherwise—"

"—and fumble bug Norris takes over from there," Granny Bert pitched in. "Clumsy as he is, he has a fall, or catches food poison, or some other false ailment that he can sue over."

Virgie picked up the conversation. "After the business goes under, Quagmire steps in and sells the property to a select set of clients."

"And where does Mr. Nieto come in?" Madison asked, pretending not to know the answer.

Derron supplied the answer, "Oh, Mr. Nieto is one

of those select clients. Along with the late Anastasia Rowland, bless her fashionable soul. I truly regret that we never had an opportunity to share our favorite boutiques with one another." His handsome face was sincere in its expression of regret. "By the way," he added, "Nieto approves Mr. Norris' questionable actions before they move forward. That way, a waiting buyer guarantees their efforts."

"So, where does Shilo Dawne come in?" This question was in earnest. Madison still hadn't quite pegged Shilo Dawne's part in all of this.

"The way I figure it," Granny Bert said, her eyes squinted as she studied the attractive brunette, "she was doing the books for *Fresh Start* and got wind of something fishy stinking up the works. She probably knew that her bosses weren't only customers of Quagmire's, but major shareholders in *Greater Lone Star Development*, the outfit that spearheaded this whole thing. She probably wanted in on it."

Shilo Dawne shook her head in denial. "I knew something was going on, but I hadn't figured out what. The books weren't adding up. I thought the owners were skimming off the top. But I wasn't blackmailing them, if that's what you think." She swung her gaze to Norris. "But *you* were, weren't you? You were blackmailing Anastasia, threatening to reveal her part in this *thing* if she didn't pay you to stay silent."

"You don't know what you're talking about." Norris brushed off her claim in a cold voice.

"I saw your name on a slip for petty cash. Not that I call a thousand dollars petty, but I didn't question her. I didn't understand what it meant at the time, but you were blackmailing her. I remember seeing the two of you in the parking lot one day, and she looked upset."

"Mind your own business, broad," he growled.

Doyle Nieto glared at him. "You were blackmailing

her? What for, you idiot? We had her where we wanted her!"

"Yeah? She was threatening to blow our cover, you fool. She didn't know all the details, but she knew enough not to want to have any part in it."

"So, you *killed* her?" Kelvin Quagmire cried, once again coming out of his seat.

"I did no such thing," Norris denied. "I thought you killed her, Quagmire!"

"Why would I kill her? I was in love with her!"

Doyle Nieto frowned, motioning to Shilo Dawne. "While having an affair with this one?"

"We were having no such thing!" Shilo Dawne replied indignantly. "We're nothing but friends."

Quagmire nodded. "We met while she was working in the accountant pool at *GLSD*. She told me about the empty dry cleaner's building, and, in turn, I got her a job keeping books for *Fresh Starts*."

Shilo Dawne muttered darkly, "I didn't realize that nosy, obnoxious Myrna Lewis owned the building, or I would never have suggested it." She tossed Derron an apologetic look. "Sorry, Derron. I know she's your aunt and all."

He heaved a long-suffering sigh. "One of life's many injustices. We don't get to choose our own relatives."

Kelvin continued to defend their relationship. "Shilo Dawne and I had a common goal. We both wanted to further our careers and win the hearts back of the two people we loved. Nieto helped me convince Anastasia this was the perfect place to open a new location. But I didn't know she'd stay here so long," he sulked, "so I came to take her back to the city with me."

"And I didn't know she'd have eyes for Cutter," Shilo Dawne complained. "He's the reason I came back here. She should have gone while she had the chance!" she muttered thickly.

"So, *you* killed her!" Lawrence Norris changed his accusation to finger her.

"No, of course not. Why would I kill her? You should be asking her business partner that question. He's the one who took out a hefty life insurance policy on her." She threw Doyle Nieto under the bus to save her own neck.

"*I* didn't kill her," Nieto said in an incredulous voice.

Granny Bert frowned. "I saw you arguing with her at *Montelongo's*. She told you not to push her. She accused you of some sort of scheme."

Lawrence Norris wasted no time changing his tune. "Which makes you a prime suspect," he said. "So, *you* killed her!"

Madison raised her voice to be heard over Nieto's protest. "So far, Mr. Norris," she pointed out, "you've accused all of your associates of killing her. I think thou dost protest too much."

"Why would I kill her? Nieto was paying me off the top, and she was paying me blackmail money."

"Shut. Up," Nieto ground out.

Heeding the dark warning in his voice, Norris changed his accusation once again. "The broad," he insisted. "The broad definitely did it. She wanted both Anastasia and the wife out of her way so she could have the guy to herself. *She* killed Anastasia, using the wife's own knife so the cops would suspect her."

"No! No, that's not what happened at all!" Shilo Dawne protested. She panicked, seeing seven pair of accusing eyes turned upon her. "Yes, I—I framed Genny, but I didn't kill Anastasia. I'm not the one who stabbed her. You have to believe me!"

"Wait. Back up," Madison said. "*You* framed Genny? Why? How could you do such a despicable thing, Shilo Dawne?"

"I—I didn't mean to. Not consciously. I... Kelvin called me, all hysterical because he found Anastasia dead, and I just... reacted. I didn't think, I just acted."

"How? What did you do?" Madison demanded.

"I admit, I went into the kitchen to confront Genny. Cutter said some cruel things to me, and I wanted to get even by lashing out at his precious wife. But she wasn't there. I saw the knife on the floor and picked it up just as Kelvin called. He was inconsolable, so I told him to stay there, and I would come to him. I took the secret passage, the one Granny Bert just used. I knew it came out here in your office. Kelvin met me at the side door and—and I gave the knife to him. I knew it would buy him time, plus it would cast doubt on Genny, everyone's golden girl." A bit of defiance curled around her last statement.

"Buy him time for what, exactly?"

Those same eyes turned on Kelvin. "I—I know what you're thinking," he said, backing away. "But I didn't kill her. I swear, I didn't kill Anastasia. I loved her!"

# 24

Madison glanced at her grandmother, who slowly eased her way to the front door. With a discreet move, Madison disengaged the door locks and alarm. It must be time for their last guests, and things hadn't gone as expected so far.

Her goal today was to connect the four people sitting before her to the sleazy new councilman and his sketchy backer. She simply wanted to establish possible motive for anyone other than Genny. If she discovered the big "hush-hush" project in the process, all the better.

Part of her plan had worked. The quartet had turned on each other, blaming their associates for taking part in the scam.

But she had gotten so much more. She hadn't expected Shilo Dawne's admission to framing Genny. It was the best possible scenario, of course, but left so many things still unanswered.

Was she sitting in the room with a killer this very moment? She had been so certain she knew who had killed Anastasia, and in her scenario, it wasn't any of these four. Did she have it all wrong?

"Can we go now?" Lawrence Norris demanded.

"You can't keep us here! None of us killed her. You can't pin her murder on us."

"Really? The police may see it differently. I know I do. I realize now that each of you have motive to want her dead. I still don't know what this mysterious 'big deal' is you keep alluding to, but I know you all stood to make money off it. Nieto, I think you were the one behind this project, whatever it was. From the sounds of your argument in the restaurant, Anastasia didn't want to be part of it, which would ruin all your carefully laid plans. Norris, you were blackmailing her so that it didn't put the project in jeopardy. Kelvin, you may have loved her, but it didn't keep you from making money at her expense. And Shilo Dawne, like Norris pointed out, this gave you the perfect opportunity to get rid of Anastasia and Genny at the same time. Even though you didn't know all the details, and even though you deny it, you could have blackmailed the others to let you in. So, yes, you all had motive to want her dead. And you all had the opportunity to do so here, where wearing a disguise was expected."

"You can't prove I was here," Lawrence Norris jutted out his jaw, "because I wasn't."

Derron challenged his claim. "Really? Then why did you come to reclaim a credit card that must have fallen out of your pocket that night?"

"I came because you said you'd involve the police. I never said I was here."

Virgie suddenly yelled, "Watch out! There's a bee!"

While the others only dodged sideways, Lawrence Norris covered his head with his arms and looked frantically around him.

Madison winked at Virgie's quick thinking and good memory. Granny Bert must have told her friend that the man in the Venetian mask was allergic to bees, the same way she told Madison.

"You had a good disguise that night," Madison told Norris. "But your conversation with my grandmother revealed more than you intended while you were dancing. For one thing, you're deathly afraid of bees."

"I'm allergic," he sniffed. "Doesn't mean I killed Anastasia."

"But you were here—all of you were— and you each had motive and opportunity to kill her. That's reason enough for me to call the police."

Movement at the door heralded their latest arrivals. Granny Bert came in first, followed by Reggie Carr. Joel Werner lumbered in behind them.

He stopped in his tracks when he saw the others in the room.

"What is the meaning of this?" Werner demanded. "What are all these people doing here?" He glared at Carr. "You said we'd have the place to ourselves!"

"That's what she told me! And she said she was ready to throw in 100K! What was I supposed to do?"

"You were supposed to keep your mouth shut," he growled.

When he turned his glare upon the others, Norris was quick to say, "She doesn't know a thing." He nodded toward Madison. "Not really. She's just guessing."

"I think I know enough," Madison contradicted. "I know whatever this big project is, you needed to buy up as much land in The Sisters as possible. That's why you wanted to buy part of Hank and Virgie's place, and why you planned to take over *New Beginnings*." She saw the surprised look on their faces. "You're right, I don't know that last part for sure, but it makes sense. Nieto, you and Kelvin were seen discussing the building, and Kelvin, you kept asking Dierra all sorts of questions about it. Norris, you planned to sue, presumably so Genny would go bankrupt and sell the building. Which

Kelvin would then sell on behalf of *Greater Lone Star Development,* and *back* to one of its own. How am I doing so far?"

"You're not making any sense, as usual," Werner said. "I'm not listening to another word. I'm out of here."

"Don't you want to hear the rest? I know that Nieto and Anastasia hold shares in *GLSD* as *Anato, Inc.* And that you, Joel Werner, are another of their stockholders, and that you sit on the board. And don't look so surprised," she snapped. "I know how to do my research."

"Then by all means," Werner smirked, "go on with what you think you know."

"I know that our sleepy little town is hardly a hotspot of activity. I always wondered why Anastasia chose The Sisters for a new restaurant location. It doesn't fit in with her typical business model."

Nieto offered an answer. "Opening a new location is always risky, but sometimes the gamble pays off. Entrepreneurs are risk takers by nature."

"Why all the interest in Genny's building?"

"Our gamble paid off. It never hurts to be thinking of expansion. If business continued to go as well as it started, we were considering buying her out."

Shilo Dawne had something to say about that. "Then you were *definitely* keeping another set of books," she accused, "because the official books beg to differ! And like Madison said, this town is hardly a place to get rich."

"Maybe not now," Reggie Carr said. He wanted to sound smart and contribute something to the conversation. So far, Werner acted like he ran the show. As always. "But it's time this town started to grow," he said. "The new resort can change all that."

"What did you just say?" Madison asked

incredulously.

"The new re—"

"Shut! Up!" Joel Werner charged forward to stop the train wreck unfolding before his eyes. He pulled Carr up by the collar of his shirt, spittle flying over the councilman's face. "Don't say another word, you idiot! Don't *any*one say another word."

"Why?" Carr argued. "We know we need backers for this project to work. If the old broad is willing to put in 100K, don't you think there could be others who want in, too?"

"I said to shut up!" He pushed Carr, ramming him up against the wall.

Shilo Dawne recalled her snooping expedition. "I found a map in Anastasia's office. I didn't understand it at the time, but there were copies of deeds attached. Is that what all this is about? Is that what *Greater Lone Star Development* has planned? A resort here in The Sisters?"

"Just tell them and get it over with, Werner," Carr snapped, "before this whole thing blows up in our faces! People like their community the way it is. No one wants a huge resort and a hi—"

"Highway?" Granny Bert finished for him. "You're right. We don't want a highway coming through here. That's what the political rally is this summer, right? For Senator Macintosh."

Virgie's voice was scornful. "Isn't he the one pushing to build that new interstate that will swing through this area? Like we don't have enough asphalt crisscrossing through our farmlands already! How are people supposed to eat if they sell off all our ranches and farms? Some idiots think it all comes from a grocery store, but it takes honest-to-God dirt to grow every bit of it, from beef to beets."

"Now you've done it," Granny Bert groaned. "You've

gone and riled her up. She and Hank can talk for hours on how the city is encroaching on our lands, snuffing out our food sources. And I wholeheartedly agree. We don't want no more city messing up our country."

"It may be too late," Kelvin Quagmire spoke up. "That's the plan. *GLSD* plans to buy up as much land as they can, so they have a foothold here in River County. They'll start with a big resort and a takeover of the town. *New Beginnings* will become a shopping destination. Restaurant on the bottom floor, shops and boutiques on the top two. Then—"

"Shut that man up!" Werner demanded.

"Why? Carr is right. We should schedule a town hall meeting," Kelvin said. "We could—"

Nieto came to his feet. "We could knock the hell out of you! That would shut you up." Without another word, he buried his fist into Kelvin's face.

He crumpled like an old dollar bill.

Shilo Dawne squeaked, attending to her friend. "Did you kill him, too?" she shrieked.

"For the last time. I. Didn't. Kill. Anastasia." Nieto pointed at his associate. "Norris did!"

"I did no such thing," the man denied.

"I guess you had nothing to do with that landowner over in Walker County, either," he sneered. "The one whose death was ruled a suicide by our deputy friend right here." Nieto motioned toward Joel Werner. "I don't mind ignoring a few rules and regulations or erasing a few figures. But count me out when it comes to erasing lives."

"She was going to turn on us," Norris reminded him coldly. "You told me to do what it took to make the problem go away."

"I meant pay her off. Let her pay you off. Create a diversion. Find another backer. Anything but this. For God's sake, I didn't mean to kill her!"

"I don't take orders from just you," Norris said, sliding his gaze toward Werner.

"Hold on," Joel Werner warned Norris. "Don't say another word. Not without my lawyer present."

Granny Bert goaded him. "It's that bad, huh, that you have a lawyer on call? You're even dirtier than I thought. And everybody hates a dirty cop. Especially the other prisoners."

"I'm not going to prison. I didn't do a thing. I wasn't even at the party."

Something clicked in Madison's mind. "That's not true. You didn't buy a ticket, not in your name anyway, but you were there. You were the man in the blue suit. Your wife was wearing the veil."

He opened his mouth to deny it but then shrugged. "So? It's not like we crashed the party. Someone gave us the tickets."

Kelvin Quagmire roused, slowly coming to his feet. No one paid him much mind as Madison continued.

"I watched the surveillance cameras. I knew there was something familiar about you. Your mask hid your face well enough, but I had a feeling I knew you. I saw your wife on the walkway, watching the shadowy corner where I found Anastasia's body. She just kept standing there, waiting for someone. I saw a man—you, obviously—come from the shadows and hand her something. She then hurried down the path, out the gate, and disappeared. She disposed of the first knife, didn't she?"

"What knife? You don't know what you're talking about!"

"I think you do," Madison said, narrowing her eyes. "I think you stabbed Anastasia, handed the knife off to Sharese, and the three of you..." she pointed to Werner, Nieto, and Norris, "...left before Kelvin found her. He saw that she was dead, panicked, and called Shilo

Dawne to help. Shilo Dawne had Genny's knife, gave it to Kelvin, and he stabbed her again with the butcher knife. Then he managed to get away before the estate went on lockdown."

She shivered when she realized she must have missed all of them by mere seconds, including Shilo Dawne, who had snuck in and out of her office via the secret passage.

"You're crazy," Lawrence Norris insisted.

Madison arched her eyebrow. "Am I? When I first found her, there wasn't a knife. By the time Brash arrived, there was one sticking in her body."

Quagmire was now fully alert and standing behind Nieto. Werner looked at him in disgust. "You stabbed her after she was dead? That's just sick!" It seemed as if even a worm like Werner had limits as to how low he would go.

Seeing the accusation in all their eyes, Kelvin Quagmire grabbed Nieto around the neck in a chokehold, threatening to strangle him to death.

"You aren't pinning this on me!" Quagmire yelled. "I didn't kill her. Anastasia told me to meet her at midnight. But the crowd was too thick, and I was a few minutes late. By the time I got there, she was just lying there, surrounded by blood. I—I didn't know what to do. I guess I panicked. I didn't kill her, but I knew how it would look. I called Shilo Dawne, and she brought me the knife. I swear, I didn't stab her. I—I just put it in the hole that was already there." Tears streamed down his face as he revealed the horrendous act, but his hold on Nieto never slacked. "Nieto had the most to gain from her death," he accused. "He was her partner and wanted her share of everything. He killed her, and he deserves to die!"

As his chokehold tightened around Nieto's neck, the man in the chair choked out, "I—I didn't kill her.

Norris did."

Norris shook his head, jumping from his chair. "That's a lie!"

"He's telling the truth," Joel Werner agreed. "Norris killed her." He crossed his arms and took a defiant stand, ready to block the man's flight.

Realizing he was cornered, Norris tossed Werner a defiant glare. "But you took the knife. If I'm going down, you're going with me. You *and* your wife. You planned this entire thing out. Said you knew it the minute you saw the poster. It was the only bright side to the ice storm, you said. Why you were out in it I'll never know, but you said the masquerade party was the perfect place to get rid of Anastasia. You told me to make it happen, then you took the knife from me, gave it to your wife, and the two of you disposed of it. You're both accessories to murder! Her blood's on your hands, the same way it's on mine."

Granny Bert cocked her head to one side. "Boys, I think your ride is here."

The sound of sirens filled the air as three police cars, two fire trucks, and one ambulance shrieked to a halt in front of the Big House.

"I called the cops," Derron explained. He had all but blended into the shadows. No one noticed him as he discreetly called 9-1-1.

Misty Abraham burst through the door, her gun in shooting position. Schimanski came in behind her.

"What's going on here?" Abraham demanded. "We had a 9-1-1 call from this location. Is someone hurt? Why are all these people here?"

"Basically," Granny Bert said with a grin, "they're confessing to murder."

Abraham glared at Madison. "Did you disobey my orders? I distinctly told you to butt out of my investigation!"

"I solved your case for you. *We* solved your case," Madison corrected, twirling her finger to include Granny Bert, Derron, and Miss Virgie. "We all heard them admit to a scheme to murder Anastasia Rowland. You can thank us later. Just get them out of my office and out of my home."

"Is that true?" Abraham asked the others.

"Darn tootin'!" Virgie said.

"You doubt my granddaughter's word?" Granny Bert flared. "Of course we heard them!"

"They're right," Derron nodded. "We all heard them."

Madison looked over the officers' shoulders. A puffing Perry came bustling up the walk, a late third to the bust. "Where's Brash?" she asked in concern.

Abraham was busy wrangling Joel Werner's hands behind his back and cuffing him, ignoring his cries of outrage and threats to have her job. She handed him off to Perry as he finally arrived.

"I requested that Brash wait in the car. *He* respected my wishes," Misty said pointedly, slapping cuffs onto Nieto's wrists. Schimanski already had Lawrence Norris cuffed and ready to be led away.

"I wouldn't be so sure about that," Madison said with an amused smile, nodding toward the door.

Unable to stay behind, her husband bounded up the steps and into her office, assessing the situation with one sweeping gaze.

"I've got him, Schimanski," Brash said, tugging on Norris' arm. He looked over the crowded room to lock his gaze with his wife's. "You okay, sweetheart?"

"I'm great." She grinned.

Schimanski motioned to Reggie Carr. "This one, too?"

"All of them, including Shilo Dawne."

The brunette batted her eyes in exaggerated

innocence. “Me? Why me?”

“Because you took Genny’s knife to frame her for murder.”

“Mrs. deCordova!” Misty Abraham barked. “Leave the speculating to the professionals.”

“It’s not speculating, Officer. I have it all on video tape.”

Abraham jerked Shilo Dawne from her chair and told Madison, “I’ll deal with you later.”

Madison smiled, already reaching for her phone to call Genny. “You know where to find me.”

# 25

The following Sunday, Madison called for a do-over.

She and her crew were in the kitchen most of the day, preparing the traditional meal of salt bacon, black-eyed peas, cabbage, and cornbread. To please all tastes, there was also a ham, mashed potatoes, and a plate of deviled eggs.

Wanda and Sybil had forgiven their friends for leaving them out of this caper, especially when they were invited to the special meal. As Madison's way of making amends, she asked the two elder ladies to bring desserts, the highest honor she could bestow upon them.

Convincing Genny and Cutter to come had been a bit trickier. They cited Hope's runny nose as the reason, but in the end, they had agreed to come. Things were still strained between the two couples, but it helped that the meal included Cutter's parents, Tug and Mary Alice Montgomery, as well as Andy and Lydia deCordova.

Seated at the head of the table, Brash led the prayer. He thanked the Lord for their meal, the good friends and family gathered around them, for their many other blessings in life, and asked for the special favor of granting them all a bright year ahead, filled with healing, health, and happiness.

As the food was passed around and small talk flowed, the anticipated tension at the table eased somewhat. Laughter helped.

"I should have said thank you, sweet Jesus, for these black-eyed peas!" Sybil proclaimed on her third spoonful.

"I should have praised the cornbread. Bertha, is this your recipe?" Wanda asked.

"You know it," Granny Bert replied with a proud smile.

"I'm thankful Mom brought the deviled eggs," Brash said, winking at his mother. "You know you make the best." He shot his wife a look. "No offense, sweetheart."

"None taken. I agree!" Madison laughed.

"I'm not going to even pretend to be thankful about the cabbage," Blake said bluntly, "but Miss Virgie's real mashed potatoes are the bomb!"

"I suppose that's good?" Hank asked, helping himself to more of the cabbage Blake had shunned.

"It's the best!"

"Is that why you're shoveling them in like you've been stranded on an island for the last thirty days?" his twin asked sardonically.

"I may as well have been. Mom was so busy cooking supper, that we skipped lunch."

"What about that sandwich you ate, mister?" Madison asked.

The teen pursed his lips. "I considered that more of a snack."

Clearing her throat, Genny apologized in a timid voice, "I'm sorry I didn't bring anything this time."

"You brought those two adorable babies, and that's good enough for us!" Madison proclaimed.

"Plus, feel free to do the dishes if you like," Bethani added with a cheeky smile.

"Ignore her," Brash said. "It's her night to do the dishes."

"At least you only have to do them at one house," Megan bemoaned, rolling her eyes toward her mother. "I have double duty! Mom makes me do them when I'm there, Mama Maddy makes me do them when I'm here. A girl can't win for losing."

"You have two homes with loving parents, young lady," Granny Bert chided, treating her as if she were blood kin, "when many children don't even have one. Count your blessings, not your sorrows."

"You're right, Granny Bert. I do kinda have it good. And when I'm not at either of their houses, I'm at Aunt Genny's. Plus, I get to go to your house or Grammy's, so it's a win-win all the way around."

"Family," Madison said with a smile. "That's what blessings are all about. And this room is filled with family tonight. We may have our ups and downs"—she looked specifically at Genny and Cutter— "but we're still family, and we love unconditionally."

"That's the definition of family," Granny Bert agreed. "Tough times and troubles, tempered with lots of love and laughter."

"And cake!" Wanda added. "Lots of cake!"

Everyone laughed, including Cutter. He was slowly loosening up, thanks in part to 'Mama Matt' Aikman engaging him in a discussion about football.

Overhearing her husband's efforts to pull the man out, Shannon suggested, "There's probably still time to catch some of the game. Maddy, why don't we let the guys have their dessert in the family room? That way, we ladies can have a nice, long visit in here."

“Sounds like a great idea.” Madison smiled.

There had been a time in high school when Shannon Winn had been her arch enemy. Brash had liked Shannon, Shannon had liked Matt, Matt had liked Madison, and Madison was halfway in love with Brash, even then. It was a merry go-round of love, Megan called it. In the end, Madison and Shannon had become good friends, and Madison was thankful Megan had had such a good role model growing up.

While the men shuffled off to the media room and the teens to who-knew-where, only the women were left around the table. Over coffee and dessert, they swapped stories, memories, and gossip. As the conversations broke off into clusters, Madison was happy to find her best friend part of hers.

“I was serious about the dishes,” Genny told her. “I’ll be happy to do them.”

“And hog all that fun for yourself? I get to help!” When the others tried to join them, Madison shooed them away. She needed a few minutes alone with Genny.

“How are you doing, Genny? Really?” Madison asked as they piled empty dishes into the sink.

“If you mean with the depression, it’s better. I think I’m finally getting the hang of juggling Genny the wife, Genny the mama, and Genny the business owner.”

“While you’re at it, don’t forget Genny the woman. It’s important to take care of yourself.”

“I am. And I asked the doctor to give me something different. It’s not quite as strong, but also not quite as harsh. I can tolerate it much better.”

“That’s good. I’m glad.”

“As for the rest...” She took a deep breath and trudged on. “It’s weird, knowing how close I came to having my entire world changed. It makes me more grateful for what I have. I’m also grateful that Shilo

Dawne admitted she faked the attack—can you believe she actually slapped herself in the face, just so she could blame me for it? — but it also has me wondering who thought I was guilty, and who believed I was innocent."

"Does it matter? You *were* innocent, no matter what public opinion decided."

"But I have to wonder who my true friends are."

"Let me ask you something. Have you been busy at the restaurant so far this year?"

"Very. Why do you think I've been working Bethani so hard? She's been a true godsend at the restaurant, like Megan has been with the girls. I don't know what I'll do when they leave for college."

"Let's not even talk about college," Madison said, her hand to her heart. "But let's *do* talk about how busy the restaurant has been. *Those* are friends, Genny. Especially the ones who have been coming in this whole time, even before the arrests were made."

"I know," she sniffed. "And *you*. You never stopped believing in me. I just want to thank you for that." She grasped her friend's hands in her own. "I'm sorry, Maddy, for anything that may have been said. Cutter and I were just so confused and so scared."

"So were we, sweetie. So were we. But we got through it, didn't we?"

They ended up in a hug, sweetened with laughter and more than a few tears.

In time, Shannon joined them in the kitchen, and the three enjoyed a visit while the older women chatted in the dining room. By the time the table was cleared and the dishes done, Megan and Bethani had fed the babies and handed them off to their grandmother and their 'adopted' elders. It was hard to know where one family ended, and another began.

As the dinner party began to disperse and people

left, Cutter found a moment to be alone with Brash.

"Brash, I just want to say I'm sorry. And to thank you for everything you did for Genny."

"Cutter, you would have done the same for Maddy, had the situation been reversed. I only did what I thought was best for her."

"I realize that now. I'm sorry I was so hardheaded." He held out his hand for a shake between friends.

"Come on, brother. We can do better than that!" Brash said, pulling him in for a manly bear hug.

Later that night, as they climbed into bed and adjusted the covers, Brash told her, "You keep smiling."

She had a simple explanation. "I'm happy."

"Things all patched up between you and Genny?"

"I'm pleased to report that they are. I guess that's part of why I'm smiling. Things feel right again."

"I know what you mean. Cutter and I have worked out our differences, too."

"The theme of the masquerade ball was gold and silver, to plan for million-dollar dreams of a great New Year. Instead, the year started off rocky, but at least we've gotten a reboot. It's going to be a hard enough year with the kids all graduating and going off to college. I felt like we needed a do-over, to start things off right."

"I agree. And I think your idea of a re-boot was perfect."

"Just a week or so late, but not too bad."

"They're just dates on a calendar, babe. What matters is what we pack into the days themselves."

"I like that," Madison decided. "I may put it on a mug." She slathered lotion onto her arms. "I'm also smiling because I think we're finally done with Joel

Werner for good. Norris sang like a canary, admitting Werner hired him to poison that rancher so they could get his land for a *GLSD* project."

"And politicians want no part of that sort of controversy. I think it's safe to say Senator Macintosh won't pursue a route through River County after this."

"I guess we'll never know if Anastasia knew all the details and wanted out, or if the others just got too greedy to share with her."

"Either way, it ultimately got her killed."

"To be her 'friend', I heard Myrna took news of the failed deal harder than she took Anastasia's death. She had her heart set on making a fortune off this now-defunct project. And, of course, on seeing Genny and me get our comeuppance, as she called it. Something about our reign coming to an end."

"I don't think she knew about the scheme to murder Anastasia, but she knew there was something big going down, and she wanted in. On the bright side," Brash grinned, "she's now the owner of two empty buildings downtown and of twenty-five thickly wooded acres near the edge of the county line."

"Poor Don. The things he has to put up with, being married to her," Maddy empathized.

"Not me. I hit the jackpot in the wife lottery. I was going to save this for later, but I think now might be a good time to give you this."

Madison propped up on her elbows, watching him take a gift-wrapped box from his nightstand drawer.

"What is this?"

"An early Valentine's gift."

"Yeah, like six weeks early!" she laughed.

"Like you said, we had a rocky start to the year, and it's going to get harder. Maybe this will give you something to look forward to."

She unwrapped the red foil paper to find a gift

certificate. She read it silently before breaking into a smile.

"Really? A vacation?"

"Okay, so I cheated. It's both a Valentine's Day gift and an anniversary gift. All wrapped up in seven fun days at the beach."

"And at my favorite new place, *The Mermaid's Retreat*!"

"You told me how much you enjoyed it, so I thought it would be fun to go with you. Notice the unspecified number of rooms. I didn't know if you wanted it to be just you and me or the whole family."

Madison made a would-you-be-mad-if-I-told-you face. "Wellll," she said, drawing out the word. "As great as a romantic getaway with just my husband sounds, we'll have ample opportunity for that this fall. Would you be terribly disappointed if we took the kids along? If it coincides with spring break, it would be the perfect family vacation."

"It does. I already checked. And I think a family vacation is just what we need. As long as," he said, setting aside the gift to gather her in his arms, "we have a room all to ourselves."

She wound her arms around his neck. "Ooh, I like the way you think. This vacation keeps sounding better and better."

## Special Note from Author

After twenty-seven books, this is the first one my mother hasn't read. She's always been my very first reader, giving me a boost of confidence while pointing out the story's shortcomings. On September 3, my mother passed away at the age of ninety and a half years. She was a strong Christian woman, a loving wife, mother, grandmother, and great-grandmother, and a huge influence in my life. She also encouraged me to keep my books 'clean' while still delivering engaging, character-driven storylines. I hope this book lives up to her expectations and that she is reading it on her heavenly Kindle.

Thank *you* for reading it, as well.

Stay tuned for more adventures in the year to come!

Up next is *Keep Your Doors Locked*, an edgier thriller loosely based on recent events in our community. I was the primary caregiver for my mom and she was bed-bound for the last six months of her life, making an escaped convict in our area all the more frightening. No link is available yet.

For more fun and intrigue in The Sisters, Book 15 debuts April 25$^{th}$, 2023.

# ABOUT THE AUTHOR

Best-selling indie author Becki Willis loves crafting stories with believable characters in believable situations. Many of her stories stem from her own travels and from personal experiences. (No worries; she's never actually murdered anyone).

When she's not plotting danger and adventure for her imaginary friends, Becki enjoys reading, antiquing (aka junking), unraveling a good mystery (real or imagined), dark chocolate, and a good cup of coffee. A professed history geek, Becki often weaves pieces of the past into her novels. Family is a central theme in her stories and in her life. She and her husband enjoy traveling but believe coming home to their Texas ranch is the best part of any trip.

Becki has won numerous awards, but the real compliments come from her readers. Drop in for an e-visit anytime at beckiwillis.ccp@gmail.com, or www.beckiwillis.com.